6-17

Love
and
Other Subjects

A Novel

Love
and
Other Subjects

KATHLEEN SHOOP

Website: Kshoop.com
Twitter: @kathieshoop
Facebook: Kathleen Shoop Author Page

Cover design by Heidi North and Julie Metz/Julie Metz, Ltd.
Cover photos © istockphoto.com
Author photo © Jennifer Bonaroti Gold
Book design by Rachelle Ayala Publishing, LLC

ISBN-13: 978-0615724966
ISBN-10: 0615724965

Also by Kathleen Shoop

The Last Letter
After the Fog

My Dear Frank: The letters that inspired The Last Letter
(edited by Shoop)

To all the teachers who give so much

And…

Especially for

Hruska, Stewart, Consiglio, Dorn, Moody, and Buckman

1993

Chapter 1

I stood at my blackboard, detailing the steps for adding fractions. It wasn't exciting stuff. It was stab-yourself-in-the-eye boring, as a matter of fact, but it was part of the job—part of my brilliant plan to change the world. And I had constructed a downright solid lesson plan.

Said lesson was met with exquisite silence. I looked around. Thirty-six fifth and sixth graders. All seated, almost all of them paying attention. So what if six students had their heads on their desks.

I told myself my dazzling teaching skills must have finally had an impact on their behavior. The bile creeping up my esophagus said I was wrong. The truth was they had probably stayed up too late and now were sleeping with their eyes open. I ignored the heartburn. I willed myself to revel in the tiniest success.

"Tanesha, what's the next step?" I asked brightly.

Tanesha sucked her teeth and threw herself back in her seat.

I opened my mouth to reprimand her but the sudden sound of chairs screeching across hardwood filled the room. The resulting flurry of movement shocked me. Some students bolted, scattering to the corners of the room. Others froze in place. My attention shot back to the middle of the classroom where two boys were preparing to dismantle one another.

Short, fire-pluggish LeAndre and monstrous Cedrick sandwiched their chests together, rage bubbling just below their skin. Different denominators, I almost told the class. Right there, everyday math in action.

"Wait a minute, guys." I held up my hands as though I had a hope of stopping them with the gesture. These daily wrestling matches had definitely lost their cute factor. "How about we sit down and talk this—"

LeAndre growled, then pulled a gun-like object from his waistband and pressed it into Cedrick's belly. I narrowed my eyes at the black object. It couldn't be a gun. The sound of thirty-four kids hitting the floor in unison told me it was. No more shouting, crying, swearing—not even a whimper.

"It's *real*." Marvin, curled at my feet, whispered up at me.

I nodded. It couldn't be real. My heart seized, then sent blood charging through my veins so hard my vision blurred.

"Okay, LeAndre. Let's think this through," I said.

"He. Lookin'. At. Me." Spittle hitched a ride on each syllable LeAndre spoke.

"I'm walking over to you," I said. "And you're going to hand me the gun, LeAndre. Okay?" I can do this. "Please. Let's do this." I can do this. I can do this. There were no snarky words to go with this situation. There was no humor in it.

Cedrick stared at the ceiling, not showing he understood there was a gun pressed into him. I stepped closer. Sweat beaded on LeAndre's face only to be obliterated by tears careening down his cheeks. He choked on sobs as though *he* wasn't the one with the gun, as though he wasn't aware he could stop this whole mess. The scent of unwashed hair and stale perspiration struck me. The boys' chests heaved in unison.

I focused on LeAndre's eyes. If he just looked back at me, he'd trust I could help him.

The whine of our classroom door and the appearance of Principal Klein interrupted my careful approach.

"Ms. Jenkins!"

He startled everyone, including LeAndre and his little trigger finger.

**

In the milliseconds between Klein's big voice bulleting off the rafters and the gun firing, I managed to throw myself in front of a few stray kids at my feet. I can't take total credit for my actions because I don't even remember moving. Suddenly, I was there on the floor, thanking God that Jesus or some such deity had been bored enough to notice what was going on in my little old Lincoln Elementary classroom. LeAndre fell into Cedrick's arms, wailing about the gun being loaded with BBs—that it wasn't real.

My foot hurt, but I ignored it and assessed the kids while Klein focused on LeAndre. Could everyone really be all right? I checked Cedrick, who appeared unfazed. He was injury-free, simply standing there, hovering, as though guarding everyone around him.

I moved to other students—no visible harm. I hauled several up by their armpits, reassuring them with pretend authority. A firearm-wielding child usurps all of a teacher's mojo in a short, split second.

I made up comforting stuff—words of phony hopefulness that might convince them that nothing out of the ordinary had just occurred. And with each lie came the odd feeling that I was actually telling the truth. A little gun in a classroom was nothing.

Klein stuffed the piece into his pants and carried the withering LeAndre out of the room in his arms as a man would carry a woman over the marital threshold. His voice was devoid of its usual venomous tone and soothed LeAndre's gulping sobs. Perhaps he'd been shot with a dose of compassion during the melee.

Stepping back inside the room, still holding LeAndre, Klein shoved his thumb into the air, giving us the old Lincoln thumbs-up. No one returned the gesture, but I figured that was all right this once. The school counselor came into the room and announced she'd take everyone to the library while I met with the police. Leaving the room, I noticed Cedrick's face appeared to have been drained of blood and finally revealed his true feelings about what had happened. The rest of the students—their faces expressing the same shock I felt inside—wrapped themselves in their own arms, shook their heads and trailed the counselor out of the room.

It was like watching a scene through a window that wasn't mine, that I couldn't remember stepping up to. I forced calm into my voice and actions as I funneled the kids still inside the room to the door and told myself I could let the impact of what just happened hit me later. To get through the day, to be the type of teacher who could handle a weapon in the classroom, I had to leave the assimilation of the events for later.

These poor freaking kids. Where the hell did they come from and how did they end up with this life? I thought I'd known the details of their lives. Apparently not.

"Ms. Jenkins," Terri said. She stopped and pointed at my foot. "Your boot."

I gasped at the sight of the leather. It gaped like a jagged mouth, tinged with blood. I wiggled my stinging toe making more blood seep through my trouser sock. Nausea slammed me. LeAndre's shooting arm had obviously moved in my direction when he'd been startled by Klein. Had that really been just a BB-gun?

I straightened against my queasiness. "Terri, go on. I'll meet you in the library in a minute."

She left the room. I collapsed into my desk chair and removed my boot and the torn, bloody sock. "Jeez. That hurts like a mother," I said. I turned the boot over and a teeny ball fell out of it and skittered across the floor. I swiveled my chair and took my Pittsburgh Steelers Terrible Towel down from the wall. I dabbed my toe with it, staining the towel red.

I thought of the reason I'd become a teacher. That I'd searched for a way to make a difference in the world and thought, well, damn, yes, a teacher. I could save the urban youth of America. I just needed a little help and some time. I was only two months in to my teaching career, and I already knew chances were I wouldn't be saving anybody.

The footfalls grew louder as they neared my room. I knew it was her. I turned my attention to the doorway. Our secretary, Bobby Jo, wheezed as she leaned against the doorjamb. With new energy, she pushed forward and barreled toward me. I set the Terrible Towel on the desk and stood to move out of her path, but she caught my wrist and swallowed me into the folds of her body with what she no doubt imagined was a helpful hug. She gripped the back of my head and plunged my face into her armpit. The spicy fusion of ineffective deodorant and body odor made me hold my breath.

Aside from being a secretary, Bobby Jo was an emotional extortionist. She pushed out of the hug, but, still gripping my shoulders, stared at me. Her labored breath scratched up through her respiratory system. I squeezed my eyes closed in anticipation of her "I'm Klein's right-hand woman" crap. Not today, Bobby Jo. Not now.

She glanced around the room, and then dug her fingers nearly to my bones. "The boss is so upset."

I gave her the single-nod/poker face combo, as disgust welled inside me. *He's* upset? I weighed my inclination to tell her to leave me the hell alone with the ensuing sabotage that would follow if I didn't kiss her ass hard and immediately. I wiggled out of her grip and leaned against my desk.

"The boss," Bobby Jo said. "He'll be in as soon as he's off the phone with the superintendents from areas four, five, and six. They're using your sit-u-a-tion as a teaching case." Bobby Jo's plump fingers with their fancy, long nails danced stiffly in front of her as if she could only form words if her hands were involved.

Man, this school year was not going as planned. I might have been delusional to think I'd alter the course of public education in just two months, but I hadn't expected to be held up as a "what not to do in the classroom" example for one of the largest counties in the United States. Fame was one thing, scandal was another.

I looked back at my shoe, hoping Bobby Jo wouldn't

mistake my attempt to ignore her for the need for another hug. I was about to ask if I could see our nurse, Toots, about my wounded foot.

"It was only a BB-gun. You'll be fine," Bobby Jo said. "I don't know why everyone's so worked up. I heard the whole thing." She ran one hand through the other, massaging her fingers.

"What do you mean, you *heard?*"

Bobby Jo looked around the room again. "Okay, okay, you got me. I'll just spill." Her eyes practically vibrated in their sockets. "I heard the entire thing because I was listening on the intercom."

"*What?*" You can do that?

"The boss. He tells me to. Says your classroom techniques warrant that I get a handle on what's happening."

Chills paraded through my body as though they had feet and marching orders. No wonder he knew every move I made, was able to appear in my room at the worst time of the day—every day.

I readjusted my poker face.

The shuffle-clack-shuffle-clack of Klein's clown feet stopped me from telling Bobby Jo what she could do with her intercom. She shambled back toward the door. "I'll finish the report, Boss." They gave each other the Lincoln thumbs-up—Klein's way of encouraging school spirit while sucking it out of me.

I hobbled around my desk and picked up a paper that had flown off it. "I'm okay. Boy, that was something. I knew LeAndre had big problems."

"Jenkins," Klein said, "because of this incident, I have four meetings to attend before the day's over, so we'll have to meet about this on Monday."

Guess that *wasn't* newfound compassion I'd witnessed him offering LeAndre.

He crossed his arms across his chest and spread his legs, his pelvis jutting forward as though he needed the wide base to hold his slim upper body erect. "You'll have to meet with some parents. Bobby Jo will bring the police in as soon as they get finished with her interview."

He blew out a stout puff of air, the sound you heard when a bike pump was removed from the tire mid-pump. "I need you to think long and hard about how this transpired—about how I've gone twenty years with nary a gun incident and as soon as you show up, the kids start packing heat."

Please, I'd been at Lincoln two months sans gun incident. "You can't be serious. I'm not their mother. I only have the kids seven hours day. I didn't—"

Klein held up his hand to shut me up. "I don't have the whole story. LeAndre actually had two guns. The BB and another one that's convertible from toy to real. That one was still in his pants. Doesn't matter. What I need is for you to get your kids under control because there's a reason this happened in your room and not in one of the other classrooms."

"The reason *is*," I said, "I'm the one with a child who is just this side of certifiable. I love LeAndre, I feel bad for him, but he's not normal. I can't get his mother to come in to see me or call me back. Maybe now he'll be expelled and get help before he kills someone."

"I wouldn't count on that."

"Which part of *that*?"

"LeAndre won't be expelled. There are many reasons not to take that action. What good will it do him to sit at home all day, not learning anything? We can service him here."

"He talks to clouds at recess," I said. "He has conversations with himself all day. And not the kind you and I have when we're trying to remember what we need at the grocery store. I swear there is something really wrong with him."

Klein thrust his hand into the air again. "I'll see you first thing Monday, Carolyn Jenkins," he said. "And, for the last time, when I give the Lincoln thumbs-up—" he shoved his thumb nearly into my chest "—I don't care if you're in the grip of a stroke, I expect you to return the gesture."

Oh, yeah. I've got the perfect gesture for you, buddy boy.

**

Two hours into my three-hour meeting with parents, police and suited men with thick, gold-plated pens, I realized Toots, the nurse, wasn't going to swoop in and provide me with any sort of medical care. So while enjoying a lovely interrogation as to my role in the shooting, I rehung my Terrible Towel and fashioned a bandage from Kleenex and Scotch tape.

Once everyone had left, I was ready for a drink. Okay, ten drinks in a dank bar where I was a stranger, where I wouldn't have to rehash the shooting. There was nothing like a good mulling over of Lincoln Elementary events in the company of my roommates. But as I limped to my car, a no longer frequent, but still familiar blue mood bloomed inside me.

It stopped me right there in the parking lot. I'd forgotten how the dread felt, that it actually came with warmth that almost made me welcome it. Driving down the boulevard, I decided not to go to the Green Turtle to meet Laura, Nina and my boyfriend, Alex. I wanted to be alone at The Tuna, the bar where nobody knew my name.

**

I drove my white Corolla to The Tuna and pondered my most recent teaching experience. Two months ago I'd been busy dreaming about saving the world and such. Man, those were the days. This afternoon's event did not resemble my educational pipedreams in the least. I couldn't stop replaying the shooting in my head.

Okay, so LeAndre hadn't been aiming at me. And the bullet had only grazed my toe (but ruined one of my beautiful patent leather Nine West boots) and the bullet was actually a BB, but still, I'd been shot and frankly, it offended me. I loved those kids and apparently that meant shitola to them.

The further I drove from the school, the more I realized each and every county administrator and police official who'd interviewed me had implied I was somehow responsible for being shot by a disgruntled fifth grader. That left me feeling like I'd undergone a three-hour gynecological exam. The only logical next step was to get drunk.

Once in the parking lot of The Tuna, I shuffled across the pitted asphalt, squeezing in between a splotchy Chevy Nova and a glistening, black BMW. I paused and looked back at the vehicle. Who the hell came to The Tuna in a BMW? What did it matter?

Inside, I fussed with my purse while giving my eyes a chance to adjust to the murky atmosphere. The thick beer stench—the good kind—loosened the grasp of self-pity that had taken hold of me. I wove through mismatched tables and snaked a path to the roughhewn pine bar. The thunk of billiard balls punctuated quiet rhythms wafting from the jukebox. Several men cloistered at one end of the bar sent assorted, non-verbal hellos my way.

Before I reached my stool, the bartender I'd met the week before—the one with the sausage arms, overstuffed midsection and blazing red buzz cut—cracked a Coors Light and set it at my seat. I chugged the ice-glazed beer and swallowed the unladylike burp bubbling in my belly.

I blew out some air and thought about the day. Crap Quotient: 10/10. At least that bad. I'd coined the phrase Crap Quotient (C.Q.) after spending an entire day in grad school with a head cold, zero ability to smell and a hunk of dog crap on the bottom of my shoe. I'd traipsed around campus without any sweet soul letting me know I'd become the embodiment of the word stink.

I glanced at the hefty barkeep. He cracked a second beer before I had to ask. There was something precious about not knowing the person's name that knew the beer you wanted at exactly the moment you needed it. I raised the bottle to salute him. He smiled while drying glasses and silverware. I wondered if that was part of the attraction promiscuous girls felt toward anonymous lovers. It was a near-miracle that a relative stranger could serve you in some perfect way even for a short time.

I plucked at the sweaty label on the bottle with my nail, thinking about Nina and Laura, my sisters in education. The greatest roommates a girl could have, except they were forever including my boyfriend, Alex, in everything we did. I'd have to get rid of Alex if I were to reap the full benefits of having such terrific friends. Alex and I were simply not a fit and me wishing exceptionally hard that I'd fall back in love with him wasn't going to make it happen.

Because I'd missed lunch, the beer quickly did its job at anesthetizing me and eliminating the sensation that my skin had been removed and reattached with dental floss. A dark haired man slid onto the stool next to me. *Great.* Some slack-ass cozying up after the kind of day I had? I watched him in the blotchy, antique mirror across from us. He ordered a Corona then minded his own beeswax, thus, instantly becoming interesting. He was dressed in jeans and a blue, wide-ribbed turtleneck sweater, and his wavy hair whispered around his ears and neck. This was a guy with purpose, I could tell. I could feel it.

I admired someone who could communicate with nothing more than his appearance and manner—someone who had his shit together. That was exactly why we could never be a pair. I knew nothing about who I was. My shit was all over the place. Still, I was drawn to him as though we'd been destined to meet. I studied him. Maybe thirty-five years old. The cutest thirty-five-year-old ever.

This guy got points for reminding me of my eleventh grade creative writing teacher, Mr. Money. We girls had sat in class and fantasized that while reading our words, Mr. Money was falling in love with each of us.

The Mr. Money parked beside me in The Tuna made the air crackle and me want to grind my pelvis into his.

"All the parts there?" He swigged his beer.

"Hmm?" I swiveled to face him, studying his profile.

"I'd say take a picture, but that'd be wickedly clichéd." He turned fully toward me. His knees touched mine, sending sizzling energy through my body. I shivered. I was in love. I clutched my chest where just hours before, searing, crisis-induced heartburn had made its mark. Now there was a good old-fashioned swell of infatuation.

"That's a good one," I said. We lingered, staring at each other, his direct gaze making me feel as though I'd come out of a coma to see the world in a new way. I turned back to the mirror and stared at him in the reflection again. He slumped a bit, and looked into his beer in that brooding way that made men attractive and women reek of need.

I searched for something interesting to say to a guy like this. I had nothing. If I couldn't converse with a perfectly good stranger in a perfectly dingy bar, would I ever control my life? I didn't have to marry the guy. Just have a freaking conversation about nothing. Not school, not my students, not my principal. Just brainless talk. Maybe then I wouldn't feel like tossing myself off the Key Bridge.

I swiveled toward him again. "Okay. I've had a hairy day and now I'm here and you're here, too. Wearing those fantastic, understated cowboy boots. You don't look like a cowboy. And your sweater and jeans—all blend to create a look of nonchalance." I circled my finger through the air. "A man unconcerned, I might say."

His profile, as he smiled, absorbed me. I could feel him watching me in the mirror.

"Hmm." Mr. Money emptied his Corona.

"That's all you have to say?" I said.

"That's it." He swung the bottle between thumb and forefinger in a silent signal to the bartender, who brought him another one.

"Humph." I swiveled back toward the mirror and peeled the entire Coors Light label from the bottle in one piece. I must be losing my looks—the most important component of my Hot Factor. A person's H-Factor (which was sometimes influenced by the level of her Crap Quotient, though not always) rated her appearance, potential for success, attitude toward life and sense of humor in one easy-to-digest number. One's H-Factor was simply a person's market potential.

I was never the girl who drew the most attention in the room with an effervescent personality or magnificent golden locks, but I was pretty. When attempting to discern her own H-Factor, a girl had to be brutal about her shortcomings, but glory in her strengths. And like my roommate, Laura, who had an irrefutable IQ of 140, I had indisputable good-lookingness.

"Your lips. They're nice," Money said. We made eye contact in the mirror. "Boldly red," he said, "but not slathered with bullshit lip gloss. Perfect." He sipped his beer.

"That's better," I said. "Mind if I call you Money?"

"What?" He gave me the side-eye.

"Nothing. An inside joke. So you're okay with it, right?"

"Inside with *whom*?"

"With me," I said.

"Very odd."

His lips flicked into a smile that flipped my stomach.

"What do you do?" He swigged his beer.

"FBI." I shrugged.

He chuckled. The corners of his friendly eyes, with their tiny crow's feet, were not the mark of the twenty-three-year-old guys I usually spent time with. I wanted to kiss those paths of history, absorb some wisdom.

"I'm serious," I said. I feigned maturity by tensing every muscle I could.

"That's perfect," he said. "I'll go with it, Miss FBI. I'll go along with your charade, but you have to do me a favor."

"Sure. Though I really am in the FBI. Rest assured." I held up my foot. "See that hole? I took a bullet. Today, right through the leather."

He leaned over, glimpsing my boot, for two seconds. "That's a hole all right. Looks like a small caliber. Very, very small."

My face warmed. I didn't respond. An FBI agent wouldn't need to. Besides it *was* a bullet hole.

Money pulled a box of cigarettes from his pocket and emptied four joints onto the bar. "Tonight is kind of a thing for me," he said. "Don't make me smoke dope alone."

I didn't think anyone should have to do anything alone if he didn't want to. As an only child, I knew sometimes a person just didn't want to be alone.

Money shuffled the doobs around. I never smoked pot. It just wasn't me. At one point I'd gone through this whole, "I'm going to marry a politician" phase that precluded doing anything that could remotely harm my unknown, future hubby's rep. A real barrel of laughs.

Now, what if I got caught? A teacher smoking dope in a public place. What did I really have to lose? I'd been shot, for Christ's sake. Screw it. Live like I'm serious about it.

"I'm off duty," I said. "Really, what's the diff between a few beers and a few joints? Other than a pesky law or two. For your 'thing,' whatever that is. I'll do—"

He put the joint to my lips and lit the match, shutting me up.

Just a half hour later, an easy, goofy smile covered my face. I could feel its clumsiness and see its warmth in that mirror. Sort of.

We talked, we didn't talk. The silence was spectacularly warm. I still didn't even know his real name, but we connected in a way that almost made me cry. Sappy, cheesy, whatever people might say. It's exactly what happened and I'd swear on Bibles and whatever else carried that type of weight that sitting in that bar, I experienced a genuine, once-in-a-lifetime soul slip. Sitting there with him, newly acquainted, feeling like reunited friends.

And that meant it was the perfect time to leave. Mid soul slip, before things slid back to normal. Perhaps if I left at that point, a bit of him would go with me. To keep for later when real life bore down.

I called a cab. There were just so many laws I was willing to break at one time. Going home made me think of Alex. I'd forgotten about him. Proving it was time to break up. Finally, I was sure.

"Cab's here, Sweetie," the bartender said.

"Thanks." What to do about Money? I'd never see him again if I didn't act. But it wasn't like perfect would last past these few minutes, anyway.

"Give me your number, Money." I controlled my voice as it wavered.

He stood and shoved his hands in his pockets. His brown eyes shone in the darkness of the bar. He stared at me as though giving up his number was akin to sharing state secrets.

"I don't know what this *thing* of yours was," I said. "But you can't take my pot-smoking virginity and not give me your number or tell the story behind the whole, glum guy with the cool boots, alone in a dive bar on Friday night. It's simply not done."

"Give me *your* number," he said.

"No."

He looked at his feet.

What could he be thinking? He was no spring chicken. Married? No ring.

He reached across the bar to grab a cardboard coaster, wrote on it, took my hand and wrapped my fingers around it. His gaze penetrated my insides, making me shudder as he nested my hand in his. I didn't want to look away, but I had to see his hands around mine, to memorize the shape and what they said about him.

"There's something sad about you," Money said. "In a nice way." He took my other hand and I swear he started to put it to his lips before he dropped both of them and sat back down on his stool. "See ya. Careful on that case of yours. I'd hate to hear you'd been shot again."

"No need to worry, Money. Not to worry at all."

And I sauntered toward the cabbie, hoping I could do just that.

Chapter 2

On the drive home from The Tuna, the cabbie rambled about all the benefits of living in various parts of Maryland, the Washington Redskins and the traffic over the Bay Bridge. Only blocks from the house I rented with my roommates and boyfriend, a car swerved in our lane. We nearly entered some guy's home through his front window before whipping back onto the road and picking off the mailbox. I ricocheted from one side of the cab to the other.

Out of the cab, standing safely in front of my house, I slung my purse over my shoulder and patted the outside pocket where I'd hidden the coaster on which Money had written his number. I recalled the soul slip, the wholeness I'd felt.

I dug my fingers inside the pocket to nestle the coaster down deep where Alex would never see it and I could always find it. I closed my eyes against the crisp night wind that lifted my hair and cooled my hot neck. Where was it? I dug deeper into the pocket. Maybe I'd put it in the main compartment. Under the street lamp, I fell to the sidewalk, emptied my purse and sifted through lip liner, mascara, pencils, a notebook, and receipts. The coaster was gone. Gone. Gone.

Kneeling there, I ran my hands through my hair, too tired

to feel anything other than spiky pebbles under my knees and a familiar "it figures" sensation. I always lost stuff. Disorganization and I were partners in life, but losing a piece of cardboard the size of a steno pad inside of five minutes was bad, even for me.

Everything back in the purse, I stood, chuckling. Through the bay window in the wood-sided Victorian I shared with Nina, Laura, and sometimes Alex, I could see them laughing their asses off about something.

My teeth chattered. Nina and Laura were the siblings I'd never had. Our friendship was like an afghan, providing warmth, but enough space between the fibers for each of us to have our own personalities, to get some air.

Alex waved to them then moved out of my view. Laura and Nina repeatedly mimed something, falling together, laughing some more. The light in my bedroom flicked on. Alex stood in the window, took off his shirt and yanked another one back over his head. He moved out of sight. Got into bed, probably.

When I pictured Alex in my life, I wanted to cut around his body with an X-Acto knife, extricating him from the image cleanly, painlessly. But that kind of removal was far too neat for the likes of me. I'd spent the last year wanting to be in love with him again, trying to ignore that we were unsuited for each other in every way. Tonight at The Tuna, everything had changed. There was no going back. The whole soul slip deal pushed the breakup from someday to pending.

I stepped inside the door and choking laughter greeted me. Laura and Nina recounted some story about beer coming out of one guy's nose and spraying over the top of some other guy's toupee. The story wasn't all that terrific, but their laughter infected me.

They questioned me about my whereabouts, the meandering message I'd left on the machine. I waved them off, telling them I'd fill them in on everything in the morning. They were drunk enough to take my physical wellbeing as evidence I was the same person I'd been when I left for work that morning. And so they tripped off to their beds and I to mine.

I pulled on sweats and snuck into bed, barely moving the

mattress. I hung off the edge, my back to Alex, hoping he was already asleep. But it only took a minute for him to mold his body around mine. His clammy foot touched mine, making me cringe. So far, no noticeable erection, thank goodness.

It was wrong to not just break up with him. Back in my undergrad years, I thought he hadn't loved *me* enough. But as soon as I got tired of his wandering eye and cooled off toward him, he *finally* decided he was in love. By then it was too late.

He flopped his arm across my side, pulling me further into his body. His hot, boozy breath saturated the back of my neck. I held mine, waiting for Alex's trademark heavy rhythms that would guarantee he was asleep and I wouldn't have to have sex with him or be forced into avoiding it.

His hand crept up my stomach toward my breast. I shrugged it off, employing my own (fake) version of sleep breathing. I wanted to leave my body and start a new life somewhere else.

He nuzzled closer, kissing my neck in a way that felt more like licking. I stiffened then phonied up a snore.

"Mmm...Carolyn. I missed you. Here, let me see you, I missed you." He rolled me onto my back. I kept my face toward the dresser, where stacks of teaching manuals teetered on the edge. I gave a full-slumber groan.

He slurped at my cheek, my neck, my shoulder. His hand caressed my breast and then he pinched my nipple.

"Jeeze," I elbowed him away. "That hurt, Alex. Jesus, I'm asleep."

"You never complained before," he said. I could feel his face hanging over me, breathing into my ear, whistling like a hurricane.

I glanced at him then looked away again. "I'm pretty sure I never thought one caress and a nipple squeeze was a good thing."

His whiskey breath slipped into my nostrils. He rubbed up against me.

"I'm tired, Alex. I had a terrible day and I just want to sleep."

He stilled, his face hung above me. "Fine. Just don't expect me to up and have sex with you the next time you're in the mood."

I turned to him and stared at the angular bones, the strength meshed with sweetness that I knew lived beneath his skin, the combination that used to make me crumble with love and ache to have him love me back. But at that moment, examining that same face, a continent of space between us wasn't enough. Everything about him seemed wrong.

I looked away.

Alex slammed his body back on the bed. "This isn't like you, Carolyn. And if you push me too far I'll be out the door. You're not a cold person, but fuck, you're looking like one and I... Just fuck it."

I winced at every word, unwilling to engage further. Two minutes later, he was snoring. This left me relieved and sad, but at least I could breathe again. I'd like to say our relationship exploded into that mess, but it didn't. It sort of collapsed, both of us letting pieces of it fall away until we suffocated under the brokenness. At least I was suffocating.

And yet I was mired in the crap of indecision. If I couldn't love him the way I used to, why hadn't I just moved on already?

I felt bad knowing I had to break up with Alex, but it wasn't the first time I considered the fact he didn't really love me either, not in that genuine soul slip kind of way. I'd never be what he wanted in a woman. He was simply afraid of change and saw me as good enough. I frustrated him as much as I bored me. He hated that I hated cooking. He wanted me in an apron, elbow deep in cooking oil. Please. I was not that kind of girl. We were not that kind of match. He'd be relieved when we broke up.

I curled into myself and pulled the pillow over my head to block out the sound of his ragged breathing. Mentally, I went back to The Tuna, watched Money's hand slip over mine, excited by the prospect of someone new. Someone mysterious.

But the coaster. Shit. How'd I lose it? It must have flown out of my purse in the cab. If things were meant to be different, the coaster would've been tucked in my purse, waiting to be sprung into action instead of knocking around in the back of some taxi.

**

I woke at 7:00 a.m. as Alex's mucousy rasps hammered through my skull. With no chance of falling back asleep, I showered and thought about the shooting. I had to call my parents and tell them what happened. They'd want to know that I was okay. And I needed my mother. Like all daughters, I needed some reassurance that she believed in me in spite of my failures. I wanted to know that she didn't think I'd made the wrong decision in becoming a teacher. I hoped that in this one phone call she would be the mother I needed her to be.

"Oh, hey, Carolyn," my mother said over the phone. I recognized the rushed tenor. They were probably heading to breakfast at O'Reilly's. If you didn't get there by eight, you had to wait an hour for a seat. That would set off a series of unlucky events that might span weeks, at least. Don't ask.

"I know," I said. "You're running out the door, right?"

"Oh, Carolyn. Don't be snippy, please?"

"I'm being morose. Did the tone not come through?"

"Carolyn." My mother sighed.

"Mom," I said.

We were silent for nine seconds. It was my job to let her go without making her feel guilty. "All right, Mom. Call me back later. It's nothing. Unless Dad's there. Is Dad right there?"

"Nope. In the car, engine running, Madame Butterfly cranked. You know him. We'll be back in two hours. Call us then, at the normal time. Love you Caro, darling. Love you truly."

Yeah, right. I slammed the phone harder than I should have and caused a faint echo of the bell to rise from it. Was I the only person in the world who couldn't count on her mother? I adored my parents in a complicated, resentment-infused way. They thought I was all right. I know, I know, boo-hoo. Until Laura, Nina, and I started living together, I'd always felt as though I were a puzzle piece tucked inside the wrong box. With them I finally belonged.

I'd like to be able to say my frequent moodiness stemmed from a childhood of slumbering in cold gutters, draped with trash bags, head pillowed on used diapers. But I'd managed to nurture such moods while in the embrace of a whole, middle-class family with parents who taught music and read compulsively.

I knew I shouldn't complain. My parents were one of eleven couples in America who had been in love the entire length and depth of their relationship. Love like that is insane and almost unattainable but there it was with my very own parents. I was sure if I had siblings, I would have appreciated their relationship more. If I'd had siblings, I wouldn't have always felt like an outsider in my own family.

My father was more affectionate than my mom, more interested in me, and more loving, when I really got down to it. He'd always filled in the gaps for her and when she could and was in the mood, she'd be warm, too. It was as though from time to time she awoke and realized I might need her to confide in, to go to for help, to have fun with. She seemed to struggle or wasn't interested in offering any of the stuff other mothers seemed to do naturally with their daughters. I should have been used to it and satisfied with all my father did to bridge our gap, but I still wanted my mom's approval over his.

Teaching—making a substantial difference in the world—was supposed to be the perfect thing to impress my parents. And teaching in a school where twelve out of twenty-four teachers were replaced each year would make my victory actually seem victorious. I'd do something good for the world (something I'd wanted to do since I was seven) and end up providing my parents with a true, important story. I would *be* the character they'd want to read about. Except things didn't seem headed in the direction of me becoming an Educational Power Broker anymore. And that pretty much sucked.

**

Nina, Laura and I snuck out of the house before Alex awoke. By 8:45 Saturday morning we were cocooned in a booth at the Silver Diner. We perched next to the beverage station, close enough that we could serve ourselves when running low on the thermonuclear java that would see us past hangovers and into a day of lesson planning.

The girls bombarded me with questions about the gun, my foot, Klein's latest abuses and where the hell I'd been all night. Saying I'd spent the evening at The Tuna put an end to that line of questioning. They'd never suspect, for many reasons, that I'd met someone interesting there.

"LeAndre's loonier than a stuck pig. But a *gun*?" Laura drawled, drawing the word gun into twenty-three Southern syllables.

"Two guns," I said, "though I only saw one. A BB-gun and some other thingy the cops said was a convertible. You can change it from shooting toy blanks to real bullets. Don't ask me how that's possible."

"LeAndre needs a good ass-whooping." Nina smacked her hands together. "When he comes off suspension, I'll accidentally pelt him with the dodge ball a few times. Just for you, my sister."

"Sweet child of Mary," I said. "You can't just pelt kids with fucking balls."

"F-word." Nina held her hand up. I pushed it down. She used every other swear word without hesitation, like the girl who'll have every sexual experience known to man except traditional intercourse and call herself a virgin.

"The Lord—" Nina said.

"Bag the Lord stuff. For the love of God," I said. My hangover was gnawing away at my nice-girlness.

Nina looked at me, eyebrows raised. She dug her fingers into her short, tight curls and twirled a section of it around her forefinger. I knew she was silently saying *my* prayers wouldn't have a shot in hell of being answered. Laura, a full-blooded virgin, nodded. She always agreed with anyone who suggested taking the pristine, ladylike path in life.

Laura and I went to college together and then earned our Master of Arts in Teaching degrees there, but we became especially close once we realized we'd have to move to an unfamiliar state to get teaching jobs.

In Pittsburgh there were no jobs to get. The jobs there were too comfortable for most teachers to retire and they certainly didn't quit. But, the Maryland/D.C. border was fairly bursting with positions.

Laura and I had met Nina at our new teacher workshops. Twenty-four years old, she exemplified the modern teacher: strong, knowledgeable, and confident. Trouble with her was she didn't really deserve all that confidence. She didn't know a whole lot about anything other than sports.

Oh, she'd kick my ass for saying that, but still. Sometimes the truth hurts. Nina talked with administrators as easily as friends, and never seemed unnerved or flummoxed by the odd situations at our school. It was as though she'd already taught for twenty years but still actually liked it. Even with all those admirable attributes, she sometimes wore an abrasive arrogance that could put off new friends. Me? I appreciated it most of the time.

"You need to toughen up." Nina pointed her fork at me. "You're the boss of those kids." She broke into a broad smile. Not one blemish or laugh line marred her beautiful, cocoa skin. She could pass for a high school kid if she needed to.

"You mean," I said, "I should pelt my kids with dodge balls? Maybe chuck a stapler or pair of scissors at them? I can't get away with showing them I'm the boss like *some* people can."

"Like the music and physical education teachers? I overheard you say that one time." Nina said.

My head swam with fatigue and Coors Light. And thoughts of Money. But I couldn't share him just yet. Ever really, because there was nothing to share. Had he really been there? Nina's accusatory gaze pushed me further into our script.

"Honestly? Yes. You, the gym teacher, can get away with a lot more than a classroom teacher. The kids *love* gym. Let me see you teach them reading *once* and we'll see who has trouble keeping a lid on things."

"*Physical education* teacher." Nina squinted at me.

"Same thing," I said.

"No it's not," Nina said. "But you have to—"

"Nina," I hissed. "A kid BB'd up my foot and Klein yelled at me for six hours. Suffice it to say my Crap Quotient's high and anxiety-inducing." My hands shook as I sipped coffee, then slammed the cup back onto the saucer.

"Your H-Factor ain't setting the world on fire either." Nina leaned forward.

"Really? You think so?"

"*Nina*," Laura said. "Be like the old lady who fell out of the wagon." Laura's back straightened and her accent thickened. She was not a fan of a good argument between great friends.

Nina got up to get the coffee carafe. She shook her butt as she traipsed away. She looked back over her shoulder. "You just need to get to know the kids and their culture a little bit more. Read an article or two on race."

I nodded. If only there was time to read such things. "But we have white kids, too." I shook a sugar packet. Laura took it from me and put it back in the jar. I shrugged. "Katya's white. Her mother is a wreck and her dad's in jail. I know race is important, but it's not race that keeps my kids from reading. Clearly it's not that. I think they would have mentioned that in our coursework, if it were the case."

Laura rubbed my back. "Everything's going to be fine. You're a great teacher."

"Yeah, I don't know. It's hard to be good when on top of teaching, you have to run some sort of combination psychiatric ward-slash-parole office-slash-jail and social work operation."

"You worry too much, is all," Laura said. "Now let's talk about household chores…"

I shook my head. Laura needed people to tell how to do stuff like study, clean, straighten out their lives. And sometimes it suited me to be that person—especially at times like this.

For hours we sat and talked. I was grateful to no longer be talking about job woes. We bickered back and forth and finally, forever forward, Nina and I shot down her weekly chores idea. There was a lot of other nothing discussed. These moments lifted the dread brought on by all the ways I was unsure of life.

I tried to remember exactly when our friendship had locked into place like a steering wheel on a car. It didn't matter when it had happened because the friendship had formed and in it, I felt fitted.

Chapter 3

Monday after the shooting I arrived back at school at 6:30 a.m. I walked from the parking lot to the front doors. The original, elegant entrance of the former high school, consisting of a double stone staircase, offered a feeling of seriousness and importance. The halls and bathrooms were immaculately clean for a place over a hundred years old. A new addition that housed the office and primary classrooms didn't have the same character, but it had air conditioning. Enough said.

I had plenty of time to get my room in order before meeting with Klein. But once in my room, I stood in the center of it, where Cedrick and LeAndre had tussled, and I couldn't decide where to start cleaning first.

The floors were actually already clean from the night janitor's work. But papers littered the students' desktops and my desk, too. Mine also boasted an array of other items: staplers, notebooks, manuals, binders, dirty coffee cups. It was more a minefield than a useful workspace. There was definitely a disconnect between what I'd wanted the room to look like and what I'd achieved.

My happy bulletin board sayings, designed to motivate students, mocked me. *Never Say Never* and *Let's Get into the Swim of*

Things took on new meaning as my imminent drowning drew closer each day. My combination class of eighteen sixth graders and eighteen fifth graders had taught me I wasn't even treading water and that my inadequacies were boundless.

I decided the best way to approach the room was to leave it and get the meeting with Klein off the books. I walked down the hallway with the sound of my shoes reverberating off the marble floor and lockers. The echo was isolating but not as heavy as the afterschool echo that always seemed to smack of defeat.

Like the plumbing that meandered through one of the oldest schools in the county, my mind was a mass of confusion. I'd been shot in the foot in my own classroom. Had that really happened? That was not what I'd signed up for.

In the stairwell leading to the first floor, I started to limp a bit. My toe burned with the heat of the BB as though the shooting had happened right then. I shuddered and rubbed my arms. Probably post-traumatic stress disorder.

Muffled voices carried from below, surprising me. They came from the storage area under the steps. I almost kept walking. What I didn't see didn't really happen, right? I was beginning to consider that a code of conduct. It was too early for students to be in the building, so who gave a damn who was clowning around in the closet?

"Hey," I said once I reached the bottom.

I reached for the doorknob. The door swung fully open and Fionna, the music teacher, flew out.

"Oh," I said. "Fionna. What're you doing? What's that smoke?"

Fionna giggled like a four-year-old being tickled. Her eyes, circled with smudged eyeliner, looked unfocused. She giggled again. "I'm looking for the violins," she said then shut the door behind her. "That's dust in there, that's all. No one's been in there for centuries."

I was not opposed to exaggeration, but that was nuts—I could smell cigarettes. Fionna was a gifted, crazy person. Rumor had it she'd once played with the Boston Pops. I didn't know if that was true, but I'd heard her play and she was brilliant.

She giggled again and wrapped her arms around her chest. Was she braless? I looked her over, struggling to make sense of what she was wearing. Pajamas. A grown woman, educator of the country's youth, had come to school in her jammies for at least the thirteenth time. She normally slipped into school just before the kids entered her room, but here she was, chipper and early.

I wanted to see what she was up to in the closet. I was about to limp past her to investigate when the intercom blasted on. Bobby Jo's voice summoned me to the principal's office as though I was some sort of servant girl.

"I'll be back," I said.

"I'll be waiting," Fionna said.

Of course she wouldn't be waiting. But weird as she was, Fionna was probably harmless. It annoyed me that she got some sort of pass from Klein, but like Nina who taught gym, the music teacher didn't have the responsibility of turning out kids who could read the labels on their future heart medications.

I didn't think it was completely fair, but wasn't that the way life went sometimes?

**

I drew a deep breath and entered Klein's office. He wasn't there yet. Hot sun bore through the bank of windows lining the back of the office. It electrified the brilliant yellow walls, daring me not to be cheerful.

Hip-high, laminate-topped credenzas hugged every inch of wall space. A principal's office like any other. Except it was neater. Obsessively so. And disturbing. He kept a picture of himself on his desk. I think he'd actually folded an eight by ten photo in half, making whomever was in it with him disappear.

The credenza shelves housed towers of books, binders arranged by color and perfectly squared off piles of paper. That part creeped me out. Even with a breeze blowing through the windows on this mid-October morning, not one page in one stack fluttered. They knew better than to move. I should have known better than to say yes when I'd been interviewed in this very office three months earlier. But Klein had tricked me. He'd tricked us all.

Waiting for him, I realized I didn't have the answer he wanted—how it happened that a gun had turned up in my classroom. He would want to know what I'd done to screw up, what I'd done to encourage the gun incident to happen. Well, *nothing* was the answer to that, but that wasn't a response Klein would accept.

I looked at my ugly loafers and thought of the fabulous leather boots I could no longer wear. One of them bore a screaming hole through the top like a tiny anguished mouth. One hundred twenty buckaroonies out of my first paycheck. Shredded in an instant.

I traced Klein's nameplate on his desk. He'd tried to get us to call him Timothy. At first I thought it was a nice gesture, but I couldn't bring myself to do it. I had too much respect for his position. Then I got to know the prick and realized he wanted us to use his first name as a means of manipulation.

A car door slammed outside the windows. I straightened to look. There was Klein, pulling a load of crap from the back of his Mercedes. I could see his mouth moving. He was talking to someone. Who would he have in his car? I hunkered down and crept to the window. I spread two stacks of paper apart and peered over the windowsill.

A small woman with flaming red hair, stooped posture and a cane emerged. Or, she tried to emerge from the car, rocking back and forth, hoping to thrust herself out. Klein raised his voice. "Mom, Mom, don't. Let me help…here."

He positioned his forearms under her armpits and smoothly lifted her up and out of the car. He kissed her on the cheek, smoothed her hair back and walked her out of my sight line.

"The boss'll be in as soon as he gets his mother on the Metro."

I snapped around. Heat flushed my cheeks at being caught spying.

Bobby Jo smirked. "Didn't think he was human, did you?"

"That's not true." I didn't have any way to cover up my

espionage. Own it, baby, I thought.

Bobby Jo pursed her lips and waved a hand at me. She left the office, shaking her head. I sat back down.

Klein, human? That was a little generous. Anyone could be nice to his mother. Still, seeing him like that had softened me. His gestures had been slow and nurturing. They'd revealed no signs of his natural state of evil. Maybe I had been wrong about him. Whatever he had against me, he couldn't outright despise me the way I suspected. Maybe I was prejudiced against power. Who would have thought I was a bossist?

A surge of hope startled me. Maybe Klein was on my side, after all. I cheered at the thought of the encouraging words he'd offer. Maybe he'd squeeze me on the shoulder to let me know we were a team. Working together.

Klein's shuffling feet came down the hall. I cleared my throat. He came in and swept right by me, leaving the stench of his heavy cologne behind, turning my empty stomach. He stopped between his desk and the counter across from it—where I had been crouched, watching him. With his back to me, he re-positioned the stacks I'd shifted. I flinched. Had he seen me?

His back muscles contracted under his tight button down shirt of the finest poly-something blend. He was pole thin, so why was his shirt too small? I couldn't fathom. He sighed and turned. His close-set, coffee-hued, rat-like eyes were relentless in their gaze.

"So you've got how many nicks in your foot?" he said.

"One hole in the shoe. The wounds were minimal, but still it hurt. I mean I *was* bleeding."

Klein sat. His chair squeaked as he shifted his weight and wove his fingers together. Oh, boy. Whatever softer side he possessed, he wasn't going to share it with me, so it was time to be a grownup, take care of myself. I could talk to this man as a colleague. But I'd tried that. And that's what had gotten me into this mess with him—why he'd made it his first, fifth, and final order of business to harass me. One, thoughtful, collegial question in a staff meeting was all it had taken to unleash his hate for me.

I swallowed the ire rising in my throat. I could hide it. I would not let him know he got to me.

"This could have been a real situation." He drilled his finger into the desk.

I nodded.

"Luckily it was only a BB-gun," he said. "That thing looked like a real gun. And the other, the one that could be converted into a real gun in no time—Those jobbies get kids shot by cops all the time."

I blew out air. "I know," I said.

"This can't happen again." He slumped slightly.

"Yes."

Klein snapped open a notebook and put his finger on the page. "Thirty-three out of thirty-six kids said they knew LeAndre had guns. They said he'd shown them to some kids in the cloakroom in the morning. *Your* cloakroom. LeAndre is troubled, but you have to be more alert. You need to know your kids better, but not in any sort of hippy, friend type of way."

Klein kept talking, but I couldn't hear. All I could do was notice my heart folding in on itself while his words penetrated my brain. It was as though the two organs were connected.

My kids knew? They knew for half the day? Klein had to be wrong.

"Jenkins. You getting all this?"

I nodded. He fondled a set of index cards.

"Will LeAndre be expelled? He needs an alternative setting, special attention," I said.

"He'll get counseling here at school after he serves a week suspension. He's not as troubled as you've said. He behaves poorly because little is expected of him in terms of good behavior at home or in your classroom."

"He's absolutely abnormal, Mr. Klein. I'm not being mean. I really like LeAndre, despite his problems, but there're two people living inside his skin. There's something *wrong* with him. And he knows it himself. He's suffering as much as anyone he might put in danger. It's downright chilling to see him struggle with whatever is going on inside him."

"No one's in danger."

I looked at my hands. What an ass.

"Jenkins." Klein leaned over his crossed arms on the desk. "You said this was your dream to work here, with kids who needed you, whom you could open up the world for, show them their strengths. But sometimes, people just take the wrong path. Maybe this isn't the right fit." His voice trailed off.

The damn puzzle piece thing again. No. I didn't have to live my whole life not fitting in. I would carve another edge into my puzzle piece and make it fit. I loved those kids. They didn't suit this place anymore than I did and I didn't see him kicking any of them out.

"You're wrong," I said.

He knocked on his desk. "Well, then. I've come up with a plan. Number one. I'm starting observations in November. You're first. I want the following elements to be included in your lesson."

He tossed a single sheet of lined yellow paper my way. It floated over the desk. I stood to retrieve it. My gaze sped down the laundry list.

"You want to see critical thinking," I said, "math with manipulatives, reading, writing, science, and social studies, all embedded in a cooperative learning framework during *one* thirty minute lesson?" Should I bring my tap shoes, too?

"And spelling. Be sure to have your plan book out on the desk. I'll examine that, as well."

A section of Klein's bangs fell over his right eye as he wiggled into his burgundy, polyester blend suit coat. If he hadn't been making my life so freaking miserable, I'd laugh at him. A joke. He must be deeply insecure. Possibly, his peers had abused him as a child. Some terrible occurrence had to have been the seed from which he'd grown into a professional asshole.

I attempted to feel sorry for Klein, tried to think about him outside with his mother, about him gently carrying LeAndre from the room the other day. I wanted to like the guy, to see his goodness.

And I dug deep inside my imagination and tried to form a

more layered vision of Klein, one that allowed me to admire and respect him. Well, I tried, that I did.

**

Klein left the office without dismissing me, just sauntered out. I toyed with the idea of investigating who was in the other side of the folded picture or stealing a closer look at his paper stacks. Something had to be hidden behind them, right? But somehow I knew he'd pop back in and tackle me onto the floor if I made that kind of move.

Finally I dismissed myself and checked to see if Laura was in her room. She was, but meeting with her first grade partner, Suzy. So I waved and went back toward my room.

I thought about Klein's assertion that Lincoln wasn't the "right fit" for me. I stopped on the steps. My memory reached back to first grade—my mother, sitting with my teacher, whispering while I played at the next table. They didn't think I heard. "She's just having trouble fitting in, Mrs. Jenkins. We think you should try another place."

Oh, my God, I got kicked out of school for being unpopular. From that point on, all my parents did was celebrate everything about me that was different from everyone else.

My parents didn't take the teacher's recommendation. They just tried to make me fit into the original school, with all my differences, my wonderful differences: my quiet nature, my inappropriate laughing jags, and my preference for adults over kids. But the adults in Pittsburgh, Pennsylvania preferred football players to daydreaming girls who got tongue-tied when asked to solve a simple math problem.

My God, I hated school as a kid. So what was I doing teaching? The answer to that one was suddenly easy: reinventing the classroom experience so no one would ever feel like I had. And though I questioned whether I would succeed, I knew I had to continue to try no matter what people like Klein might suggest.

Chapter 4

The six rows of six desks were straight, waiting for the children who would sit at them. I pulled out my lesson plan book and wrote the daily objectives as prescribed by Klein on the board. As I wrote, I considered what the class's mood would be. I wasn't sure what to expect in terms of the kids' behavior and attitudes after the shooting.

Turned out, they just pretended it never happened. Other than them saying they weren't surprised LeAndre had brought the gun to school and then used it, they didn't say anything. Weren't they scared? Apparently, not anymore.

My classroom informant, Marvin, said they'd worry about being frightened when LeAndre returned to school, but while he wasn't there, they'd just forget about what happened. Well, okay, if you can do that, fine. Fine.

I was still upset that no one told me about the gun beforehand, that they didn't trust me. But there was no time for discussions like that. I had six reading groups plus language arts to teach before lunch.

I made sure the thirty kids who wouldn't be in the first small group had their seatwork and understood what to do with it. Back with the small group, seated at the table, I turned to the page that would walk me through this particular lesson.

Tanesha, Terri, Katya, Crystal, and Evette weren't seated yet, but hovering around me, their hot breath searing my scalp as though they were searching for something on top of my head. For people who disliked me so much, they sure spent a lot of time invading my personal space.

I should've hung a white flag from one of the floor-to-ceiling windows, burrowed under my desk and covered myself with incomplete math worksheets while waiting for someone—I didn't know who—to rescue me, to put these kids and me out of our misery.

Yes, surrender seemed a fantastic option. But there in my chair, teacher's manual in my lap, lesson plan and lofty dreams for my kids in my head, I decided I would not give up. I wasn't that smart but I wasn't that weak either. I'd teach these kids something even if the process stole my breath and shriveled the skin around my bones.

"You need style, Ms. Jenkins." Tanesha flipped the ends of my hair.

"What I need is for you all to sit down so we can do this lesson. We're down to twenty minutes," I said.

Terri *tsked* as though I had stomped on her dog. She looked down at me, asserting power that wasn't supposed to be hers. I resisted the urge to push her into her chair. Her braids jingled and clicked, reminding me that she wasted at least four hours each night weaving intricate patterns into her hair. She should have been doing something constructive, like her homework.

I pushed my shoulders down and straightened my spine, fighting to expose my teacher persona. It was in me somewhere. None of my grad school professors had mentioned what to do when students conducted critiques of their teacher's hairstyle and fashion sense rather than read devoid-of-context stories in their readers. And that handy, five-pound teacher's manual in my lap? Useless.

"Okay Tanesha. Where is Misty standing in the story?" Jumping into the lesson would force them to sit. Worked once, anyway.

Shoulder shrug. Tanesha's.

I wanted to shrug back.

We were losing time—invaluable, would-never-get-it-back instructional time. Beads of sweat sprung from the pores at my hairline, causing me to scratch my head. I held my breath to give Tanesha the prescribed wait time students supposedly needed to form coherent thoughts. Ten seconds was recommended. Grueling pause. Clenched teeth. Unbeknownst to the professors of the world, wait time in real classrooms was wasted time.

My circle of girls "reflected" while I searched the room for potential trouble brewing with the other kids. They were in charge of themselves because some genius had decided small group instruction was the optimal way to teach. Maybe if you had eleven kids in a class, but with thirty-six split between two grade levels and six reading groups? That meant for most of the morning, the kids were on their own doing busy work because anything meaningful was too hard for them to do alone.

Kenneth wandered the room mumbling about a conspiracy to hide his reading folder. And since he actually used the four-syllable word 'conspiracy' in his ramblings, I let it pass. Meanwhile, Laronda brushed her hair while reading. Clayton paced in circles, in one opening of the cloakroom and out the other, wearing a path into the already worn floor. But everyone else read or slept behind their books. Things were going well. At least it was quiet. Except inside me. My esophagus bubbled, and heartburn screamed.

"Girls?" I cleared my throat and poked at my manual. "Where's Misty standing in the story?"

Tanesha's head tipped forward, jaw lax. "Misty at the corner. Any old chili pepper can see that." She finally slammed into her seat. The other four girls followed suit, exasperated with the idiot teacher who sat in front of them.

I stifled amusement at Tanesha's word choice. It had been a stupid question, yes. But it was in the freaking manual. Klein had ordered us teachers to follow the manual at all costs. Sinewy Evette raised her slim hand. She had told me the first day of school that she hated her velvety, dark skin and the "boring, bunned hair style" her mother made her wear. She had no idea she was the definition of beauty come to life. Thank you for volunteering, Evette—my go-to girl, enemy of peer pressure, my pre-adolescent hero.

"Umm. Ms. Jenkins. You ain't never gonna get yo-self a man with *that* style." Evette poked a long finger at me and looked away. The others snickered. Well, damn it. The final girl had crossed over to the bad side.

I have style, ladies. And I have a man. Not that I want him.

"And yo hair. *Umm, umm, umm.*" Blond-haired, blue-eyed Katya—a lanky, white mirror image of Evette who was equally unaware of her shocking beauty—cleared her throat. Dirty blond-haired Crystal scolded me with her expression. Terri sucked her tongue until it clicked with disdain.

I did a quick check of the rest of my students and leaned in toward the girls.

"Girls, like I've said before, if you're going to toss out an insult, hurl it in book language as well as neighborhood language. Remember I demonstrated Pittsburghese and you did street and then we did book language? I need to hear book language during groups. I need to hear proper English, otherwise none of this matters. Where Misty is standing in the story doesn't matter at all."

"You should work a little harder with your clothes," Terri said. "And that hair. Here." She freed the hair I had pushed behind my ear. It settled in front of my right eye. Freaking wait time.

Terri was exceptionally smart. But being pretty meant more to her than intelligence. In the way Evette and Katya were not cognizant of their beauty, Terri fully understood her attractiveness and what it might deliver in life. And boys. Oh, she was interested in the boys.

She leaned toward me. "Yo hair's triflin.' You need to find a style that says, wow. *That all we sa-yin.* That is all we are saying." Terri bobbed her head, her beads clicking, a percussion symphony as she over-enunciated the 'ing' in 'saying.'

I smoothed the dangling section of my bob back behind my

ear. "Well. Yes, that was certainly book language. There at the end. Good."

"Sure." She nodded, finally settling in.

I blew out air and poked at the manual again. It read, *Look at students. Ask the following question.* So I did. As if I wouldn't.

"What is Misty holding?"

The girls fell over the books like rag dolls, exhausted by the plain, stupid question. Could I really blame them?

And so the morning went. Painful for all of us. In different ways, yes, but we shared the same agony. That much was true.

Chapter 5

The week flew by uneventfully, meaning I suffered for the art of teaching only mentally and emotionally. There had been no shootings or weaponry stowed in my cloakroom and there'd been only the occasional wrestling match and pulling of hair.

I'd begun to use the thought of Money, our time at the bar, as salve for the school day. When I wasn't using beer—okay, *while* using beer—I recounted every word we said and found my down-in-the-dumps ego soared a little higher. I plotted ways I could track him down, including heading back to The Tuna to interrogate the bartenders who might remember him.

I was determined to break up with Alex that Friday afternoon, but when I got home from school, there was a note from him saying he and his friend Rocco had gone to meet some friends in D.C. They'd be gone all night. Since the intention to break up had been there, I viewed myself as having made progress.

I cooked up a special surprise for Laura's birthday. I'd invited her friend from home, Paul, the guy she never stopped squawking about when she got tipsy, to go out with us. He lived in Virginia and was thrilled to help us celebrate. The other part of the evening was for me. The festivities would take place at

The Tuna. Oh, well, Laura would have to take the good with the bad and all that. I couldn't be the only one who had to learn that lesson.

"Why don't you wipe that silly grin off your face, Carolyn," Laura said. "Spill the surprise right now."

I shook my head and chomped on a pretzel. Leggy, six-foot Laura folded her body onto the couch next to me while Nina cracked open some beers. Laura weighed the same one hundred and eight pounds as me, though she was five inches taller. She had gorgeous, wide set denim-blue eyes and long, poker straight black hair.

Her H-Factor was a ten out of ten as far as she was concerned. To me, she was an eight out of ten. I docked her points for the Southern crap. Not that I'm prejudiced or anything. But I couldn't always stomach the belle bit and knew her thick Southern charm often hid her real thoughts and feelings. No one was that nice or proper.

"Well," Laura said as I swigged my beer, "if we have to sit here waiting for my surprise to arrive, then I'll just move onto *my* plan to bring some order to our happy little domicile."

This took a little of the fizz out of my buzz. Laura's plans always meant I had to change something about myself.

Laura stretched her legs, then tucked them up to her chest. Her height was definitely the first thing people noticed about her. Then her graceful, classic looks. With Nina, it was probably her sculpted cheekbones and strong jaw first. Then her scathing diatribes, which sometimes sent people running before they learned about her sincere, generous nature. People often assigned her an H-Factor of six out of ten due to her abrasiveness. I scored her higher.

I sipped my beer.

"Honey." Laura turned to me. "I've been aiming to have this talk with you for weeks." She took a sip of her whiskey. White Lightning, she called it.

"Talk?" I chugged half my beer. Laura's talks sometimes resulted in feeling like she was scraping my brain with a wire brush, but I loved Laura and didn't want to spoil her happy birthday. I would be quiet and listen. I sipped my Coors Light and swallowed hard.

"I constructed something," Laura said. She pulled a large piece of paper from her school bag. It was actually four pieces of paper that had been taped together to make one big chart. She held it up. "On here, I have names and a corresponding chore. Including the boyfriend. And over here, I have dinner mapped out. Who is cooking which night and some suggestions for what to make."

She scrutinized it for God only knew what. It was kind of nice she'd waited two whole months before taking action.

She conveyed such confidence. Apparently, she'd been one of those kids who was always treated as though she were five years older. People paid attention to her because she was tall and organized. And okay, she'd been more mature at sixteen than I was at twenty-two. One drunken night in college she'd said, *Caro, you're cuter than the most charmin' two-year-old I ever did see.* Only in the sober light of Sunday did I realize she sort of thought I was an idiot.

I touched the chart. "When do you find the time for this kind of crap?"

She recoiled.

"Not crap," I said. "Stuff. I can barely get my lesson plans done on time and you manage to finish all your work at school and construct this kind of life-map thingy. I mean. You're just so... you know."

So much like someone's mother. Which was good for me in a lot of ways. I wanted someone to keep me going in somewhat the right direction, but I didn't want assignments to complete. Not after such trying days at Lincoln. Maybe if I were a sales associate at Ann Taylor then yes, that might work.

I almost said I didn't want any part of her plan. She could have taken it. Though she cried more than a person ought to, she had a toughness that undergirded her weepy nature. In grad school, she was one of those annoying people who managed to arrive at her internship every morning with stellar lessons and a smile on her face. Upbeat even after having been up all night doing her grad-school homework. In our tutorial, Laura would always raise her hand at the last second of class to tell a story, ask a question, offer six points that illustrated how her experience was going so freaking great. A collective groan would permeate the room. Classmates plotted her murder. She knew it. She didn't care. She had something to say and we often learned from her.

"I can't do this," I said. "On this timeline, anyway. And I can't cook. I can't think about that right now." I'd be breaking up with Alex tonight or tomorrow. I resisted the urge to dig a pen from my purse and scratch Alex's name from the chart.

She grimaced. "Well, I'm as busy as a stump-tailed cow in fly-time, too."

What the hell did she just say?

"Maybe," I said, "if you'd forgo the graphic organizers for all the days of our lives, you'd have more time to clean if that's what's important to you." I blew out a laugh, loving that I slipped "Days of Our Lives," into my sentence, thinking she might find it cute, too.

Laura narrowed her eyes. "I end up doing everything while you guys plant yourselves on the couch watching 90210 and Mentrose Place—"

"Melrose Place," I said.

Laura sighed and hunched her whole body. "Sometimes you're meaner than a pack of rabid raccoons." Tears welled in her eyes. She looked even prettier.

That Southern stuff must have been part of her secret to success in the classroom. I didn't have a shtick. Laura wiped a tear and I couldn't have felt worse. I'd never made her cry before.

"I'm sorry, Laura. You know—"

"Your bitty bit H-Factor, *sans* personality, *sans* refreshed complexion is about two out of ten." With that, she slammed her drink onto the table and stalked toward the bathroom.

She was making fun of my use of the word "sans." Uncalled for, considering I hadn't used it much lately.

Crap Quotient: off-the-charts.

**

I was good for three beers by the time Paul arrived. At the sight of him, Laura began to swoon. She glistened. Pheromones and lust seeped from her skin like never before. It was like seeing Mother Nature at work, saying, for the love of Mary, Laura, get some sex on, sister. You're way too old to have never been touched.

While it charmed me to watch Laura in action, I was still a little pissed. The judgmental tone of her H-Factor comment spoiled the spirit of the assessment and so I wouldn't re-engage just yet. I wasn't normally a grudge holder, but I wasn't a carpet remnant either.

Laura left Paul to talk with Nina and sat back with me.

"Carolyn?" She held up a beer. I nodded. We usually just ignored each other until any bad feelings absorbed into the atmosphere. I wasn't opposed to facing problems head on, but Laura was. She thought discussing trouble would bring her more. She twisted off the bottle cap and handed me the beer.

This was her apology—her invitation to forget our snipey exchange. And that was fine. I didn't like sappy emotional operations that involved hugging, touching, and tears. And I needed Laura, so this was good enough for me. Who gave a damn what she thought about my H-Factor?

She smiled at me and clinked my beer with her whiskey tumbler. Paul excused himself to use the bathroom.

"Hey." Nina wiggled her butt in between Laura and me. "While Paul's using the John, spill it, sister, before your judgment is clouded by your sexual repression. What's Paul's H-Factor?"

"He's charming. Sweet as good butter—"

"Cut to the number." Nina popped a cheese puff into her mouth.

"Looks: eight," Laura said.

"Eight?" We screeched back.

"Dylan on 90210 is an eight," I said.

"Not in my book," Nina said.

"You can't be trusted to say." I bumped her shoulder with mine and felt light and happy in my friend cocoon, any holes plugged up tight.

"Hey y'all," Laura said. "It's *my* job to decide."

We nodded in agreement.

"Looks: eight. Personality: ten. Academics: ten. So his average score is? H-Factor: A smokin' *nine*."

"You're off the freaking deep end of love if you think he's a nine." I looked into my beer, wishing the object of my own obsession was here. Damn it. I'd lost Money like I lost magazines on the Metro.

"I'm not in love with Paul. We're just friends," Laura smoldered with God knew what—maybe a soul slip? No, soul slips were quiet murmurs of greatness, not this big flashy display of happiness. Nina and I smirked at one another with the knowledge that Laura was deeply infatuated.

We—Paul, Laura, Nina and I—stood outside our house waiting for a cab to take our drunk asses to The Tuna. Nina and Paul were immersed in a discussion of what was better: lacrosse or soccer. I daydreamed about seeing Money again.

Laura ran her hands down my arms then squeezed my fingers. "I know why you want to go to The Tuna. You met someone." She released me and stepped back as though my coat had caught on fire. I raised my eyebrows.

"You're softer," she said. "Sweeter. That's why I agreed to go to that rat hole Tuna on this very special birthday." Laura smiled. Boy, Paul had warmed her up good. At first I figured it was just her own hot swell of lust she was feeling, but then I thought about Money again, the lines that appeared at his eyes when he smiled. Being lost in thoughts of him might have made me appear more good-natured than usual.

"I did meet someone," I said. "But nothing happened. I took his number, but I'm not even going to call him. Well, I lost the number, actually. And knowing him for one night was enough. No use tempting fate."

"You took his number and you lost it. Hence the trip to The Tuna."

"Hence." I shrugged.

"Well, shut my mouth. I knew it." Laura stared at me as though I'd grown a second nose. In a way, I guess I had.

Chapter 6

Scrambling out of the cab, I reminded myself that showing up at The Tuna was futile. Money was gone, like a sliver of reality, lost in a parallel world. Even still, the place had grown on me. The low-key atmosphere would be a nice change for everyone.

"Isn't this a mafia hangout?" Laura scrunched up her face.

"Mafia?" I said. "The last time I was here...wait just a minute. There *were* a few lumpy looking types. I don't know. There's no mafia in Laurel, Maryland," I said. I held the door open for everyone.

"Mafia's everywhere, Carolyn," Nina said.

I scanned the bar for Money. No sign of him. Disappointment. Where'd it come from? Did I really believe he'd been showing up here every weekend since we met? Looking for me?

Laura and I played pool while Paul and Nina commiserated at the nearby jukebox. Laura grew up with a pool table in her rumpus room and she was good. With the right amount of alcohol, I could hold my own. Like that moment, right then.

Two cute guys watched us and asked in for the next game. No harm in that. We introduced ourselves. Tonight, Laura was the FBI agent. I was a stripper.

"Her name's Sugar!" Nina bellowed through her cupped hands.

Nina slipped a coin in the jukebox and the heavy opening notes of *Pour Some Sugar on Me* by Def Leppard pounded. Apparently, it was my signature song. Laura ran her hand down my body like I was a refrigerator up for bidding on *Price is Right*.

"Don't be fooled by her school teacher, white-bread looks, fellas," Laura said. Her speech was slurred with booze, her Southern drawl souped up. "She's a stripper through and through. Look at her little bitty body. Runs marathons and dances all night. Any wonder our sweet Sugar looks like this?"

I tried to keep from laughing at Laura. She was finally relaxing and releasing some of her pent up energy. I balanced my butt on the side of the pool table and took a shot behind my back while everyone chanted, "Sugar, Sugar," to the beat of "my" song. I smiled as the cue ball hit the number three red and it disappeared into the pocket. There was nothing better than drinking beers with friends you knew so well, you could make up lies about them without even clearing them first.

Nine pool and two whiskey shots later, the game was over, and Laura and I were fifty bucks richer. Paul ran into three fraternity brothers from Penn and was yapping with them— never peeling his gaze from Laura, mind you—giving Laura and I the chance to talk. We clinked our beers at the bar and settled in.

"How are you doing it, Laur?"

"What?"

"Managing at school," I said.

"Well," she stretched the word. "First, I have Suzy. The only thing separating us is that accordion wall. We might not be friends outside of school, but we're supportive of each other. You have those moon-goofy partners constantly giving you the short end of a smelly stick."

"Those two supposed grade level partners of mine are irritated that I draw breath," I agreed, feeling comforted. "All they do is watch me stumble and fall. Snickering. I wouldn't mind if I physically fell and they laughed. That's funny, but finding humor in my inability to teach kids? *That* is a travesty. I'm playing with the lives of living, breathing people who need skills I'm supposed to teach and I have no idea how to do it."

Laura lifted her chin and settled into advice-giving mode. "Maybe consider taking your focus off of work. You're like a dog with a bone. Take up cooking. I know you want to save the world. But that's impossible. We could take some sewing classes, some cooking classes. I know you met some guy, but really, isn't Alex for you? I've never heard you say word one about him not being the one. There's a domestic side of you just bursting to get out."

I squinted at Laura. There was no domestic anything inside me. "Alex? We're not right. I kept my doubts inside. Until I was sure. The encounter with the guy I met here confirmed it. Alex and I are *not* meant to be." I sighed. Laura had done nothing to answer my school question. But really, that was the answer. She didn't pine over dreams, the kids, the way things should be.

She just did her job and cried to rid herself of toxins. I surmised that her frequent weeping made her appear vulnerable, encouraging Klein to like her. But she didn't really need the tears. She simply was a teacher. She didn't have to go into overtime to figure it out. She was the essence of everything I wanted to be in the classroom.

"Fancy stuff, Sugar," a deep voice interrupted me. Laura leapt in surprise. I didn't turn around, but I knew who was standing there. I tried to stop the smile spreading across my face.

Swiveling on my stool, I inventoried every inch of Money's handsome face. Crisp, clean deodorant or aftershave wafted from his body. Not too much. Standing there, he seemed like the most familiar person I'd ever known.

H-Factor: 10/10. His. Mine? Didn't matter.

"Money." I gave him a casual nod. "How's it going? This is one of my roommates, Laura." I forced some poise to the surface, dug out that powerful indifference I'd tapped into the night I met him.

Money lifted his beer toward Laura. "FBI, huh? Sleepy old Laurel, Maryland's a real FBI hot bed," he said. "And Sugar?" He lifted his beer at me. "That one of your covers? A stripper, huh?"

"You're so smart. I could feel it when we met." I tried to will him to sit. To touch me. *Take my hand again.* I wanted to tell him I had lost his number. But that would have seemed irresponsible and un-FBI-like.

A woman—a blond Cindy Crawford, mole and all—slung her arm around Money and plastered her boobs against his chest. Any chance of her being his sister or first cousin was gone with the combination hug/nuzzle/boob thing.

"Who're your little friends, baby?" she asked.

I crinkled my nose. I wanted her to use his name. If I had that one piece of information, our relationship would move forward.

"Oh, this is Sugar. And her roommate, Laura," Money said.

"Sugar. That's interesting. I'm Precious," she said. Her gaze picked away at me, scrutinizing. I straightened against it.

"I'll bet," I said, feeling like I was starring in *Gidget Meets the Debutante*. She pulled Money away.

Once they were out of earshot, Laura leaned into me. "I do declare."

I let out a gust of breath and slumped over my beer. "What's that phrase mean, anyway?" I said.

"You don't have to be psychic," Laura said, "to feel the heat blistering between ya'all like bacon on Sunday morn. Who cares if he's as old as our daddies?" She elbowed me.

"No way, no sizzle. But, he's not *old*, old. Not over…thirty-five?" What was I doing? I had to shake off all thoughts of him because clearly he was taken.

Laura swiveled around and stared at Money and the Cindy Crawford lookalike.

I pulled her back. "Stop staring."

"There's someone else with him. Another filly," Laura said.

I spun around and back. "That's a broad. Not a filly."

"He's not over forty," Laura said.

Nina stepped into the conversation. "The geezer?" She signaled the bartender for a beer. "Sixty at least. H-Factor: two. I can't believe you'd be interested in that guy. He's okay. But come on. Shoot for someone at least semi-young."

"Finding true love isn't about shooting for someone," I said. "It just happens. Not that Money over there has anything to do with love. He's a fantasy for a poor sad, girl who's nearly newly single. Nothing wrong with a little fantasy now and then."

"That's a horrible fantasy," Nina said.

"The H-Factor is relative, suited to our individual needs. Consider Laura's ranking of Paul as a nine. For some reason, slackers suit you and old men suit me at this particular juncture."

"So." Money slid onto the stool next to me. Laura and Nina moved away to argue over whether Nina did indeed prefer slacker men. I ignored Money. My cheap fantasies about him falling madly in love with me had met their demise upon the appearance of the Cindy Crawford lookalike. The puzzle piece image came back to me. If these were the people Money hung out with, there was no way we were a match, no more than I was a match for Alex.

"Where's Cindy?" I could give him one crappy sentence.

"Cindy?" he asked.

"Crawford. You know. Supermodel?"

He threw a peanut into his mouth and electrocuted me with his smile. The only thing ruining the moment were my friends and Paul standing there pointing, laughing and giving me the Lincoln thumbs-up. I examined my beer bottle.

"There you go again." He picked at the label on my Coors Light. His fingers looked muscular. Protective and gentle. Touch me, I thought. Fuss with my hair. *Something.*

"Being mysterious. Dark," he said. "And I don't mean all the FBI/stripper horseshit. I wasn't born yesterday, my friend."

"I can see that," I said.

His smile flashed, then disappeared.

"Seriously," I said, "as mysteries go. How's the case of the missing supermodel going?" I swiveled toward him and leaned my arm on the bar. Arching my back just slightly enough to (hopefully) appear casually seductive. Cackling from the girls' direction made me come out of my pose a little. I tried to block them out.

"She means nothing." He seemed to be choking on his words.

"Cliché" I said.

"Touché." He leaned so close I could feel my skin leap toward his.

Then his gaze lifted and fixated on something behind me. A bump to my arm broke the seduction. Cindy.

"Come on, Jeep." She toyed with his amazing curls. I imagined her fingers were mine.

Another woman stood beside blonde Cindy Crawford, tapping her foot. "We're late picking up Mary Lisbeth." She looked at me. "I'm Mary Colleen. MC for short. Mary Lisbeth's one of our five other sisters. Jeep's and mine. We're," she circled her hand to include Jeep, blonde Cindy Crawford and apparently a bunch of invisible sisters, "a close-knit bunch."

I raised my eyebrows at his name. "Jeep?" I decided if I wasn't going to have a chance with him, I might as well go down tough.

"Family name," his sister couldn't say fast enough. She stepped in between Jeep and me, making my stool spin.

He handed blonde Cindy Crawford an envelope from his back pocket. "Give this to Ernie. He's over by the door. I'll be there in a second." The women looked at me, then headed toward the exit.

Where are you going? What are you going to do? I wanted to shout at him. But I kept my poker face. Panic welled in my belly, fueling heartburn. I couldn't believe I had lost his number. How could I tell him?

I couldn't keep my gaze from locking with his any longer. His eyes weren't brown like I had originally thought. They were hazel. Like mine. Though his were more brown than green. And mine were greener with amber tones. We were so destined to be together, I couldn't believe it. Hazel eyes, both of us.

He swept the tip of his finger down my nose. "Catch ya later, Sugar." And he walked away. Crushing me with his absence. This must be how stalkers got started. Luckily I was too swamped with work to trace some guy's movements. I hadn't even managed to keep track of a coaster bearing his number. How would I manage an all-out stalking operation?

"Hey?" A new bartender snapped his fingers in front of my eyes. "That guy left this for you." He slid a Coors Light toward me. And a cardboard coaster. Messy printing on it said, "Don't work too hard. Call this time. Final chance."

My fingers traced the words and numbers and I was filled with oxygen-producing infatuation. Life itself.

Crap Quotient: 0/10

H-Factor: 10/10

Soul slip: Hell, yes.

Chapter 7

The morning after Laura's birthday celebration, I slid into my seat on the inside of our booth at the Silver Diner. I waited until everyone had their coffees before slapping the coaster on the table. "What do you make of this?" I said.

Laura ran her finger around it. "Good, strong vibes. Testosteronish. Masculine."

"No shit, Laura," I said. "I mean in general, what do you think? This character Jeep. Some sort of family nickname, his sister claimed. I can't use that name, Jeep, it's too strange. But, he left the coaster for me. After he swept his finger down my nose like I was eight years old. After the whole Cindy Crawford sexual tension situation. And his sister. Seemed a little attached for my taste, but what do I know? I'm an only child. What the hell am I supposed to make of all this?" I sipped my coffee and let the questions percolate.

Laura moved a coffee ring around her saucer with her spoon.

"He bought you a beer. He can't view you as a child," Nina said.

"Who does that?" I said. "Run their finger down someone's nose? In what context is that remotely sexual or exciting?"

"You're repressed. The act of breathing, if you look at it right, can be sensual," Nina said.

"Yup, repressed." Laura nodded.

"You're repressed, too." I lifted my coffee mug to Laura. "You've yet to have sexual relations."

"See," Nina said. "Repressed. Who says that? *Sexual relations*." Nina stirred cream into her coffee.

"His hands." I closed my eyes to envision them.

"Here we go with the hands." Laura sighed as though someone had set a car onto her shoulders.

I refocused on the girls. "I'm serious. His hands are magic."

"He only touched you once," Nina said. "He's a little old to be feisty, but who am I to judge?"

I stirred my black coffee. "He touched me more than once. The other time was when he passed me the coaster the first time, back when I was there alone." A chill raced through me. I shook it off. "Magic hands. He's got them."

"*This* is your problem," Laura said. "You fall hard and fast and then wonder why you've fallen out of love. This is exactly why you should steer clear of sex."

I shifted in my seat. "This time is different. So different than with Alex."

They stared at me.

"I had my first soul slip."

"What?" Nina said.

"That's not like—" Laura put her hands over her ears, "—a Dirty Sanchez or something, now is it, ladies, because I can't handle another sexual description like that."

"It's not sexual." I shook a sugar packet I wouldn't be using. "It's the instant fitting of one life into another's. You don't know it until you feel it and then there's no denying it."

They'd never heard of such a thing. My explanation that Nina and I had a friendship version of the soul slip didn't help elucidate the matter. Apparently our soul slip was one-sided.

"It sounds lovely. It sure took us a lot longer to grow into our friendship, but I get it," Laura said. Her expression told me she understood. "What about Alex?"

"I should have broken up with him a long time ago. This has nothing to do with him, really."

We were sitting in silence, waiting for our food, when the diner door flew open and the stabbing sunrays made us flinch. Even before my eyes adjusted to the sudden light change, I knew who had come in. In the spotted haze I could make out Alex's body. I'd had three years to memorize how every inch of it hung together, his gait, the way he held his shoulders and hands.

"Alex?" My eyes watered as I squinted up at him. This wasn't good. His lips were tight, his eyes angry.

"What's this?" He held up a piece of notebook paper with Jeep's phone number scrawled across the top in my telltale chicken-scratch. I'd written the phone number on five pieces of paper and stashed all of them in great little hidey-holes, or so I'd thought.

"I, uh… Well, it's a phone number. Sit down, Alex. Let's calm down."

He bent over the table, his knuckles on it. Spittle flew from his mouth. "I knew something was up."

"It's nothing." I don't know why I bothered lying. This was it, my chance to get out of things. No more putting it off. Just get on with it.

"I. Called. It." Alex clenched his teeth as he spoke.

"Oh." I felt a surge of hopefulness at the thought that the number had not been fake. "It worked?"

"If you wanted some character named *Jeep*, of all fucking things, to answer the phone, then I'd say it worked."

The tendons in my neck tensed as I grimaced, then I shook my head. I looked into my coffee then back at him. "I'm sorry, Alex. The number is nothing. But you're right about something being wrong. I… Can we talk outside?"

He stepped aside and swept his arm outward to create an invisible path to the door. Outside, my shoulder bumped his as we trudged toward his car. He jerked away. He leaned against the trunk and lifted his hands, signaling it was time for me to explain.

"I think it's time for us to split," I said as fast as I could and still have my words be understandable. Sudden, sharp wind came up and burned my cheeks. "Cold front came in last night."

He rolled his eyes.

I shrugged.

"Just like that?" He stepped toward me.

I stepped back, hugging myself—holding things together now that I was letting everything out. My teeth chattered. "You're not in love with me. You're scared to be without me because you hate change. I'm afraid to be without you because I'm sentimental. I collect things, attach meaning to them and create histories that don't allow me to make objective decisions. Like keeping my grandmother's china, even though it's ridiculous."

Alex gritted his teeth, barely opened them to speak. "So now I'm relegated to the same status as some old china?"

"No, no, no. That's a horrid metaphor." I took his hand. I traced his lifeline and gathered up my big girl courage. It was time. "I'm not what you want. And I don't know what *I* want."

He pulled me forward, into his body. "You *are* what I want. A wife." He kissed the top of my head.

My shoulders hunched up at the mention of the word.

"We can move back to Pittsburgh when you've finished teaching here. They'll hire you in a second after working in this hellhole. Can't you picture it? Me and you, kids, home, happy?"

"What do you picture me doing in this happy home scenario?" I spoke into his chest.

"Teaching, being the great wife and mom I know you'll be."

I felt a twinge—I was softening—but I had to be strong against these ideas. He really was a good guy. I pushed out of his embrace. He reached for my hand. I snatched it back.

"Thanks for that." I said. "For thinking that. But you want me to be a good wife in the old-fashioned way, to be all things to our family, to love it and to do it all tomorrow."

His eyes seemed to brighten. I stepped back further. I felt like running.

"I can't be *one* of those things, let alone all of that stuff for you.

"Carolyn—"

"I'm not the one for you."

He looked toward the road.

I needed to end the conversation before I gave in to trying to make it work. "And you're not the one for me."

Alex's jaw clenched. He knew I was right. He just needed time to process it. He hadn't struggled with the thought of breaking up for a year like I had. He'd feel like hell, but not because I'd broken his heart. Because I'd broken his dream. Not that it could ever come true. Life would teach him that over time.

Alex made a disgusted, I-give-up motion with his hand, then traipsed toward the front of his Accord. I couldn't move. He wrenched the driver's side door open and turned back to me.

"You're wrong, Carolyn. You just don't know it yet."

I lifted my hand to wave and nodded. I could let him leave thinking he was right. It was the kind thing to do. He tore out of the parking lot, driving angry. I said a little prayer he wouldn't kill himself on what was quickly becoming an icy road.

And then I went back to my friends with trembling hands and a shaky spirit. I could barely breathe.

"Looks like that went well," Nina said.

"Yeah," I said. I was emotionally drained, but the tears I expected never came.

Laura squeezed my hand a few times, telling me I didn't need to reiterate what was said, that they understood my need to just be.

They busied themselves with a discussion about soul slips. Had Laura experienced one with Paul? Listening to them calmed me and led me smack back to the truth. The soul slip—that I'd had one and it hadn't been with Alex, ever. Even if I never saw Jeep again, for those few seconds during both our encounters, I'd known exactly what it meant to belong to someone in a deep and wonderful way.

We lingered over omelets, waffles and coffee, giving Alex ample time to clear out of the house. It didn't matter that hour upon hour of lesson planning was waiting for us, that I wouldn't be able to show my face at Silver Diner brunch until Klein's observation of my teaching was over. There was that much work to be done.

Somehow I needed to convey to Klein that I knew what I was doing in the classroom even when what was officially expected made no instructional sense whatsoever. I could do it. But I needed this morning to stretch on a little longer, long enough to feel as though everything was as it should be.

Chapter 8

Over three weeks had passed since Klein had informed me I'd be the first teacher to be observed. From Laura's post-party debriefing at the Silver Diner on, all I did was work. At home, at school, during lunch. Gone were my favorite extra-curricular activities: running, happy hours, weekend brunches and dinner in front of the TV.

I missed our Silver Diner discussions of love, the week's happenings, our students and the red flags that should have warned us to run from such a ridiculous profession.

By the time the observation rolled around, I was sure I would earn Best Teacher Ever status in Klein's eyes. I'd been prepping the kids on what to expect, been extra consistent with discipline and had propped them up with all the confidence-building words I could summon.

They seemed to be excited about proving they were better students than Klein thought they were. The only thing standing in my way of a first-class observation was the appearance of my classroom. I'd already cleared out some of the debris—handouts I hadn't used and wasn't going to and supplies that always found their way into a mess by the end of the week—but I wanted the space to sparkle.

I'd planned to get to school by six-thirty a.m. to finish organizing, but there was an accident on the beltway and my three cleanup hours shrunk to one. Still plenty of time. I told myself to relax. I'd done the important work. I had planned an effective and engaging lesson.

In a rush, I used the kids' bathroom before heading to my room. I stepped in the stall and started to undo my jeans. My wardrobe had taken a significant nosedive since the first day of school. I'd started out wearing Ann Taylor sheath dresses with coordinating cardigans and pumps; they'd seemed the perfect way to tell the world I was serious about teaching. But I barely had one dress left to wear. My class had destroyed my beautiful outfits with an accidental stab with scissors here, a slash of a marker there.

I read the bathroom walls beside me. Someone had written about Tanesha. "You're a big mama, like your chocolaty chip Gramma." Terri's bubble printing with smiley face dots over the "I's" gave her away. Tanesha must not have seen this yet. There'd be a brawl when she did, best friends or not.

I buttoned my jeans. I didn't understand these kids, though sometimes I felt I knew them like they were my own. I washed my hands and noticed words beside the mirror.

"Ms. Jenkins a bietch. An ugly wite bietch."

I outlined the letters with my finger. LeAndre's words. When had he been in here? They were his letters, all right. Too-perfect and round. Afraid to make mistakes, he was painstaking with his printing. Must've taken him thirty minutes to do this. He might have even come back to finish it. Jeeze. When had he *done* this?

A sensation that was simultaneously numbing and painful pulsed in my chest. It was similar to the emotion I'd experienced when a good friend lied or when my mother didn't take five minutes to hear about my bad day. It was the shattering of an expectation and it hurt as badly when carried out by eleven year olds. Worse, actually.

I leaned on the sink and forced my breathing to even out.

My kids. I'd thought showing the kids I cared and believed

in them would instantaneously create learners. I poured over lesson plans and materials and had spent close to fifteen hundred of my own dollars on supplies and books. I barely did anything but work.

A tearless sob escaped my throat. This bathroom, in the old part of Lincoln, had endless height and marble that gave the quietest rustle rising amplitude that projected to the people at the other end of the hall.

"Ms. Jenkins?" The gruff voice of Ben, our head maintenance man, came from outside the bathroom.

My throat felt as though I had jammed cotton balls in it. I didn't know how I'd make it through the day. "I'm coming."

Ben was waiting for me outside my classroom door, which he opened for me when I got there. "What the hell?" I covered my mouth. The room, perfectly organized, shocked me as much as being shot in the foot had. Had Klein sent in a cleaning service? He'd want my first born for this. A limb. Or maybe my corneas.

Across the room, my desk stood in all its teacher-y glory. Wire and wood containers held things that weren't usually organized on my desk.

"I did it," Ben said. "I didn't throw anything out, just rearranged it."

"Thank you, Ben. Why?" I looked at his curly salt-and-pepper hair cut close to his head. Put him in a sweater and chinos and he'd pass for a professor at any university.

"I thought you needed help." He smiled and little lines curved at the corners of his mouth. He laid his chin atop his hands, which curled over the tip of his broom handle.

"My God. Thanks, Ben. I don't know what to say. Not to be cliché, but this is the nicest thing anyone's ever done for me. Ever. That sounds like hyperbole, but really. You have no idea how huge this is."

He scratched his chin. "The small things. Sometimes they carry as much weight as the big." He winked.

"This is gargantuan." I shrugged.

"They love you," he said.

"Who?"

"The kids."

I guffawed. "You slay me, my good friend. I thought the kids would follow me into the pits of education, where we'd uncover their strengths and talents and bury their weaknesses. Damn, Ben, they won't even follow me into the hall, let alone to hell and back."

"You think that shit? For real? You do?"

I cocked my head. "I did. I thought if they knew I cared about them, they would just do the work. I never understood the possibility that they *couldn't* do the work even if they wanted to."

Ben straightened and pushed the broom back and forth. "*This*—all this turmoil, the writing on the wall—is them recognizing authority. Opposing you is their way of admitting your authority exists. They're *almost* ready for a battle with the devil. You'll know when the time is right." He headed toward the door. "I have to finish the hall. Don't want Klein climbing up *my* back." He started down the hall, broom over his shoulder.

"You definitely don't want that." I leaned against the doorjamb. I thought of my father who taught music at my high school for thirty years before retiring. He always said the janitors and secretaries knew everything. Here's hoping Ben knew more than I did, because if this was the kids liking me—recognizing my authority—I didn't ever want to see the alternative.

**

Sitting in perfect rows, my students were ready. They folded their hands neatly on their desktops as the clock struck ten. They were ready. Klein was fashionably late. I paced. My heart beat like jazz music, in choppy, fast rhythms. We practiced turning sentences from Pittsburghese to street to book language while we waited. I needed them occupied but didn't want them overtaxed before delivering the equivalent of a performance at Sea World.

The door swung open and slammed into the wall. I took a deep breath and let it out as Klein entered the room. He scowled, weaving his way to my desk, stopping to address this kid and that, pointing at stuff on their desks, moving on before they could even respond to his questions.

The kids shifted in their seats, cleared their throats, tapped their pencils and averted their gazes from Klein's, but it was still ungodly quiet. So far so good. I nodded at them, letting them know everything would be great. They *could* impress Klein. Show him how smart they were.

I'd artfully jammed each item on Klein's Observation Expectations list into the half-hour plan even though I knew having so many different components would just confuse them and lead to a watered down, incongruent experience.

Klein sat at my desk and I focused on my kids, feeling calm. Most of them stayed quiet and participated. I thought I saw Klein smile a few times. Maybe I should invite him to observe more often, I thought. I almost felt as though I was teaching in a real classroom, with kids who respected me and wanted to learn. Maybe this was just what we needed in order to start over.

Once the lesson was complete—thirty minutes on the dot—relief surged and my mood soared. It was over. Over. I nodded at Klein. He caught my gaze and held it for a moment before looking back at his notes.

Get up, Klein. I willed him to leave the room. I stared at him, waited for him stand, to at least shuffle his papers in preparation for leaving. Anything to signal he'd finished. The screeching of my kids' chairs, their sighs and murmurs, made me realize I must have been staring at Klein for some time.

Within another half a minute, my wave of relief that the lesson had been successful and we were finished was replaced with suffocating shock as Klein rocked back in my chair and flung his clodhoppers onto my desk. What was he doing?

My throat closed. He's staying. My freaking God. The guy is kicked back for the duration. He looked as though he was about to light a ciggie or pop a picnic lunch onto his lap in order to get really comfy. He shot me the Lincoln thumbs-up. I offered one back, barely stopping myself from giving him the Jenkins middle finger.

Two hours later, he was still there. Picking through my desk, over the desk, under it. Was that legal? Where was the union? Shouldn't the union bosses have alarms for this type of thing, notifying important leaders that one of their underlings was having the life sucked out of her right in front of the kids she was supposed to be teaching?

Klein's famous sneer never wavered. His plaster-y skin glistened as though watching me work was a burden on his very ability to live and breathe.

As for my students' glowing good behavior? At the one-hour mark, something snapped. Like Cinderella back in rags at the stroke of midnight, the kids were suddenly back to their normal, short-fused selves. They bickered and intimidated one another by standing up and launching their chests into each other.

Kenneth looked at Larry and he looked back. Crystal breathed too loud. Tony mentioned Katya's mother and her lack of hygiene and something about food stamps and the social worker who frequented the home in between visits paid by burly police officers. Normal stuff. Up and down, angry words and no learning after that first hour. Just maintenance of student behavior.

Part of me was happy to see them act like this in front of Klein. It couldn't be just me if they weren't afraid to misbehave in front of the principal. Surely Klein would understand this. From time to time during the final hour and a half, he became frustrated with the behavior as I worked with small groups.

He'd send one kid, then another, to his office without a discipline referral, breaking his own rule about strict documentation and paying no mind to whether he was interrupting teaching or not. At some point he stopped sending kids out and just burrowed further into my plan book, disengaging from all that was happening around him.

Finally, lunchtime arrived. Klein shuffled out the door without a word. Another burst of relief. The thirty-minute target lesson had gone well and that would be the basis for my evaluation. I felt as though I had crawled through a desert in search of shade and water, finding it at the last second of life. I was done!

**

For the first time since starting at Lincoln, I dropped the kids at the cafeteria and went right to the teachers' room. No phone calls to parents, no photocopying, no preparing materials or grading papers. Just lunch with my friends. Laura and Nina were there, grading papers and writing lessons during their planning period.

The two women who taught the other fifth and sixth grade combination classes were nowhere to be found. I wished they had been there so I could tell them how well the target lesson had gone. They didn't like me much. They were both old-timers from the neighborhood. They said they'd seen "me" come and go a hundred times and were tired of being forced to baby new teachers. Well, okay, no babying needed here, fellow teachers. I did it. I'm good.

Nina and Laura stopped talking as soon as I entered and looked at me as though I were a surgeon about to inform the family on the status of their loved one. It was then I noticed Fionna lying on the pleather couch, drool dripping out the side of her mouth onto a musty woolen pillow you couldn't have paid me millions to put my head on. I pointed to her and raised my eyebrows.

Laura and Nina shrugged and waved off my unasked question, telling me it was more of Fionna's usual nonsense. She'd arrived to school late, in her jammies, and was now catching up on missed sleep. How did she get away with this crap? If I even yawned in a teacher meeting, Klein repaid me with unplanned visits to my classroom and condescending comments in front of my students. Yet Fionna was free to treat her job as though she were at a spa for the wealthy class, exhausted from spending too much money.

I collapsed into a chair at the table. "Well, it's over. I nailed the target lesson. The kids were awesome."

"That's great!" Laura said. Nina nodded.

"But."

"But?" Nina asked.

"Klein *didn't leave*."

Nina and Laura drew back. Their mouths gaped and their eyes practically crossed.

"I know." I opened my lunch bag. "I don't know what to make of it, either. He rummaged through my desk like a squirrel setting up for a winter's sleep. And he tried to get involved in discipline. I don't know. Maybe he needed to see it's not just me. It was as though they held in all their bad habits for the thirty-minute target lesson and then, like something went off inside each of them, they were done with tidy, neat behavior."

I rested my chin on my hands. "It's like the process of apoptosis. Cells are genetically programmed to kill themselves off after a given time. With my kids, all is well for a bit, and then, in an instant, everything begins to shred in front of my eyes and I can't stop any of it from happening. Klein can't get mad at me. It was an act of science. Nature. Something."

The girls nodded.

"I bet he actually likes me after all that. A little, anyway."

I felt optimistic as I said those words, actually looked forward to our after-school debriefing. I imagined him saying, "Wow, Jenkins, I can't believe you're getting as much done as you are, considering how difficult your class is. I'm glad I chose you to teach one of the fifth and sixth grade combination classes." I imagined him nodding, his expression filled with awe, and finally, respect. We'd be colleagues, just as he said we would be in my interview.

Laura cocked her head. "You really think he'll come around like that?"

Nina looked as though she didn't buy into my optimism. "Not after the way you embarrassed him with that test data," she said. "He's not letting you off the hook."

The last staff meeting. Yes, that. It had been a simple statement regarding the fact my fifth and sixth graders needed different instruction than was prescribed in the manual. When he brushed me off, I hit him with a pie chart showing which skills they could employ and which they had no idea how to use. They were below grade-level in nearly every area. Many could have been classified as illiterate if someone felt the need to throw around labels.

"I didn't *try* to embarrass him. I just want my kids to do well. He said we were a team. Should I feign stupidity or something? We're talking about people's lives here, folks, not the selling of fine leather goods. If what he said to do worked, I wouldn't question it. I'd love to spend my afterschool hours on things like, say an older mystery man, or run more—I haven't run more than four miles in a row in a month."

I went to the vending machine and got a bag of pretzels and a Peppermint Patty. When I returned, I said, "No. I think this is a turning point for Klein and me. I know it went well."

Nina went back to her plans and Laura forced a smile before doing the same. I hated their lack of optimism. Laura taught first grade. She'd become Klein's pet teacher and although I knew she hated him, it burned my ass that she was having a much easier time.

She worked with another new first grade teacher, someone our age, and they collaborated on everything. Shared the discipline, the trouble, the occasional good stuff. And their good stuff seemed to snowball into huge golden eggs of good teaching moments.

My shit stuff seemed to snowball and explode exponentially, sending tiny shit-balls out to explode and create even more classroom messes.

I nudged Fionna to offer her a pretzel. She responded like a corpse. I turned to the girls. "Any idea why Fionna's forever wearing bedclothes to school and napping instead of doing lunch duty like the rest of us?" I bent down and sniffed her for booze.

"I think she's narcoleptic," Laura said. She didn't look up from her papers.

I leaned in again to get a whiff of Fionna. Nothing decisive. "Not to be rude, but I've never heard of anyone actually having narcolepsy."

"Maybe she's partying with all that money she inherited last year," Nina said.

"What?" I said. Laura stopped writing.

"Yeah," Nina said, "she got a hundred grand from her

parents. They died in an accident. Who knows? Maybe she's out late finding ways to spend all that cash. It could be tiring to come into money like that, to not know what to do with it."

"Yeah, exhausting. I wouldn't want an inheritance or anything," I said.

Fionna stretched, groaning, and then said clear as anything, "Ohhhhh, Timothy. That's a thumbs-up, baby."

We froze, waiting for her to open her eyes and realize what she'd just said.

But she turned to her other side and folded into the fetal position, her crack peeking out from her pajama bottoms.

Oh my God, we mouthed at one another.

Then we ran from the room like kids, laughing in the hall, knowing we'd heard Fionna right, but not knowing how she could possibly, even in her dreams, associate Klein with anything good, like sex. Laura wouldn't accept that Fionna was referencing Klein and accepted the task of researching whether Fionna had a boyfriend named Tim. Imagining Fionna dreaming of Klein made me envision his hands on my body and my skin tingled with disgust. No. There was no way anyone in her right mind would willingly cavort with his slimy self.

**

I sat in Klein's office after school waiting for my observation debriefing. I teetered on the verge of professional ecstasy. I'd climbed past optimistic by late afternoon and was now experiencing true happiness. I believed the combination of my having taught a brilliant target lesson and Klein seeing just how unwieldy the class was would mean a new dynamic for us, a rediscovery of the team concept he'd gushed about when I interviewed with him.

He strolled in, mouth turned up in what I think he intended as a smile. But I found myself flinching at the sight of him. The crooked smile brought out the Satan in him and my spirits sank a notch or two. Still, things had gone well in the lesson. He would have to recognize that.

There was no friendly banter as he breezed by me and

rolled his chair snuggly to the desk. I cleared my throat and realized that every bit of confidence I'd felt existed on a fault line. And Klein's next words would either initiate a massive quake of failure or let me live with a smidgen of hope that I could, in fact, be a good teacher.

I held my breath, then quietly let it out as seconds, then minutes dragged on. Why didn't he say something? Klein paged through his legal pad. Then he finally looked up at me with a hard expression and began to read aloud every word I had said over the entire morning. I didn't remember forming half the thoughts he read back to me, taunting me with them. It was quickly clear he had characterized my lesson—the whole morning—as a disaster.

"You said," Klein sneered, "'Terri, go ahead,' and then you gestured with your hand toward the door in an effort to guide her from the room. Don't you think it would have been better to say, 'Yes, Terri, you may use the lavatory now?'"

"Uh," I said. No, asshole. "I was in the middle of helping Kenneth sound his way through a three-syllable word. I thought I should remain focused on the children who were sitting in front of me, considering they're in small group with me for such a short time. I think she understood exactly what I meant."

He stared. I cleared my throat and straightened in my seat. Klein's silence clamped on tight. Sweat broke out over my scalp as though my body knew I was holding back disrespectful words but it had to let the tension out in some way. How dare he? I was a good teacher, no matter what else his scribbles suggested.

He hunkered back into his notes. "Here. After Kenneth said he thought the character in the story named Marcel was angry, you asked, 'Kenneth, what makes you think Marcel is angry?'"

I nodded, remembering asking that one. Good question.

"That question isn't in the manual. It said to ask what color shirt Marcel was wearing."

I glanced away from him. I'd thought this through quite a bit while planning. "I wanted them to think beyond the words. The question in the manual required an obvious—may I even suggest, moronic—response. It required nothing of the students in terms of thinking, digging into their grey matter, connecting the new information to old. *Learning*," I said.

He rocked back in his chair so far he almost whacked his head on the windowsill. He crossed his arms across his chest and massaged one bicep, then the other. As he rocked, his body covered and exposed the clock behind him. An hour and a half had already passed.

"Do you realize," he said, "the amount of money that goes into creating these text books? They have *experts*, troops of them, write the stories and questions and create activities. And *you*, who can't even find a pencil in or on or around your desk, think you have a better question to ask?"

I shifted in my seat, put my arms on the armrests and leaned forward a bit, trying to convey relaxation without appearing as though I was spending a day at the beach. I knew my lips were pursed, but I couldn't stop that. Yes, that's right, I felt like saying, it appears I know better than the experts. My head pounded with fatigue. Right then it became clear.

There wasn't going to be any collaboration between us. No collegial support and brainstorming to improve literacy and the love of learning in my classroom. My place in his school was clear. I sat back and crossed my legs.

"Of course not," I said. "It wouldn't be remotely possible for me to ask a better question than what was in the manual. You're right." I said this in a monotone with a poker face.

He squirmed as though deciphering the meaning behind my words. "Well. We're clear then."

"Yes sir." You freaking prick.

I stole a look at the clock. Six-oh-four p.m. I pulled my bag onto my lap, ready to pack up my notes and put this meeting behind me when Klein pulled my plan book from under his legal pad. He wiggled his finger, indicating I should put my bag back onto the floor.

A two-and-a-half hour meeting apparently wasn't going to be enough to cover all my shortcomings.

"What's *this*, Jenkins? I can't make heads or tails of it. It's unclear. It's a disaster. I can't read a bit of it." He poked at something in his notes, nearly bouncing out of his seat in excitement.

I wanted to gash his eyeballs. Tell him he didn't need to make sense of it. It was *my* plan book. I couldn't speak. I tapped my pen, waiting for him to answer his own question as he had done through much of this meeting.

He stared, silent. Guess he *did* want an answer. It wasn't that he needed this information. It was that he wanted to spit on me. He was disgusted to simply share the air with me.

"Um, with six reading groups, plus the work each group needs to do when I'm with one group in particular, I can't fit it in the little blocks. I have longer versions of the lessons in a planning binder at home," I said weakly.

"I'd like to see those. On your desk with these, everyday."

"Do I need to do the block plans if I submit the long ones instead?" I pointed to the block plan book in his hand.

"Do both." He knitted his fingers and put them under his chin.

I stared.

"And there's the matter of your walls," he said.

My eyes widened before I could stop them. I hadn't done anything to the walls. Nothing harmful, at least. What the hell was his problem with the walls?

"Your store decorations and inspirational sayings are fine, but you don't have any of the county mandated signage on your walls."

"Signage?"

"You did attend the new teacher workshop, didn't you? I saw your name on the list."

"Yes."

Crap Quotient: 10/10.

He swiveled to the shelves behind him and pulled out a six-inch binder. He flipped it to somewhere in the middle. "Right here: tips on comparing and contrasting and QAR, sequencing, graphic organizers, higher order thinking charts. All missing from your walls. How are the kids supposed to perform on the state tests without seeing the reminders over the course of the school year?" He slapped the page in the binder.

They can't *read*, asshole. I wanted to scream. They *can't* peruse the freaking signage and apply the ideas to the tasks at hand, because half read like second graders. The sudden mental image of me ripping LeAndre's gun from his hand and spinning around to use it on Klein made me smile. Rumor had it the year before Klein had to employ armed guards for weeks after a gun-wielding father threatened to shoot him. I understood that man. Whoever he was. I could've killed Klein. If it wouldn't have permanently affected my Overall Life Satisfaction Score, I would have.

"Are you smiling, Jenkins?"

"Yes," I said. "I guess I am."

And I guess that was stupid. But I was apparently overflowing with stupid. I knew more than Klein gave me credit for, but clearly I didn't know as much as I needed to. Everyday, I learned that more and more. And each day I thought I hit the bottom of my ignorance pit. Yet, there I sat, looking at my feet, realizing that the pit was, indeed, vast and subterranean, and I just might drown in it before half the year was over.

**

I dragged myself into the house at exactly eight forty-five p.m. There was a note saying everyone had gone to the Green Turtle. I looked at the coaster I'd secured in between the mirror and wood frame. I should call Jeep right now. But what did I have to offer as a woman, a human being? I'd been stripped down to my bones. There was nothing left of me, of who I was. But the pre-observation me wasn't terribly attractive, anyway, so maybe now was the perfect time to call. What did I have to lose? I dialed the phone. No answer. Fate.

I was fine with fate at that moment. I grabbed a six-pack and collapsed on the couch. I chugged half a can of beer and stared at the blank TV. I was even too tired to turn it on.

I ran my hand over the leather couch and lay down against the armrest. After receiving our first paychecks, we had gone furniture shopping. We thought leather would last forever. The lacquered, mirrored coffee and end tables came with the couch in a package deal. An area rug with red geometric shapes defined the living room space and influenced our decision to splatter red paint on the wall above the TV.

Nina and I loved it and everyone who came in stopped in awe, though not always the good kind. It had impact, despite Laura's constant bitching that it appeared bloody. She'd wanted feminine and happy. I thought the redness filled the room with life and balanced the black furniture.

Before I dozed, I said a silent goodwill prayer for Alex. I'd never felt freer than I had since breaking up and even though he was gone physically, I still thought of him often, as though he would walk into the house at any point. For all the awfulness I'd experienced that day, I was relieved that I wouldn't have to deal with Alex later that night, that he would not appear wanting something, taxing me even further.

**

The next morning I woke up with Nina shaking me. I'd fallen asleep on the couch.

Laura's expressive blue eyes were wide in her signature 'Something horrible is happening here' expression. "How'd the post-obs debrief go?" she asked cautiously, as though she already knew the answer.

"The colonoscopy, you mean?" I rose up on my elbows. "I don't know where to start except to say I have all the information you need to conduct perfect observations. Consider me your lab rat. I have four hours worth of helpful hints to offer you and Nina so you can be successful in every way I wasn't."

Laura cleared her throat. "Timothy retained you *four* hours?" That's our Laura. We made fun of her for using his first name, but now, she seemed smart. She knew how to play the game. Until recently, I hadn't realized there was a game to play.

And I hadn't meant to piss off Klein. The failures of our curriculum were clear very early into the year. I didn't know asking a question about the effectiveness of the curriculum was equivalent to saying "Your mother's a ho." For Klein, the

71

curriculum was a living, breathing thing he felt obligated to treat as a loved one, even if a totally dysfunctional loved one, alive, but hamstrung by ineptitude.

I fell back against the couch and groaned. "Oh, my God it was awful."

Laura played with the fringe on the edges of the afghan. "He wasn't...you know," she scrunched up her nose, "feisty?"

"He was feisty, all right. Feisty with scathing, searing, unfair opinions and ridiculous mandates. He beat me like a dog."

"Huge cliché," Nina said.

"It fits," I said.

I recounted the entire torturous session and when I couldn't think about it one more second, I took a deep breath. "Okay. Let's not think about Klein anymore. It's bad for my health."

"Well, we're glad you're okay," Laura said. "If it had to be anyone, you are the one who could handle it. Me? I'd have quit if that were me."

"I wouldn't quit. I'd let him have it if it were me, but I feel for you, sister," Nina said. I was too tired to tell her a gym teacher wouldn't ever be in my position.

"Thanks," I said.

I didn't like being the guinea pig, but at least my own failures could help my friends not suffer. I told them, it didn't matter what they taught. If they posted the right signage and adhered to the manual, they'd be fine. In fact, they just might be brilliant.

Chapter 9

I almost called Money three times. (I couldn't think of him as Jeep. I just couldn't.) But late night planning sessions and early morning attempts to organize the room that couldn't be tamed got in the way of my being really proactive in the dating arena.

However, any time the kids ignored me or criticized my lessons—or my wardrobe or the way I walked or talked or breathed—I could mentally return to The Tuna. The place where I'd created the person I wanted to be, who sat with the guy I wanted to be with.

Not that I ever stayed in my fantasy long. I didn't want to. I actually wanted to be the best teacher possible and have people refer to me as such. Taking extended mental trips to Fantasy Island wasn't going to help me accomplish that. It had been weeks since I'd last seen him, and the more time passed, the easier it was not to leave a message.

In addition to the aforementioned reasons for not calling Money, there was the risk of the fantasy being blown if I finally reached him and he didn't recall who I was. I'd never even given him my real name. Really, what was I to say? Hi, this is the fake stripper? Or, What's up, this is the faux FBI agent? None of it seemed right. So every once in while I looked at his number, picked a date and time to call him, then was happy when he never answered.

Laura, Nina, and I were nearing the end of the first quarter of the school year when we learned we were now required to allocate at least nine percentage grades per child for behavior. Two days before the quarter ended we made behavior charts that could be translated into percentages. Pegging who was well behaved was simple. Parsing behavior into percentages wasn't.

We were also required to fill out pacing sheets. The sheets mapped out the speed at which we moved through the reading book. Without exception, this was the easiest task assigned to us. So when Klein called me to Sissy Serra's room for the pacing meeting, I was calm and confident.

The load of books in my arms felt like shale slabs. I waited for Klein to move his crap over so I could set mine down. I watched him handle his materials. Bony, white fingers. His nails were short and too manicured. His single status wasn't surprising. Not only did his personality suck, but those fingers. They made me shudder. I blocked out the image of him touching a woman. I couldn't be involved with him. Not for one second.

Sissy Serra, a middle-aged reading specialist, sometimes revealed a giddy inclination toward Klein while simultaneously disgusting me. It occurred to me that maybe she was secretly in love with him. Why else would she still be here when she could've been long gone to one of the quiet suburban or rural schools in the county? She oddly preferred this crazy place. Maybe she was the person in the picture on his desk who had been folded out of view.

"Jenkins," Klein said. "Here's the pacing chart you handed in the other day. Let's. Take. A. Look. I assume you made a copy?"

"Uh, no. Sorry."

"What? Didn't they teach you that in your master's courses?"

I looked into my bag, distracting myself from his tirade. The pocket where I had put Money's number was empty. I just wanted to touch the numbers to give me the confidence in myself I'd felt in the bar with Money. I couldn't find the number. Bad omen.

He snapped his fingers under my nose to get my attention. "Well, think about it next time." He pulled some forms from a folder. "I happen to have an extra copy."

I stole a look at Sissy. She was buried in her notes.

My stomach clenched. Feeling ten years old for the thousandth time this year, I waited for Klein to start.

"Looking at your pacing sheets, I'd say things aren't good." He tore up the sheets I had so diligently filled out a few days before and tossed the papers into the basket. It was loaded with other teachers' pacing sheets. At least I wasn't alone. Laura's were right below mine. I was confused. I looked back at him as he intertwined his fingers and leaned on fresh pacing sheets.

"You need to redo these. There's a problem with your pacing."

"Problem?"

"You're a month behind. At least. Pacing and attendance— the two areas in which Lincoln is proficient. According to the state, if we lose those proficiencies things will get bad."

I nodded. Now it was clear to me why he couldn't expel LeAndre, why having him in the classroom, even if risky, was a better alternative in his eyes: the school's attendance.

He pushed the clean pacing sheets to me. "So we're clear." His hard, close set, eyes bore into mine. I shot a look at Sissy, who was nodding.

I wiggled in my seat the way the kids did. "Mr. Klein, I can't move faster. Not with six reading groups per day. And not when they can't even read the stories in front of them now. How can I move faster?"

He glared as though I'd suggested it might be fun to pull his nails from their beds.

"The only way to move faster is to *say* I'm moving faster," I said. "Who cares if I *say* they read all the stories if they *can't read*?"

Sissy and Klein stared at me.

He tilted his head. "That's right. You understand perfectly. Sissy will work with you on some of these smaller details you're referring to. Fill out that pacing sheet the way you just said."

"Details? Little things like how half of them don't know their letter sounds?" I said.

"Those things work themselves out if you just follow the curriculum. Some kids develop slower. They'll catch up if we stay the course set forth in the manuals," Klein said.

That sounded like a really good solution: just proceed. Reading problems eventually smooth themselves out. But I knew that was wrong. If these problems fixed themselves, I wouldn't have sixth graders who couldn't decode the word 'couldn't.'

He stood and looked at his watch. "Lunchtime. I want the sheets tomorrow."

He left, then stuck his snake-like neck and head back through the doorway. "And you're over the copy limit by about two-thousand units. So whatever you're copying, cease and desist." He knocked on the door before leaving again.

Whatever I'm copying? My ass. I'm making Christmas cards featuring my ass. I sighed.

I looked at Sissy. "It sounds like he's saying I should lie about how quickly I'm moving through the curriculum."

Sissy breathed out heavily. "It's hard to understand. You being new. Coming from those suburban Pittsburgh schools. We see it all the time with you girls. Here? It's survival. Period. And those letter sound issues you're concerned about. I'll get you some stuff on that, though there isn't much you can do for them except wait for things to click."

"Okay," I said. Sissy left for lunch. I remained in my chair. She couldn't be right. There had to be plenty I could do. I knew I was failing as a teacher. But I wasn't the only one failing. The students had to have been failed by many more teachers before me.

I snapped out of my fog when I remembered that Fionna (dressed in a tutu, tights, ballet shoes and Pearl Jam T-shirt) had been assigned to watch my class and that I needed to get back there to relieve her. But I couldn't move. Lie about what we were doing? Yucko. I had to figure this out.

And I'd start by chucking those six reading groups. If he

wanted me to lie, I'd lie. And the first big fat one would be to him. I'd have two sets of lesson plans. One for me, one for him. If I was going to lie it'd be to help these kids actually learn something. Not to help Klein keep his job.

**

I gathered my materials, including the fresh pacing sheets, and trudged into the hall. Distracted, I nearly ran right into Klein and a student. I apologized and squatted to pick up some of my scattered papers as they kept walking. I stood and saw they had stopped. The student—a third grader—had wet his pants right there in the hall.

He was eating sobs, nearly hyperventilating. I couldn't let Klein work his evil so I went toward them, calling the boy's name. But by the time I got there, Klein had knelt in front of him, blotting at the puddle with his papers, telling the boy there were spare clothes in the nurse's office.

I nearly choked on sight, struck with sadness that this person who hated me so much had this wonderful side he wielded only so often. With his mother, with LeAndre, with this kid. Don't get me wrong, I'm glad he wasn't mean to kids in need, but shit, I was in need, too, and compared to Klein, I was a kid. So what the hell? I left them to their private moment and headed back to my classroom.

A student office helper stopped me and handed me a note. It said I had twenty minutes to call my parents or they'd be out the door to the airport to begin their world tour. Sigh.

The teacher's room was empty when I called my parents. "Hey, Dad. You're leaving again?"

"Yeah, I got home from the library and your mother had found a flight to London, cheap. We haven't been there in so long. We'll pretend to be locals, hide in old rented rooms, bring back good memories," he said.

"That sounds soooo good." I leaned against the wall and twirled the phone cord around my finger.

"What's wrong, Sweetie?"

"Things aren't going so well. I didn't want to tell you," I

said. Suddenly, I didn't care about *proving* I was important, I just needed my father to *tell* me I was important, no matter how good a teacher I was or wasn't. "I'm in hell, Dad. I can't get anything right. It's not like teaching at home. Where everyone is the same. Well, we know I wasn't the same as everyone else at school, but I wasn't a problem, either."

I coughed into my hand, trying to steady my quaking voice. "I don't mean to be insulting, but it seemed like teachers had it so easy in our district. Just show up, do your job, go home. I really wonder if I made a horrible decision."

"The first year is always hard," he said. "You're doing great. You're a person who perseveres. It's who you are."

"I'm a disaster." My throat burned and felt as if it were closing on the sob I was fighting back. "You couldn't make up the stuff that's happening in this place. It's as though we're auditioning for *One Flew Over the Cuckoo's Nest* or something."

I looked over my shoulder to be sure no one was in the vicinity. "But as bad as the kids are or I am at dealing with them, Klein is the problem. Nothing I do is right in his eyes. And he doesn't do anything to help. I may not know the answers, but he doesn't, either. And, he's been snooping in my room. He went through my desk and, he and the secretary listen in through the intercom."

My dad sighed. "A person becomes a principal, it's Instant Asshole. Does your union rep know any of this? Klein can't rifle through your things."

"The union leaders here are more like social directors and shepherds than anything else. And that's not all bad. No one runs around citing the contract to reduce the amount of work that needs to be done. And though the kids have problems I love them. It's Klein who makes it awful," I said.

"Should I come? Your mother and I can put off our trip. If you need us, we'll be there."

"No!" I said. "I didn't mean to make you worry. I know Mom wouldn't want to change plans. That's not her thing, changing plans." His offer made all the difference in the world. "I'm fine, really."

"Mom wouldn't mind. You just say the word, but you *can* do this," Dad said. "You can do whatever you set your mind to."

We wrapped up our conversation. I sent my love to my mom, who was out on last minute heading-to-London errands, then tramped back to the classroom to assess the damage. I hoped I'd be able to make my dad proud. Because even though I wanted to be the greatest teacher ever, he actually was.

What he said about doing whatever I set my mind to was typical of him. He set that mantra inside my skin from birth and that part of me, the optimist, often directed my goals.

But coming from the reclusive (not withdrawn as in they didn't leave the house, but solitary in their coupleness) pair they were, my pursuits were wracked with uncertainty. Wracked to the point I wondered if I had some sort of diagnosis lurking there, waiting to be discovered.

I was forever swinging between "Yeah, I can do this, I can fit in, I can make a difference in the world," and "Oh for shit's sake, what was I thinking by getting up in the morning?" Walking down the hall I reminded myself that I was lucky to have had my parents, my upbringing. At least they had always returned calls to teachers who needed to talk to them.

I took a deep breath. I had work to do and hell if I'd quit before I'd done it because deep in my very being, living amongst the depression or sadness or whatever it was, lurked the idea that these kids were more important than my potential to fail. For them, I needed to succeed.

Chapter 10

Saturday morning we gathered around our usual table at the Silver Diner. Nina and me. Laura stayed behind to do some *Leave it to Beaver* act for Paul. She was auditioning her housewife skills in some bizarre attempt to make him realize she was a catch. In love already, any dope could see Paul didn't need to be convinced. The charade made me uncomfortable.

Who wouldn't want to be married to smart and organized go-getter Laura? I mean, besides me. I'd kill her. If she didn't kill me first. But really. She was the kind of person the world was always looking for. Seeing her run around our house wearing an apron, serving Paul as though he was bed-ridden, seemed wrong. But Laura declared it the Southern thing to do and therefore right.

Maybe I was prickly about it because Laura doting on Paul was a signal she was pulling away from Nina and me. She wasn't just falling in love, she was fertilizing the earth and laying down roots with another person. Which only reminded me of my own rootlessness and called further attention to my alone-ness.

I knew this was immature. It was life. I was grossly underdeveloped when it came to finding joy or expanding my circle of friends. Nina and I lapsed into a quiet brunch, segregated by our private thoughts.

I also suspected Laura skipped brunch because she was a bit mad at me. The pacing meeting and the conversation with my father had resulted in my employing a super-subversive reading curriculum. Instead of teaching according to some publishing company executive who'd never laid eyes on my kids, I'd developed lesson plans based on my internship experience and common sense—in reading, especially.

I didn't really know what I was doing, but I knew no one else at that school did, either. And I found it amazing that when all the crap is shaved from a day and students are provided interesting literacy activities, teaching didn't seem so bad. Best of all, the kids were actually learning. I could feel it.

Nina and Laura weren't so sure about my surreptitious lesson plans. They knew how much pleasure Klein got from attacking me for stupid little things, but now I was breaking the rules, big-time. Laura, especially, was a rule fiend.

Secretly, Nina admired me, I knew it. So, there I was, gently lifting myself out of my friendship cocoon, not wanting to, not wanting their disapproval, but knowing there were bigger things at stake. Things they'd hopefully understand at a later time, when they knew exactly what it felt like to be me. I mean, didn't everyone, at some point in their lives have to be the puzzle piece that didn't fit?

Chapter 11

Every Monday morning Klein held staff meetings in the school library. He made us give him the Lincoln thumbs-up to start things off. Nothing but crap filled the meetings most of the time—more ridiculous things we were expected to do to achieve high state test scores.

Twelve Lincoln teachers had been there at least two years. The other twelve were brand new to teaching. Only one new teacher, Nina, was black. Seven of the veteran teachers were black.

Unless directed otherwise, I always sat with Laura, Nina, Suzy, and Fionna (who, today, arrived late wearing a fur stole with a silky, though not totally sleazy, nightgown overtop leggings).

At the meetings we segregated ourselves—by seniority, mostly. My "partners," the two other women who taught the other fifth and sixth grade combination classes, ignored me most of the time. They were more of a fixture at Lincoln than Klein. They'd gone to the school as kids, still went to the church down the street and they didn't trust me. "You young girls…" was how they started every sentence. When not ignoring me, they told me I was screwing up. But no one made anyone as miserable as Klein did. If pushed, even my partners would stick up for me in front of him. That's the level of asshole he was.

Klein rocked on his heels then up on his toes. "I'd like to start the meeting by congratulating Culpepper, Fitzsimmons, Parker and the entire third grade team of rookie teachers. I am pleased with what I saw during my observations. The veterans performed okay."

I felt a pang of jealousy at Nina and Laura's success. I hated not being on the list. I despised giving my kids a sub-par education. But I was glad my friends weren't going through what I was. An emotional stew brewed inside me.

Klein actually smiled at the staff. His eyes lingered on Fionna, who giggled. I glanced around the room to see if anyone else had caught it. No one indicated they had. Maybe I was suffering from hallucinations now. Klein's smile faded when his gaze touched on me.

"So, people." Klein latched his hands behind his back, suit coat riding up his forearms. "Two items on the agenda. One is art. You're supposed to be teaching it. I'm not seeing it in your plans or objectives." Even the gilded teachers began to squirm and shift in their seats at this statement. In between reading and math, preparing for tests and breaking up fights, there was no time for non-art teachers to teach art.

"Which brings me to the second issue." Klein continued. "Objectives. I was in two rooms last week where there were no objectives on the board. The kids had no idea what they were doing in their lesson or why they were doing it. For once, it wasn't Jenkins. Miracles never cease."

He paused and everyone stared at me. Had that been a compliment or an insult?

No time to think about that. He went right back to blustering about keeping an emphasis on objectives. There were so many things wrong with that, I didn't know where to start. One, my kids didn't give a shit what the objective of a lesson is. Saying, "Hey jackasses, this is what you're going to learn in this lesson, so now let's learn it," wouldn't ensure learning took place.

Two, due to my super subversive curriculum, the objectives didn't match what we were doing. I wrote the objectives to match the required curriculum instead. If the kids noticed, they never said. I didn't tell them what I was up to. I wouldn't put them in the position of lying.

Though on one level I hated using—and certainly didn't want to get caught employing—an alternate curriculum, it had made a difference and for me there was no going back to Klein's way of instruction. The students were learning how authors chose words and constructed sentences to make readers sad, excited, and curious—the power in being able to do that.

We used music—both theirs and mine—as text. And they wrote. About everything. Their spelling was horrible and it took major effort to get their pieces cleaned up to the point at which they could be displayed, but the amount and kind of writing they were doing made them feel important. Official, they had said.

They were actually learning and there was a semblance of peace and optimism in the room. I'd take on the guilt if it meant making a difference in the kids' educations. I just hoped Klein would stay clear of my room. He'd already been in there since I'd started the program and not noticed anything was awry. I didn't want to be fired before I had a chance to make a lasting difference.

Klein drew me from my thoughts by telling me I was first on the list for art observations. Art observations? Please, I could give him my failing evaluation without even having to go through the torture of a lesson. I was many things, but an art teacher, I was not, nor could I even pretend to be.

Chapter 12

Heading toward my classroom, wondering how I was going to teach art in any kind of formal way, I felt drained. I heaved myself up the steps that led to my room when laughter from under the stairs—the storage space where I'd seen Fionna hide—caught my attention. I crept around the stairs and headed toward the closet. Smoke billowed from behind the door. Okay, it was just a few small snakes of cigarette smoke, but in a school, the snakes might as well have been billows.

I held my breath and peeked around the door. Fionna stood, eyes closed, head back, blowing smoke out of her nostrils.

"Fionna! What the hell are you doing?"

She leveled her gaze on me as though I'd invaded the privacy of her home. "Getting ready for class, that's all."

"You can't smoke here. You know that," I said. I looked around the storage closet. Boxes were stacked on the floor, and a makeshift table with a teeny lamp on it held Fionna's plan book—and some white powder on a small mirror. Cocaine? I'd never seen cocaine before. Why did my mind go there? Fionna was a teacher. Chalk dust.

"Fionna, don't smoke here. I don't want to—"

"What? Tell on me? Please. The girl who can't even pile

papers in an orderly fashion. That's rich."

"What's that?" I wiggled my finger at the white stuff on the tiny mirror in front of her.

Fionna shrugged.

Come on, Fionna. Tell me it's chalk dust, regular dust, fairy dust. Anything.

"It's not cocaine, is it?" I whispered. She dropped her head back again, sucked her ciggie and blew smoke rings. "I mean, *honestly*, Fionna, no."

"Don't be so self-righteous. We can't all live on the fumes of indignation. We're not all products of perfect homes and high expectations. I'm here to bring music into the lives of unfortunate souls. I mean, I'm supposed to be traveling the world with the symphony of my choosing. You know that's how I started out my life? At eight, attending the High School for Performing Arts. High school, Carolyn. Now I'm just here. Can you imagine?"

"It *is* cocaine?" I ignored her characterization of my upbringing. What did she know?

"What difference does it make?" Fionna said.

"The difference is there are kids here. They could find it, use it. You could hurt yourself. Them. It's *illegal*," I said. I ignored the mental reminder that I'd smoked pot a few weeks before.

Fionna dug her cigarette into her violin shaped ashtray and glanced at the powder.

"If you tell anyone about this, Carolyn, no one will believe you."

"I think they'd believe me before you. I can't be the only one who's noticed you've squirreled your drugs away under the main staircase of the school."

"I've got pull." She rolled her eyes as though she'd explained this several thousand times in a row. "You've got a messy classroom and even messier instructional methods. I've got twelve kids playing concertos and you've got thirty-six kids reading Curious George instead of grade-level science books. Don't make me embarrass you."

"What the hell do you mean, you have pull?"

She smirked at me, clearly not feeling obligated to elaborate on what she meant. The morning bell, which, at that moment, I learned was located in the storage room, clanged, piercing my skull. I stumbled from the closet, cupping my ears. The rising sounds of kids heading to class followed. I'd have to get to my room without resolving this with Fionna. "This isn't over, Fionna. You can't keep doing this."

"Phhhft." She swung her cigarette at me, telling me to move along.

She was right about one thing. Even in her jammies, she got a lot of music out of her kids and they flourished in her room. If not for the drugs, she might have been my idol.

**

I arrived at my room as the students were shuffling in. At my desk, I rearranged my mess and came across one of the papers I'd written Money's number on. I stared at it and wondered if Laura had been right that night at The Tuna, the last time I'd seen my fantasy man. Maybe I should focus less on this job, more on my social life. I'd call him. That would cheer me up. I shoved the paper into my pocket. This time I would leave a message.

I dug in my closet for some art supplies. I figured I'd better have my kids produce something to satisfy Klein's new demands. Craziness. Anyone who'd seen my splatter-painted TV room wall would immediately rip the art supplies from my grasp, forbidding me to even think about art, let alone try to teach it. I'd get the kids to respond to the story we were reading today by drawing. My focus would definitely stay on reading instruction.

I ordered the students to get into reading formation. They quickly, quietly, *surprisingly* moved their desks to the outer edges of the room, retrieved their carpet remnants and sat in the middle on the floor.

This welcoming setting signaled we were getting down to the business of comprehension. I created my own questions that made them think. And not just about how the story reminded them of a movie on TV, but real thinking about what the author was trying to convey. Using the text to inform their thoughts, they were empowered by the process. I was exhilarated. Feeling as though I'd moved from the act of babysitting to the art of teaching. In just a short time, I'd seen some changes in the kids. For instance today, it only took three exchanges about my hair and clothes to get Evette and company to settle into our novel, *Bridge to Terabithia*.

Hand raised. "Kenneth?"

"If you lived back in the day, would you have slaves?"

I sighed as though someone had just set fifty pounds of sand on my back. Two steps forward and one step back. This had nothing to do with *Bridge to Terabithia*. What was I supposed to do with this?

Lately, each day, Kenneth came bearing a new accusatory statement or knife-sharpened question. I always answered. Encouraging discussion seemed the right thing to do.

"Would I have had slaves? Well, really, I have no idea. I want to say, no, of course not. But if I had been wealthy and living in the South, I might have."

"Kenneth?" Evette said his name so it sounded more like Kinnith. "You cra-zay. No women had slaves back then. Only men."

Kenneth straightened in his seat and pointed at me. "Say you were a man. You'da had 'em."

"Why're you so sure of that?" I asked. "Maybe I'd have been one of the people helping with the Underground Railroad."

Evette put her hand up. "Ain't none of the whites in this room woulda had slaves. Not Katya, Jimmy, Crystal or Ms. Jenkins. Why you say that, Kenneth?"

Kenneth put on his best menacing expression. "Cause Ms. Jenkins's white. Pure and simple. Whites had slaves."

"She ain't white," Jamaica yelled. "She *black*. Light skinned, but black." The students gaped at normally mute Jamaica.

"What do you mean, she's *black*, Jamaica?" Terri broke the silence, her face screwed up as though she'd just swallowed a bug. "She looks like Ricki Lake. She and Ms. Hooper, they twins.

And I know Ms. Hooper's white as the social worker who visits your mamma everyday."

Jamaica flinched.

"Hold on there," I held up my hand. "First, I don't look like Ricki Lake. Second, Ms. Hooper has blond hair and sapphire blue eyes and is a whole year younger than me. We're not even from the same state. And about me being black..." I leaned forward and almost whispered. "Why'd you say that, Jamaica?"

She stared at me. Her lips started to move, then stopped. "You can't be white. You too nice."

"She *ain't* nice," LeAndre mumbled. He cackled at the ceiling, his rolling chuckles steadily rising in volume, then stopping abruptly. He jumped up onto the chair beside him and then back onto his square of carpet. He looked back at the chair with a surprised then confused expression on his face that seemed to ask, "Did I just do that?"

Once he settled back into a rocking chant, we got back to work with the novel. The others just proceeded as though it were perfectly normal for him to behave in such a way. They seemed to view him with a kind of frightened awe. They weren't going to provoke whatever misunderstood instinct lay below his skin. There were few fights these kids didn't think they could win, but LeAndre was one of those fights. And besides the day with Cedrick, this was the only fight I'd seen them back away from, ever.

**

There was a stillness, a calm all that morning as we read and discussed the novel. I reveled in the peace, the unforced harmony. Something important sat in our circle of instruction as the silence remained, something that told me I had made the right decision with the subversive curriculum. At one point I opened my mouth to ask the students a question, but a small click sounded above our heads before I spoke.

We all looked to the ceiling. The intercom. *They* were listening. I'd completely forgotten what Bobby Jo had said the day of the BB-gun debacle. It had never been quiet enough for us to hear it before. Dammit, I thought. I leapt from my carpet remnant. I wasn't going to let them do this. I pressed the intercom button by the door.

"Yes? Do you need something?" I said.

A small gasp caught in Bobby Jo's voice. "Uh. No. No. Um. Yes. Don't forget to hand in the sheets Mr. Klein put in your— oh, check your mailbox. That's it. Check your mail for some forms."

"Mm-hmm. Thanks, Ms. Carpenter." I let go of the button and wiped my brow with trembling fingers. I went back to my chair.

"They listening in on you? On us?" Marvin asked.

"I don't think so. I think—"

"Now, Mr. Klein, he *white*," Jamaica said with so much emphasis the whole class erupted in laughter, hooting. I put on my best poker face. Boy, I wanted to laugh along with them. If white meant asshole, he was the whitest ever born.

"Okay. Inappropriate. Okay. We have work to do. None of this will mean anything if we don't actually learn to read. That's so important," I said.

"More than math?" Kenneth asked.

"Well, no. But for now, reading is our emphasis. And writing. We're going to explore some of the ideas we were talking about in writing. And start a project. But for now, let's just finish this chapter."

They nodded enthusiastically. Thank God in Heaven. They were smiling and it wasn't because someone just cracked on another's mother. They were actually happy to be there reading and learning.

As we finished our chapter, pinging sounds from the windows drew our attention. Another interruption. But one I was grateful for—Cedrick's uncle. Each day he checked in on Cedrick's behavior via the window. I gave him the okay sign and turned back to my still silent class.

I jumped at the sight of Klein standing in the middle of the room, glaring at me.

"Well." He threw his arm out toward the blackboard. "Your

objectives are on the board."

I nodded. I balled my hands to make them stop shaking. I knew my secret curriculum was right for the kids, but I didn't want to be fired. I waited for him to notice the books in their laps, to realize we were not doing what the objective on the board stated for that time. But he'd only glanced at the board. If quizzed I was sure he wouldn't be able to recall the content of the objectives. He in fact seemed to be focused on something completely different than what I was worried about. What that was, though, I didn't know.

"I'll see you at three. In my office." He flicked on my lights as he left.

My stomach knotted. Now I'd have to worry until the end of the day. But that was probably part of the fun for Klein.

"I'd kill that man if he was chillin' me that way," Jimmy said.

"I'd take out my nine," LeAndre added.

"No, no, no. That's not how you handle things like this. This is exactly why you learn to read and write. To become powerful. No one can ever take your education away. Ever. It can't be stolen. It becomes part of who you are. Or aren't."

"You don't seem so powerful," Kenneth said.

Ouch.

"I am. Trust me."

I knew Klein was pissed at something but, I also realized we may have fooled him. He hadn't noticed the *Bridge to Terabithia* novels. He may have realized we weren't spelling, but that was all he knew. If he'd had any inkling I was up to something instructionally subversive, he wouldn't have hesitated to pull me down to the office right that moment. I wasn't dumb enough to think he wouldn't kick my ass if he caught me, but it was good to know he tended not to catch what was beyond the end of his nose.

I gathered the materials for the next lesson as the kids shoved their desks back into rows. No skirmishes during the process.

Despite progress with comprehension and engagement

during lessons, my kids were always one word, one sardonic expression away from a wrestling match. This might lead to someone throwing a chair—or whatever was handy—across the room. Other times, they did the macho dance: two boys circled each other waiting for me to break them up so no one would have to back down.

And then there was the general yelling out—threatening me with lawsuits for having them do homework, calling them on their non-compliance, noticing their unwillingness to walk in a line quietly and so on. Unless Klein was there. That was the only time they followed my directions. At first I thought they behaved in front of Klein because they were afraid of him, but it had become clear they were doing it for me. I felt stupid being grateful, but I was.

**

I gave my instructions for the assignment to the class—a writing assignment that would keep them on-task much of the time because writing was constructive, not passive in nature. This allowed me to take a small group of the non and slow readers to work with them in peace. The most basic part of reading—decoding—was still a problem for them. I could get great discussions going, but none of that would matter if these students weren't fluent, independent decoders.

I didn't really know what I was doing. This was beginning reading instruction after all, not intermediate instruction. And asking for help, stating that the prescribed reading materials were horrible and worthless, would be met with yet another round of harassing interactions with Klein.

Five out of six of the low-functioning kids came to sit with me as requested. LeAndre was missing. I glanced behind me and saw he was still at his desk.

"LeAndre, come on. We're ready." I passed out the materials to the children who had gathered. The room was still relatively quiet. God, I thought, I've actually made headway.

I began to think about writing an article for *Teacher* magazine on how to muddle through the first year of teaching when the sound of scuffling made me look over my shoulder. Some kids dove under desks and others scattered to the outskirts of the room.

Please don't let LeAndre have a gun again, please.

I turned slowly, chilled by the prospect of what could be happening. LeAndre stood on his chair, holding my huge pair of teacher scissors open, with one point poised at his eyelid, under his brow bone.

His shoulders heaved with labored breath. His hand shook, causing the point to nick him and a spot of blood to appear. More of a scratch than a laceration, I told myself. That's good. Stay calm.

"LeAndre." I stood. He didn't respond so I went toward him wishing I could make him stop, wanting to give him whatever was missing from his life. If I only knew exactly what he lacked.

Sweat beaded at his hairline, then dripped onto his cheeks. He'd seemed mentally unstable all year, his moods swinging like a trapeze. He'd threatened to kill a classmate with a disturbing mix of remorse and conviction, crying while threatening. That, the gun incident and countless behavior referrals to Klein had yielded nothing in the way of support for me, other students or LeAndre himself.

Across the room, by the door, Marvin's hand snaked up the wall toward the red button—the emergency button. I nodded to let him know he could press it.

I crept closer to LeAndre, not knowing what I'd do once I got there. "Could you put those down, LeAndre? We don't want to see you get hurt. Please."

His voice seemed disembodied, scratchy, not his. "I *can't*. I want to, but I *can't*." I could see the battle below his skin, behind his eyes. His mind wanted to stop his dangerous behavior, but his body wouldn't let him. It was as though he were being held captive by himself.

"Put down the scissors," I said. "Will you give them to me? We don't want to see you hurt, LeAndre." My heart heaved and quickened as his desperation stabbed at my soul, bled through my body.

"I'm already hurt."

"I know, LeAndre. I—"

The door swung open and Klein sauntered straight to LeAndre as though he were blowing bubbles and singing nursery rhymes instead of threatening to impale himself. The kids who were still standing hit the floor and rolled into balls.

LeAndre turned the scissors on Klein. The balled up kids covered their heads with their arms. Klein hesitated. He raised his hands in surrender. "Ooooo-kay. Let's get Miss Tucker in here. And everyone else out."

He backed up to the door and pressed the intercom button. He asked Bobby Jo to send the counselor down, that it was an emergency. He motioned for the rest of the kids to move out of the room.

Miss Tucker arrived and asked me to leave. LeAndre was hyperventilating. I didn't want to leave him, didn't want him to think I'd leave him alone, not knowing what would happen next.

"Your class needs you, Miss Jenkins," Miss Tucker said firmly. "LeAndre and I will be all right. I can take it from here."

I nodded. It. Take it from here? Exactly what that meant, I had no idea.

Chapter 13

Hauntingly bad described the rest of the day. The boys felt the need to spread their pre-adolescent testosterone all over the library in response to LeAndre's breakdown. We stayed there until paramedics delivered him to the hospital. Klein was due at a principal's meeting but had given me a quick, scathing reprimand in front of the kids. He'd actually had the balls to ask me why I hadn't reported LeAndre's odd behaviors.

Luckily, the orange copies of all the three-page forms I'd filled out were safely stowed in my desk. Just because Klein hadn't acted on any of my referrals didn't mean I hadn't written them. And it didn't mean I'd thrown them out just because he didn't care enough to help. And there was my journal. I documented everything every kid was up to in my class. Not for the reasons Klein wanted me to document things. I actually cared. LeAndre's attempt to stab Klein finally got his attention. It had offended him, apparently.

I wanted to tell the kids to go back to the room and just read. Or write. Or draw cartoons. Whatever. Just stay quiet and get through the day. But unstructured time was a recipe for brawls, spats and girls pulling out each other's weaves by the handful.

That was one of the hardest parts of teaching. There was absolutely no down time. Not one minute. My mind wandered back to Pittsburgh where I'd done my teaching internship. My mentor would have been having lunch right then. A whole hour. No lunch duty, no recess duty. She would have been in the teachers' lounge eating slowly, discussing the upcoming sale at Saks. Camelot. That was how they referred to their school. They didn't know how right they were.

Once we were permitted back in our room, the kids ambled through the hall, but for the first time it was a straight line. One of my grade-level "partners" was leading her class to gym. She couldn't resist smirking at me. She was obviously aware of the LeAndre situation. One of her kids, Marcell, started hopping on one foot, squealing about something in his shoe. My partner strode over to him, took him by the collar with one hand and gently, but firmly moved him back against the lockers. She didn't hurt him, but I thought the act was inappropriate and embarrassing to the student.

I shot her a scolding look. She shook her head and walked into her room with her class trailing behind.

Inside my room, I flicked on the lights. Kenneth was the first in the classroom behind me. "You touch me like that, I'll call my daddy's lawyer."

"And you should, Kenneth. You should."

**

When Nina and Laura realized I wasn't coming down from my classroom at the end of the day, they searched me out. I knew they must have already heard the story several times over. I was wandering around my room, picking up the remnants of the day, organizing it into piles of garbage and stuff to save.

"I feel like I'm living in the twilight zone," I said. "My heart's broken about LeAndre. Broken. In little pieces. I've never seen someone in such visible emotional pain. It was the equivalent of watching someone saw off a limb with a dull blade."

"You see, they know that about you," Nina said. "The

minute you sat them in that crazy friendship arc the first day of school your number was up, sister. They know you have no idea who they are and they're exploiting that like a con man in an old folks home."

"Pshaw," I said. "What about Laura here?" I shoved my thumb in her direction. "Don't tell me *she* understands any more about these kids than me."

Nina balled up a paper from my desk and shot it into the overstuffed garbage can. "Her blockheads? They barely know their names. They have no idea what she knows or doesn't."

"*Nina.*" Laura laughed. "Mine are just so much younger than yours, Caro. Four or five years make a big difference. They're still little sweethearts in first grade. I'm starting from ground zero with them. That's very different."

I crumpled up a piece of paper and bounced it from one hand to the other. "I'm starting to think it's partly because I'm white. Kenneth brings up race nearly every day." I shot the paper ball at the wastebasket. It hit the rim and bounced off.

"That little thing? Race just occurred to you now? What have I been telling you?" Nina balled up another sheet and sunk it into the basket.

"Well, skin color isn't supposed to matter." I tossed another balled-up sheet and it ricocheted out. "But Ms. Soto across the hall took Marcell by the shirt and moved him back into the lockers. I wouldn't say it was a push, but I would never do anything like that." I snapped my fingers. "Her whole class snapped to attention. I'm starting to think she can get away with that stuff because she's black. No one threatened to sue her like Kenneth did to me. Me, who's never laid a hand on any of them."

"Soto," Nina said, "has leeway because she went to school with her kids' grandmothers. A black teacher who was more like you than Soto would have just as much trouble with your kids."

"So it's *not* just me or my race?"

Laura gathered some papers and stacked them. "Course it's not you."

"Oh, it's you," Nina said. "Though your problems are not

completely because of your color."

"I can't change that, Nina." My heart sank. If it were as simple as my race, I would have to quit now. "What am I supposed to do about my race?"

Nina grabbed me and squeezed me into her body. "Quit obsessing, for one. You just need to understand where they're coming from a little more. So let's go out and get some beers. Maybe you can call the geezer. What's his name? Bike or something? I was thinking I should start a serious campaign to find the love of my life since you're both moving in that direction."

I was fine letting her change the subject. I was tired of thinking. "I wouldn't say I'm moving that way. I haven't even talked to Jeep since, well, The Tuna." I fired another balled up piece of paper into the basket, finally sinking one.

I raised my hands in victory. "A guy like him wouldn't have time to listen to a whiny, down-in-the-dumps-about-her-job girl, would he? Besides, Laura has chores for me, right? Does that sound like a line from Little House on the Prairie or what?"

"Relax. Laura's in love. She's loosening up," Nina said.

Laura stopped organizing my papers and looked up, face reddened.

"Paul's coming again tonight?" I said.

Laura balled up a paper, tossing it into the garbage can.

"Oh, he's coming all right," Nina answered for Laura. "I can hear everything that goes on in that bedroom and it's not pretty," Nina said.

"As if listening to you having sex with your latest paramour would sound like Mozart," I said.

"Is that all you can talk about?" Laura said. "Some folks are oversexed."

"Paul must be sporting some serious blue balls." Nina pushed aside a stack of papers and sat on the edge of my desk.

"You have to give it up someday. Right?" I said.

Laura grinned. "I did."

"Really?" I said.

"Nah. Just wanted to see what it felt like to say it." Laura smiled deviously.

"The cat that ate the canary," Nina said suspiciously.

"Nah," I said. "She didn't do it yet. She'd tell us. At this point, we're as much a part of her sex life as she is. She'd have to tell us."

"Let's not get dramatic," Laura said.

I moved to sit on the desktop with Nina, scooching her over with my butt. "Do you think LeAndre will be all right?"

Nina smiled, no sign of sarcasm. "I don't know. But there's nothing you can do about it."

"I hate answers like that," I said.

"I know. You like to wrestle the world into submission."

"Don't we all?" I replied.

"No," Laura and Nina said at the same time.

Then, affectionately coerced by my friends, I called Jeep from the teacher's room. They stood beside me like I was in high school and I ended up leaving a giddy, nonsensical message on his machine. Then, due to my painfully ridiculous message, I had to call back and proclaim that the prior message was left while I'd been undercover. Yeah, I know. Stupid. But that's just how it was.

Chapter 14

A full week after LeAndre flipped his lid, I still didn't know how his treatment was progressing. Getting information from his mom, Klein, anyone, was like trying to penetrate a six-inch cement wall with your fingers. LeAndre's mother returned one of my calls, but had no information. That was typical. I hadn't been able to get in touch with her all year. She was never available to discuss her son and I had to fight hard not to think bad thoughts about her, to assign the label of negligent to the image of her in my mind.

Klein had no information and didn't care. Even the guidance counselor, Miss Tucker, was useless in terms of information. We'd eventually have an Instructional Support Team meeting where everything would be sorted out. Until then, LeAndre went with me everywhere. On my mind. In my heart.

On the positive side, his absence seemed to calm the class and after a few days I began to think we were cresting over the worst of the school year. Things were actually going well, great, actually. The kids quietly filled their backpacks at the end of the day. I would begin to clean my room like a normal teacher, though it was still a holy mess. There were no more crises, no meetings with Klein.

"Hey, Miss Jenkins?" Kenneth said one afternoon. "That big old secretary's chiming in again."

"Polite, book language, Kenneth."

It *was* odd that Klein wasn't doing the end-of-day announcements. But it had been a good day and I wouldn't let it be ruined with thoughts of Bobby Jo and Klein.

Before Kenneth could rephrase his statement, the classroom door creaked open. Klein waltzed in with three men. Two were dressed in Secret Service vests. One wore a suit. He was familiar. No, I thought. It couldn't be him.

Breath left my chest. It couldn't be him. Money? I looked away and back again. It *couldn't* be him.

His gaze worked its way around the room, the kids, the mess. Then me. We stared at each other. I shook my head. This couldn't be happening.

Money's expression changed from serious to delighted, then back to dire. He looked at a note card, then back at me. "Ms. Jenkins," he said. He nodded as though we ran into each other in my school all the time.

My throat constricted. Money's gaze left mine and again traced every inch of my messy room. Shelves were piled with books, papers, binders. There was crap everywhere. I felt utterly nude—exposed for the super-fraud I was. Stupid that I thought another day could end on a high note.

Klein shuffled around poking students, telling some that they needed to come with him and the other men. There was no discussion about the nature of this invasion. Another weapon situation? That would warrant the Bureau of Alcohol, Tobacco and Firearms. Not the Secret Service. It was a confusing mess and as Money left the room with four of my boys in tow, he turned. "Nice room."

What the hell did that mean?

Terri stepped beside me and squeezed my shoulder. "He your father?"

"Who?" I said.

"The suit man."

"No." Jesus God, no.

"Your lover?" Tanesha stepped up to my other shoulder.

I hated that word. I cringed when an adult used it. I almost puked to hear a child employ it.

"What? No." I said.

"Your brother?" Cedrick asked from across the room.

"Of course not." I signaled the kids to line up for dismissal.

I couldn't have been more mortified if Money had opened my head and read my thoughts. How childish was the whole "pretend you have a cool job" game my friends and I always played? Not that he'd bought it. But I'd picked the FBI, for Christ's sake. And now he'd seen my atrociously messy room. If he ever had an interest in me, it was gone now.

"Ms. Jenkins." Marvin shuffled his feet as the class walked down the hall toward the doors. "You said you wanted to talk to me after school."

"I do. But Mr. Klein wants to meet with me about whatever this situation is and I have no idea how long that's going to take. Tomorrow?"

"I ain't got nothin' better to do." He threw his backpack over his shoulder.

"A born leader like you. Good athlete. You must have all kinds of stuff going on after school."

He shrugged. "Don't worry about Mr. Klein," Marvin said as the line of kids snaked out the door and down the stairs. He stayed behind and spoke quietly. "It's just Old Ms. Holloway making funny money again. The boys, they spent the money at lunch. Ain't got nothin' to do with you."

I was stunned. I was glad to have this information before meeting with Klein, to know that this type of activity could not be pinned on me in the least bit. I shouldn't have been surprised no one let me know it was common for some students' family members to make counterfeit money—why would they tell me before this point? What would I have done if they'd told me? We certainly didn't have an action-plan for what to do if I heard rumors about funny money.

"Thanks," I said. "For the heads up."

"Yo," he said as he started outside.

"Marvin." I thought about the way everyone in the class knew about the gun before it grew into the shooting incident. I considered all the improper, sometimes frightening information they carried around with them. "Why don't you guys tell me this stuff *before* someone gets caught?"

"We don't want to disappoint."

"Oh." I pushed my shoulders down and back. "That's not your job. I'm the adult."

He nodded and readjusted the backpack straps over his shoulder.

"Be careful going home," I said. I watched him leave the building, whistling. They didn't want to disappoint? That would imply some sort of respect. But that didn't exist as far as I could see. Up until now, they merely tolerated me, only did what I asked when in the mood. Perhaps with what Marvin said, I could begin to see things differently—perhaps in fact, they were finally getting ready to learn.

**

I reached the office to find Bobby Jo waiting for me. She had an exasperated expression on her face and jerked her head toward Klein's office as she arranged papers without even looking down. She hit the stapler with her fist then plopped the new set onto the finished pile and punched again. The drum-like pattern of sound stamped through the quiet of the office.

Standing just outside Klein's office I took a deep breath and let it out. Thanks to Marvin's information, I was at least semi-prepared for this meeting. No way could Klein blame me for this. I'd fake confidence. Be the girl at The Tuna. Think FBI. Think Girl At The Bar. I knocked on the doorjamb.

"Enter," Klein barked.

I put on my poker face. Having Money see my classroom was similar to having a one-night-stand and then, in full light, having to walk across the room naked. No way to hide faults. Every last bump and dip in your body visible to someone who may or may not give a shit about you.

This was worse. I looked good nude. My nightmares

revolved around people seeing the disorder that ruled my existence. Poise. Communicate poise. I relaxed my hands at my side but felt like they were pulling my shoulders forward so I held them at my waist, as though I was about to sing opera.

Klein chewed the inside of his mouth and tapped his fingers on the binder in front of him. "Another acrimonious event. This is becoming way too common."

I nodded.

The uniformed guys were expressionless. Jeep smiled, melting my insides. I'd die if I actually had sex with him. Maybe I should. Just to do it. I was falling in love. With an image. Not an actual person. What? Did I always have to be in love? Think I was in love?

"Jenkins!"

"Huh?" I sounded like one of my fifth graders.

"Huh?" Klein said. "Four boys in your class are passing counterfeit bills. That's huh."

I narrowed my eyes and glared at him.

"Your class is running like a pack of wild animals—"

I held up my hand. He shut up. "With all due respect," I said, "I'm not anybody's mother here. I didn't raise them. I take exception that you would imply in even the tiniest way I have sanctioned or contributed to the passing of funny money."

I turned on my heel and stopped, looking over my shoulder. "I have my weekly lesson plans to get to. I'm not trying to be rude, but...I have to go." And with that, I walked out the door. My heart sped with all the energy and abandon he'd ascribed to my class.

Bobby Jo puffed out her cheeks then blew out her air as though she'd had a rough day herself. I caught her smirking as I went by.

"And you can stuff it, Bobby Jo." I didn't stick around to see her response, but I knew without looking I would pay for such hubris. She and Klein would certainly make me pay.

**

With long strides I headed to my room. My spine

straightened as I moved, even while knowing I'd locked myself into many more months of principal-inflicted hell by not submitting to Klein's abuse in front of Money. I couldn't breathe. I felt dizzy and collapsed into my chair, where my body settled but my heart rate didn't.

I leaned back in my chair and realized I had never really sat in it. There was never an opportunity to. I laughed at my gall in Klein's office and stared at the ceiling. It was then I saw them. Fifty spitballs adhered to the ceiling, splattered around in such a way that in another context they might be considered abstract art. When'd they do *that*? I was asking that question way too often.

My door creaked open. I didn't look away from the ceiling. I was off the clock, officially, and so Klein could officially kiss my ass. I had to take advantage of what I knew would be momentary boldness.

The feet coming toward me weren't Klein's. The sound of Klein's shuffling feet were forever embedded in my brain, sure to torture me when I was old with Alzheimer's. Or maybe in hell. I'd just float around some creepy place, sweating my ass off, listening for the sound of Klein's feet.

Money's face appeared above mine. He peered down at me. I stilled. I was sitting in the most unattractive slouch in the world. My legs were parted. Luckily my skirt hadn't hiked up too far up my thighs, and with opaque tights, I didn't look obscene. What was left to hide, anyway? He had seen all this. H-Factor: 1/10.

"I guess the jig's up." He smiled.

"It appears to be," I said.

"The Holloway boys—their mother and aunt running bad bills, you, the FBI stuff," he shook his head. "I should clean up this shithole once and for all."

I swiveled the seat back and forth, hand resting on my head. "Shithole? You blind, my friend?"

"This is some operation you have going here," he said.

"Funny, funny, funny, Secret Service man." I sat up. "Now what am I to call you? Money? Jeep? G-man?"

"Jeep'll do."

"So. You busted a big one. You know the real me. What's next? Hightailing it back to the Cindy Crawford lookalike? What are you still doing here?" I didn't have time to be pissed on by yet another person, especially someone who thought I was a big asshole. That was going to be my new motto. Pissed on no more.

"I'm asking you for a date."

I sat up. A date?

"Tonight," he said.

"I have plans. I mean lesson planning."

"I'll pick you up." He walked toward the door.

"But you don't know—"

"I know where you live."

With that, he left. His boots reverberated down the hall. He knew where I lived? I ran after him. "Hey, Jeep." The name was growing on me. "Wait." I stopped just inches from him, looking into his face.

The lines near his eyes creased. "What?" His voice was patient. He looked at me as though there was nothing in the world he'd rather do than share space with me.

I went up on my tippy-toes and touched his stubbly cheek. That smell again. So familiar, yet specific to him. A guy I'd only met three times. He grabbed my wrist, pulled me into his body and kissed me hard, our hands, clasped between us. His tongue was warm and gentle. My body came to life.

Static burst from his radio.

He pulled away. "Be ready at seven."

I fell against the lockers, watching him walk away. He knew I'd be ready. Dear God in Heaven, I was ready.

Crap Quotient: 3/10 (pending further harassment from Klein).

H-Factor: Holy shit, it's high.

Chapter 15

After a quick stop at Ann Taylor for a great pair of pants and a sexy but not-trying-too-hard top, I dressed for my date. I could go almost anywhere in the outfit with the exception of an Aerosmith concert or formal ball.

I leaned over the sink and studied my face in the mirror. Carefully, I sponged on just enough foundation to even out my skin tone, lined my upper lids with chocolate eyeliner and also used it to just slightly darken my eyebrows. Mascara was the final touch.

Next I used the cheapest Wet and Wild lip liner in the world. Smashing while understated. Number 666. I filled in my lips with it, and voila, color that never wiped off. If I woke up beside Jeep the next day, I wouldn't look any different than I did now.

But that wouldn't happen. I wouldn't have sex again until I was married. Laura had it right. I leaned in close to the mirror and stared at my face, trying to figure out what I looked like to Jeep. Had he noticed one of my eyes was greener than the other? That they changed colors depending on...I don't even know what, exactly. If he didn't notice this type of thing, I was bagging him. No more wasting time on guys who don't notice things. No way.

**

Waiting made me nervous. The type of insecurity that had led me to stay in a relationship with Alex for three years was sitting firmly inside me, just waiting to spring back into action as though only pretending to have gone away.

I sipped wine and told myself there was nothing about me that was "less than" this guy except at least a decade of age. The roommates weren't around to talk me down so I had to do it myself. I'd banned them from this event. If they were around when Jeep arrived, we'd all end up at the Green Turtle. It had happened to every one of the guys that they had dated. There was no first-dating one of us. It was all of us. And so far, none of the first dates at the Green Turtle had yielded a second.

A soft knock at the door caused chills to run up my neck. I opened the door. This was nothing. No big deal. Pretend it's the only date with him. Have fun and nothing else. Above all, sex. None of that. As if he'd asked to have some.

"Hi." He beamed.

"Hi." I stepped aside. "Want some wine?" I cringed. Not exactly a graceful welcome.

"Sure. But not too much. We have someplace to be," he said.

"Mysterious."

He held out a small, carved box tied with a brown velvet ribbon. Not pink, white, or red. Brown, the perfect color for velvet. The box still in his hand, I felt the ribbon. Backed with silk. Who was this guy? Sent by Satan himself—someone to trick me. Had to be.

"Carolyn? Here. Open it." He put the box in my hands. We sat on the couch.

"That's some paint job. Splattery," he said.

"Cool, huh?"

"It's unique," he said sweetly.

I raised the box to him. "I can't believe you're proposing already. Was it my frightening tidiness? The stunning amount of respect from Klein? Or how I'm ever calm, effective and full of the right answers with my students?"

"No." Jeep took one of my hands and kissed it. "It's the opposite of that," he said. "The opposite."

Screw my pre-marital sex rules. We should have sex right now, I thought. Even if I had no idea what "the opposite of that," meant. It sounded freaking fantastic. I couldn't move.

"Not that I'm proposing," he whispered. "That'd be immature."

"Yeah." I looked at the two by four inch wooden box, ran my finger over its curved carvings. I glanced at Jeep then pulled the bow free. The ribbon fell into my lap. I lifted the hinged lid. Empty.

I looked up from the box and met Jeep's gaze.

"For your dreams." He shrugged. "Your worries. Your darkness." His quiet words were matter of fact, as though everyone in the world gave corny, beautiful, totally perfect gifts every day of the year.

I realized I was holding my breath. "Sex," I said. "We should have sex. Get it over with. I can't take the tension." I couldn't handle such depth of sincerity and thoughtfulness.

He laughed.

"Ha-ha…kidding." I retraced the carved box, trying to compose myself. "The gift. It's so beautiful. I'm kidding. I don't want to have sex with you at all."

"Of course you don't," he said. No sign of hurt. We looked into each other's eyes, my knees touching his.

"That's what I like about you," he said, "you don't want me at all."

"Well, shit. Don't tell me this is all about some crazy chase."

"Carolyn. Put the gift in your room and let's go."

I felt wobbly as I set the box below the mirror on my dresser. Alex had bought me one thing the entire time we dated. A sweater. And I had to pick it out and remind him forty-two times before he showed up with it.

I wound the velvet ribbon around my finger then placed it beside the box and looked into the mirror. Jeep didn't need to notice anything about my face or eyes. He already knew every inch of my soul. My eyes burned. I wiped my lower lids and pushed the feelings away.

They were good feelings, great as a matter of fact. But I couldn't trust them. They would consume me if I let them settle in. It told myself to enjoy the moment, that I didn't have to let my fantasies take over. This was merely a chance for fun and if anyone deserved some amusement in life, it was I.

**

Forty minutes after Jeep gave me the gift of a lifetime, we arrived at his home in Chevy Chase. Pulling into the driveway of his white Cape Cod, I'd already doomed the relationship. Based solely on the perfect gift. I mean, where do you go from there? It's a jagged fall from grace after that. There's no way to meet those heights again, let alone eclipse them. But still, I could have fun for one night.

The home was cuter than I imagined—handsome, grown up. Very grown up. The yard was neat. A gently curving brick walkway led from the street to the house. A complementary curving garden lined the walk and must have given way to extraordinary color in spring. My nerves pricked at me. I should have opted for the group date.

He opened my car door and reached for my hand. I couldn't focus. I had never even considered love at first sight, but here it seemed to be.

Infatuation, dummy.

We walked up to the porch where the light flicked on and a woman opened the front door.

His sister, Mary Colleen. I'd met her at The Tuna.

She put her hand out. "Hi. We met at that seedy bar."

"Yes. Hi, I'm Carolyn. Good to see you again." Tell me they weren't living together.

"I'm just picking these up for Tess," Colleen shook a delicate set of towels at us. "His ex-fiancée. She needs them for her new place. Don't forget about tomorrow. Mary Helen will kill you if you're late for dinner. Big plans to work through. The extravaganza." She glanced at me.

I hid the grimace I felt at knowing Jeep had an ex-fiancé. It shouldn't matter. I wouldn't let it matter.

"Okay, MC. See you tomorrow." Jeep kissed her cheek and shut the door behind her.

Extravaganza plans? MC seemed to be pissing all over Jeep. Letting me know he wasn't unattached even if he didn't have a girlfriend. But I could be paranoid, so I decided to leave that assessment up in the air for a while.

"This is it." He waved me farther into the foyer. It featured a green, blue, and reddish slate floor and a gorgeous mahogany writing desk. The stacks of mail on it tempted my nosy gaze. Sage green walls complemented the floor. A crystal chandelier was the finishing touch. The cozy feel of the space made me want to move in.

Everything that was wrong with my house suddenly flashed through my mind. Its garish obviousness. My *God*, the red splatter paint, for the love of Mary. He must have thought we'd hired some of our kindergartners for the job.

Jeep's comment that the red-splattered wall was "unique," suddenly took on more meaning. What could he possibly think was worth knowing about me? Talk about the wayward puzzle piece. Trouble was, I didn't know if it was me who was in the wrong box, in this case, or Jeep. What could he possibly see in me?

The dining room to the left and the living room to the right were outfitted with gleaming, dark hardwood floors.

"You stealing from the government or something?" I said. "Maybe putting some of that counterfeit money to use?"

"Family money. Can't escape it no matter how I try." He shrugged. "It's not overdone, is it?"

"Uh. No. You don't even have anything in here." I walked into the living room and spun around, arms out to my sides. It was cavernous and empty. Further confirmation of the cheesiness of our house.

"I don't need the living room, so I didn't think I should do anything with it. I watch TV in the den." He wrapped me in his arms from behind.

There were so many things I wanted to ask. I should have requested an interview instead of agreeing to this date. I hated all the not knowing. What were his favorite TV shows? Songs? Just how much money did his family have? What in hell's half acre goes on during the private family dinners?

He led me into the dining room. The polished floors were covered with an Oriental rug in brick red, ruby red, burgundy and other reds I couldn't put names to. A traditional dining table stood bare with ten chairs around it. Brick red walls warmed the room. "You don't mind if we eat in the kitchen? It'll be more comfortable."

"Afraid I'll spill on the Oriental carpet, are you?"

"That, too." He pulled my face to his. No warning. Just the second most magnificent kiss imaginable. It was softer than the one in the hallway at school. His spicy smell and gentle lips lingered on mine, making the rest of me melt into his body as though we'd been made for each other.

He pulled away. "I'm making you dinner."

I nodded. I was glad he wanted to take it slow. He had just learned my name that day, after all. He took my hand and we went into the kitchen. Exposed brick walls gave way to floor to ceiling windows and professional quality appliances. The walk-in fireplace and rough, hewed pine mantel contrasted artfully with the lustrous floors. This guy had some balls. Who the hell used hardwood in a kitchen?

The space that ran the width of the back of the house was divided in half. Part kitchen, part den. Homey wooden blinds covered the windows. An old trunk served as the coffee table. A leather couch, loveseat and chair beckoned to me with promised comfort. Bookshelves marched around every square inch of wall holding academic books and paperbacks—thrillers, murder mysteries, courtroom dramas. We had more in common every second. And he'd clearly read them all and wasn't one of those types who could read but chose not to.

Still more shelves held beer steins, mugs with faces, and stacks of Sports Illustrated and others displayed classic tomes by

Austin, Wharton and Dickens, et al. I thought of my parents. They loved those authors.

How long had I been gawking? He was busy at the sink. Maybe he hadn't decorated all this himself. The fiancé. This must have been her handiwork.

"I made dinner," Jeep said. "And without asking what you like. Don't take that as a sign I'm controlling or anything."

I nodded and sat on the stool at the marble island. I shooed my insecurities away and they shuffled back in.

"Carolyn. You're supposed to say it was the definition of controlling to plan a meal for a woman I barely know and not ask her what she likes to eat."

"Of course you're controlling. You're a man," I said.

"There's that sass I've come to know and…"

The word didn't come out. I should have wired myself up so the girls could listen to the date and interpret it. The whole family money thing was freaking me out. It wasn't as if I'd grown up poor. Or that my parents hadn't given me the most important things: education, creativity, independence, but this kind of stuff was different.

He slid a glass of white wine into my hands.

"So what's for dinner?" I said.

"Why don't you go check the guest bathroom?"

"Bathroom?"

"The tub, to be specific," he said.

He led me to the hall bathroom, pointing out his office, guestroom, and master bedroom along the way.

I waited at the door while he entered the room and pulled the shower curtain open. "Ta-da!" He grinned.

What the hell? I stepped into the bathroom, noticing the gorgeous towel and soap displays and finally I peered into the tub. I grasped the towel rack to steady myself. There, plain as anything, as though perfectly normal, were two flopping lobsters.

"Lobsters?" I stared at them so I didn't have to look at him.

"I figured you for a seafood aficionado," he said.

Not when I got to see said seafood frolicking in someone's bathtub.

KATHLEEN SHOOP

"They're not pets?" I said. "Boy, I'm relieved because I don't like animals." I ran my hand across my forehead dramatically.

"You do like seafood, right?" He looked anxious.

"I love it," I said, walking out of the room.

"Good. I'll boil these up and we'll be eating in just a few minutes."

I forced a smile to cut through my grimace. My heart plummeted in my chest. That was reassuring. A strike against him. Thank God. Though still terrifically interested, I no longer wanted to have sex with him. Very, very good. Cut down on the chances of me making a complete ass of myself to eighty-two percent. At least that.

**

I was unsuccessful at ridding my mind of the image of the frolicking lobsters in the tub, so I employed a tactic normally reserved for six-year-olds. I hid my serving of lobster tail in my napkin.

Then I'd feel guilty about wasting food and I'd attempt to eat it. Even drenched in butter, every time a piece of lobster neared my lips a wretch would grip my throat. But, the salad was great. I ate an enormous amount of salad.

After dinner I excused myself and dumped the lobster into the toilet.

"You're not bulimic, are you?" Jeep said through the door.

"What? No. Believe me. If I eat something, it's staying in. I just run it off."

"That would make you an exercise bulimic," he said as I came out.

"How do you know about that stuff?"

"My sister, MC. She's got it bad. Doing better. But... Oh, sorry. Why ruin things by yanking family skeletons out of the closet too soon, right?"

"Yeah, right," I said, wondering if he was already seeing the end of our budding relationship.

We snuggled into the love seat in the den. He was on my

right. I turned so my right leg was bent against his and the left fell over his knee. He pushed buttons on the remote.

"What're we watching?" I said.

"*About Last Night.*"

Of all the movies in all the world, he'd picked that one? It was the corniest of the corniest, in the way that I just loved.

"All right. All right," I put both feet on the floor. "What's going on? You wiretap my house?"

"What's the problem?" Jeep asked.

"This movie. It's my favorite."

"Youch. You're kidding." He turned it off.

I raised my eyebrows and waited for a response.

"I didn't have time to run to the store. And this one was here. My ex-fiancée, Tess. It was *her* favorite movie." He looked bemused. Clearly this kind of coincidence was meaningless to him.

"Oh, my God," I said. "That's it. Chemistry's gone. Let's do us a favor and break up now. Not that we're together. But come on. This movie, haunting us? We'll end it now. But before we do. Fill me in on a few things?"

He nodded and pulled both my legs over his. I fell back against the arm of the loveseat. "Shoot," he said, massaging my calves.

Fireworks. Electric man. That's what I should call him. Not Jeep. Not Money. That was too cheesy given his family status. Who could have guessed that?

"Okay," I said. "Tell me about the fiancée. She decorated the place? That why there's no living room furniture? She took it with her? I'm not going to find her diaphragm lying around, am I? I'm not up for any sort of love triangle, you know. Even though we're breaking up."

"The fiancée," he said. "Tess. You met her at the bar. She was great. Perfect, actually. A lifelong friend of my family. But no spark. Very dull. Our relationship, I mean."

"Perfect? The opposite of me?" I said.

"Exactly." He lay down beside me.

My insides flipped out of my body and found their way

back in.

We kissed forever. And when it seemed as though we should stop for a second, we stared at each other, taking each other in via our skin, our fingers, our eyes.

"Can you stay?" he asked.

"Well." I bit my lip. "I can stay. Of course. But do I want to?"

"Quit doing that. Analyzing. Your house is crazy. Your job is crazy. You work for a complete lunatic. Can't one thing in your life just be whatever it is? Not what you think it should be?"

I laughed a little, thinking about my roommates. Nina would tell me to stay. Laura would tell me to get the hell out, fast. But not before cooking him a meal to put in the fridge as a thank you for his hospitality.

"I'll stay. But no sex. I'll write that down if you'd like. Just so we're clear."

He lifted me like a groom carrying his bride and walked me to the bedroom. "How about nakedness? Can we work with that?"

"Naked? With no sex? I'd never even considered that. You're onto something, Jeep. I can't call you that. I thought I was getting used to the name, but I just can't. And I certainly can't be naked with someone whose name I can't use. What's your middle name?"

"Sylvester," he said.

"You're kidding," I said.

"Serious." He plopped me down on the comforter.

"My God in Heaven, your parents should be arrested," I said. "Now."

"They're dead," he said.

"Oh."

"It's been ten years."

"Last name?" I asked.

"Flannery," he said.

"Flannery. Flan. That's a food. Won't work. Jeep it is. Reluctantly."

"Whatever you say, Carolyn." We kissed as though we

hadn't spent the last few hours twined together on the loveseat.

Every once in a while he removed a piece of clothing, or I did. We touched every inch of each other. But no sex...no fruition of any sort. And no feet. I don't do feet in any way. I kind of thought I was going to die. We didn't say a word for the next three hours. Just kissed and touched and looked. And finally, slept. Perfect.

**

Perfect lasted just so long. I was awakened in the night by the sound of paper ripping. I ignored it twice, then was fully awake, realizing the rips were Jeep passing gas. I winced. Sometimes people did that in their sleep. It wasn't like he was ripping one out during dinner or something.

I started to fade back into sleep. Another rip. But it wasn't Jeep.

No. Not Jeep. Another moment of almost falling back to sleep and I realized it was *me*. Booming, echoing off his sparsely decorated walls. So loud, they woke me out of a sound sleep.

Oh. My. God. I held my breath. What was happening? The freaking salad. Nothing but veggies and wine and my ass was home to one mean mixture of gaseous chemicals. He stirred, but didn't say anything. Maybe he didn't hear. Or he was being polite. Ignoring the farting on my behalf. Nice of him, but still humiliating. There was no way I could stay after this. I couldn't blow ass all night as though I'd known him for sixty-three years or something. This was the breakup.

I snuck out of bed and called Nina. She could tell I was panicked and didn't pry for details. She just came to get me like the best friend in the world. By the time she arrived I'd convinced myself he was glad I was leaving. He had to have heard the farts. I couldn't fathom anything more mortifying. It was for the best. It put a quick end to what likely would have been a rocky relationship.

I refused to discuss the matter with Nina. I couldn't do it right then. In the car with us was some Random Man she'd met at the Green Turtle. I wasn't about to embarrass myself in front of what's-his-name in the front seat. And so I was free to mentally lament my fall from grace, my booting from the world I'd finally felt good to be in. Done, finished, finito. It figured.

At a stoplight, I looked out the window and saw Klein's black Mercedes. It could not be him. What would he be doing out at this hour? He should be at home devising ways to kill me so no one could pin it on him.

I sat up and rolled my window down. It *was* him. He was talking to someone beside him. With brassy blond hair. I ducked down so only my eyes peeked over the edge. Klein threw his head back, laughing at something. I didn't know he was capable of laughter. Real, emotional laughter—an outburst of sorts. Not choreographed or evil. Not him at all.

"Nina, look," I said. But she had leaned over to Random Man and looped her arms around his neck. They were making out as though tomorrow would never come.

The light changed and Klein pulled ahead and I saw, very clearly, despite the noxious gasses that had addled my brain, Fionna was in his front seat. Fionna. That was her leverage right there. That couldn't be. Yet it was. Well, holy moly, this was some bit of information, I thought as we turned to head toward our house.

Klein was a lot of things, but cavorting with Fionna the pajama queen just didn't make any sense. Then again nothing made much sense anymore.

Chapter 16

The next morning we gathered at the Silver Diner.

I laced my hands around my coffee mug. "There I was blowing ass," I said. "Loud. Like cars backfiring. I had to leave. It was a crushing development."

"Was it like 'plhh,' you know, like a baby?" Laura asked.

"Or a 'weeeee,' kind of high pitched thing?" Nina suggested.

"No. It was like 'riiip, riiiip.' Just the freaking loudest harvest of hot ass air you could ever imagine." I made the noise again and we laughed so hard we were wheezing. "I thought it was him at first. It was so *male* sounding."

The girls laughed so hard they couldn't speak.

"I've never been jolted awake by a fart in my life. And to have that happen at this very delicate time in our relationship."

Laura was the first to gather herself. "I still don't get the whole nekkid, no sex thing. Nothin' happened? That's what I'm to believe?"

I pointed a piece of toast at her. "I divulged the symphony of ass air thing," I said. "Would I lie to you about having sex?"

Laura lifted her coffee mug in a toast, nodding.

"We floated on this incredible plane of understanding

without even saying a word. Like we both wanted the exact same unarticulated thing." I closed my eyes, reliving the moments.

"You could have oral sex," Nina said to Laura. "With Paul."

I opened my eyes to see Laura's reaction.

"Fiddly dee." Laura scowled. "I think that's more intimate than sex."

"Your virginity will be safe. It's a nice option for someone like you." I sipped my coffee.

"Ya'all are making my skin crawl. I'll never grow accustomed to your crass northern ways." She sipped her own coffee.

"I love oral sex," Nina said. "Being in control of someone's pleasure...umhmm. Not that I've done it in ages."

"So the manhunt's not going well? Random Man looked promising last night," I said.

Nina shook some salt onto the saucer under her coffee. "Nah, Random Man's a dead end. Cute, but stupid. I can't handle that combo."

We nodded. I took a pinch of the salt Nina had dumped and tossed it over my left shoulder.

"I still don't get why you bolted from The Bike's place," Nina said.

"Did you miss the whole blowing ass thing?" I said. "Laura, you blow ass in front of Paul yet?"

"Get off this topic." Laura pushed her plate to the side. "My grits are clumping cause I can't bring myself to eat. And ya'all are keeping me from sharing my precious news."

"News?" I shook ketchup onto the spot between my home fries and omelet.

She thrust her hand into the middle of the table. Squealing followed a collective intake of air. A rectangular diamond ring shimmered on her finger. Sparkly tears to match the diamond welled in her eyes and trailed down her cheeks.

I put the ketchup bottle to the side and took her hand, staring at the glittering gem. Seeing her so moved made me surer than ever that Alex had not been the man for me. I would not have reacted like this to his proposal.

"It's an emerald cut." She sobbed, turning her hand back and forth, scrutinizing the stone. "I mentioned it once. Said I hoped I could have one like Granny's and here it is." She flung her hand toward us again. "Big as a credit card."

Paul had surprised her with it at the Green Turtle, after everyone else left. He said Laura should remember the proposal in the context of one of her favorite places, even if it wasn't the most romantic. But of course the proposal ensured the Green Turtle would be, from then on, romantic to Laura.

I sighed and realized I wanted that, too. To be sure. In a relationship. To trust it would last forever. Jeep came to mind. Ridiculous. As though we were right for each other. Really, the farting situation had just saved me from a lot of messiness. I wouldn't have to suffer through finding out he was all wrong for me.

Besides, I was far too childish to be married. And I wasn't sure you could change that about yourself.

"I'm so happy for you, Laura. When's the wedding?" I said.

"In June. Right after school ends. A June-bug affair. Just as I always dreamed about. And I would love it if ya'all would be in it. It just wouldn't be right if you weren't."

Nina and I oohed and ahhed, genuinely thrilled to be in our first wedding. Excited to see our friend so exquisitely happy with her life. But at the same time, I felt a twinge of discomfort. With this news, I knew my blanket of friendship would be slowly pulled from my body. Leaving me exposed to the elements.

We rounded out brunch with my information regarding Fionna and Klein. We all agreed it made sense—explained why Klein would cut her breaks. If Fionna serviced him on a regular basis, he might be willing to overlook that she showed up regularly in her jammies.

She had to be damn skilled, because she'd been cut a hell of a lot of slack. And I hadn't yet decided whether I should turn her in for her drug use. Not to Klein. Clearly I'd have to go above him. But I wasn't sure I should do anything. No one was getting hurt. And she was weird even when she wasn't high. Who could say when her weirdness was fueled by artificial means and when it wasn't?

That day, the first full day of Laura's engagement, passed by in a flurry of excitement. Laura phoned her family and other friends. We paged through five-pound wedding magazines, dog-earing the glossy sheets that depicted the most promising bridesmaid dresses. Suddenly nothing seemed more fun. Planning a fantasy event full of beautiful things with people who wanted nothing but the best for you.

And then I got depressed. No way was it worth it to go through all that happy shit just to be hit by crap when it was all over. It would be impossible to live up to a day like that. And whoever was stupid enough to meet me at the other end of the aisle would suffer along with me.

Lying down on the couch, bridal magazine balanced on my knees, hiding behind its misleading promises, I shrugged off my negativity. I didn't know where I got all these horrible ideas and assumptions about life. They were just there. Maybe there was something to reincarnation—that layered in my skin were prior experiences still influencing my life.

Or my parents. They had chosen to have only one child. Me. And I had spent a lot of time alone. Not in a neglectful I-might-burn-the-house-down way. It was that they were their own unit. They loved me. I could feel that. But they shared an impenetrable layer of being that I couldn't enter.

It had left me with darkness. Even Money-Jeep-Sylvester had noticed my blue mood that night we met.

I went to my room and touched the box he had given me. I pulled a scrap of paper from a notebook and wrote: 'Horrible Attitude Toward Marriage', folded it and closed it inside the box.

Chapter 17

Jeep called Sunday, but I let the machine pick up. He was clearly happy about our date and disappointed that I had left in the night. All good signs. Then I got mad that I left. I should have just shrugged off the gas situation and laughed about it. Who cared if he had heard? Up until then it had been the most magnificent date ever. The perfect example of why I couldn't get married. First thing wrong and I'd be out the door.

He said he was going to be indisposed for a few days. Secret Service crap to do. What a line that was. Anytime things get touchy at home, pretend the President needs you. Jeep could be back snuggling up with Tess, for all I knew. I bet she never even farted in private. Probably had the gas surgically removed when necessary.

Monday morning didn't allow me to linger on thoughts of Jeep. I walked into school and was notified that LeAndre's Instructional Support Team (IST) meeting was at nine-thirty. Interrogation, Shaft, Torture. No more intrusive than your average spinal tap.

I had been keeping notes about LeAndre in a journal. About everyone. But they weren't organized and they weren't for parental or principalian consumption. I'm sure I could have been fired for what was in there. Very colorful language regarding Klein's penchant for harassing me. I made one copy of the pages that pertained only to LeAndre.

The room was filled. Klein, Miss Tucker, Sissy the reading specialist, Dr. March, one of the county psychologists, Toots, the school nurse, Mrs. Westerbrook, the emotional support teacher, and LeAndre's mother, Ms. Nardo, sat around the conference table.

I'd never actually seen her before. LeAndre was her likeness and it made me wonder if he looked like his dad at all. I nodded at her and forced a smile when I took the seat beside her. She looked away.

The room was silent except for Klein whispering to Sissy and pointing to people, then diving back into Sissy's ear. Everyone else stared at the table.

I shuffled my notes, watching LeAndre's mom out of the corner of my eye. She sat on my left and smelled like a mix of hair product, perfume and garlic. The odor reminded me that she owned a small restaurant, a popular takeout place for ribs, wings, pizza and pasta.

She tapped her short, red nails on the packet of papers in front of her. I had no idea how this meeting was to progress and I was nervous. I hadn't considered how delicate a matter this would be until sitting there with Ms. Nardo. Talk about not fitting in, being thrust into the wrong puzzle box. As much as I had questioned her mothering abilities over the course of the year, I wouldn't wish this experience on anyone.

"I can't sit here all day," Ms. Nardo said under her breath. I nodded, agreeing. I wondered how many different ways my room was being torn apart. I hoped the kids wouldn't completely destroy the substitute. It was his first time at our school. He'd brought magic tricks. I giggled when he told me not to worry. He could do almost anything, magically speaking, he claimed. So many smartass replies ran through my mind in response. But I was nice. I'd left him with his fantasies intact.

"We're all here." Klein passed around the meeting agenda. He bent over the table, employing his "make people feel comfortable by leaning in" tactic. He had that gross, fake smile on his face.

"LeAndre," Klein said. "What's going on with him from your perspective, Ms. Nardo? What did the doctors say? I'm assuming you brought the file from your psychiatrist."

She patted the packet in front of her, her hand shaking. "It's here. Dr. March read it. I assumed he shared the information with you."

Klein glared at March. March split his time between several schools. Klein had no power over him.

"No," Klein said. "I haven't been briefed. Why don't *you* share, Ms. Nardo."

She cleared her throat and began to open the file. March jumped in. "I can handle that, Ms. Nardo." March's voice was soothing as he reached for the folder. She nodded and her shoulders relaxed.

"Well, good," Klein said. "Let's get moving. Five more cases after this." He looked at his watch pointedly.

March explained LeAndre's diagnosis, quoting from the file every once in a while. Ms. Nardo balled and released her hands on the tabletop.

"In English, March," Klein said. "What's the gist? What are your recommendations for us, and of course, for Mom?"

Ms. Nardo flinched then raised her gaze to meet Klein's. She held it, jaw clenched. I cringed at him calling Ms. Nardo, Mom. At every opportunity he tried to make people feel little. A compulsion. He must lay awake every blasted night pondering the plethora of ways he could make the people he would see the next day feel like complete shit.

Klein broke Ms. Nardo's gaze and she turned hers to the file that contained all the evidence her son was not normal. I was beginning to imagine how helpless she must feel.

"We're not sure at this juncture. He's so young and his symptoms are all over the map. His mood swings look like manic depression. His paranoia presents like… Well, we're cautious about saddling a child with any diagnosis and what would be a very, very intensive drug regimen," March said.

He cleared his throat and turned a page in his notes. "For now, until we know more, his recommended course is talk therapy, some meds that are much milder than lithium, and well, we'll see. Ms. Nardo has obtained the prescriptions and LeAndre will start back when his suspension runs its course."

"But behaviorally." Klein thumped the table with his fist. "What's our plan? Jenkins is clearly in over her head with this. It could take who knows how long for the meds to be properly balanced and for therapy to have an impact. How is someone like Jenkins going to handle LeAndre?"

That was a crappy way to say it. Ms. Nardo glanced at me with an understanding tilt of her head.

"There are several routes we can take," March said. "Ms. Jenkins needs to keep notes regarding LeAndre's mood swings, atypical behavior and outbursts. Then we can start to anticipate them and give LeAndre a safe way for him to handle his shifting feelings. He needs a safety net."

"*He* needs a safety net?" Klein squealed. "What about me? Er, I mean, what about the staff? The other kids? He didn't need a safety net when he was swinging the scissors—which by the way, Ms. Jenkins, I've removed from your possession."

Disgusting, despicable creature sent here by evil beings from Hell. Not born to humans.

Ms. Nardo's shoulder's shook with silent tears. I wanted to comfort her, put my arm around her shoulder or pat her back. But I didn't know how to comfort someone whose child was suffering from an invisible chemical imbalance. Hell, I didn't know how to comfort people who lost their wallets.

Klein attempted his disarming lean-in maneuver again and lowered his voice. "Mom, how comfortable are you with the plan? What assurances can you give us that you can follow through?"

She grabbed at her neck with one hand and wiped her tears with the other. "For now it's weekly therapy. And in two months, a follow-up at the clinic with his other doctor. To discuss and monitor the medicine. We will handle it." Her voice was thin.

"Talk therapy once a week? That's enough? You think perhaps daily sessions would be optimal?"

Her jaw clenched again. Her eyes lifted and her posture straightened. "LeAndre is my only child. He's a handful. But I have to work. I can't take off every afternoon—the busiest time of the day for me. Once a week, at a hospital an hour away is what the insurance covers. If I lose my restaurant we won't have a home. What good will that do?"

Go, Ms. Nardo.

Klein pelted her with more questions in the accusing tone I knew so well.

Sitting there, watching this meeting unfold, my inadequacies as a teacher seemed to multiply. I had silently scolded Ms. Nardo for not paying enough attention to LeAndre, not getting enough help, not returning my calls. I couldn't imagine seeing LeAndre every day and not shuffling him off to a shrink the first time he talked to the clouds. Or the first time she saw him try to wrestle his rage back into his body, only to cry desperately that there wasn't any room for it. But I should have gone to her. She couldn't leave her restaurant. I should have known.

Klein tossed more papers at us for behavioral and instructional plans. I thought back to my own childhood. Age eleven. Mostly I'd been obsessed with tennis. Winning matches, being with my friends. Having fun.

The room was dead silent as people paged through their papers, hoping not to be called on by Klein.

"Jenkins!" Klein said. "I have this for you." He tossed a four-inch binder my way. "Assertive discipline. I want it enacted in your room this week. We need to keep the Secret Service and psychological experts as far from your room as possible."

I coughed.

"You're familiar with assertive discipline, Jenkins? They must have used it in your fancy schmancy Pittsburgh school, right?"

I shook my head.

Ms. Nardo looked at me then looked back to her papers. I wondered if she hated me.

"For now," Klein said, "you two work on those home/school behavior plans. I need both of you to understand the plan and what it will look like."

Ms. Nardo stared at the paper in front of her, but didn't move to fill it out. I pulled the sheet over between us. She nodded. "Thanks," she said.

"Here. We'll start with this," I said. I wanted to tell her I loved her crazy son. I wanted her and him to be okay. I cared. I finally understood her life's limitations. And all my problems seemed miniscule in comparison. Really, what problems?

"Ms. Jenkins." Bobby Jo stuck her head between Ms. Nardo and me, reading what we were writing. "The sub is gone. He only lasted twenty-two minutes. I've been holding down the fort. You'll have to finish this later."

I gathered my things from the table. "I'll call you as soon as I can, Ms. Nardo," I said. "I'll do whatever I can to help enact this plan with you."

"Thanks." She smiled and nodded.

I pushed my chair back from the table. The magician had lasted twenty-two minutes? Had to be some kind of substitute teacher record for failure. His magic? Maybe I should've warned him, let him know the kids were the magicians—the kind who could make substitutes disappear.

Chapter 18

It didn't take long to get assertive discipline going in my room. It turned out to be a smashing idea. I almost told Klein that one morning. But before I could, I went to my mailbox and found a copy of a letter that was going in my permanent personnel file. It detailed my daily practice of not turning on the lights after lunchtime. What. A. Dick.

My room had fifteen-foot ceilings and eight windows stretching right up to the top of them across the entire back wall. Ample light. Not according to Klein. He had made it his business to arrive in my room sometime during the afternoon every day. At which time I never had the lights on.

I crumpled up the letter. The county should be putting thank you notes in my personnel file for saving on their electric bills.

Other than the letter, the day started as smooth as Coors Light going down after a long week of teaching. Even LeAndre was doing better. Not as well as I would have liked, but at least he wasn't threatening himself or anyone else. Drugged and lethargic, he went to Miss Tucker's room each day after only forty minutes in our room. I suspected he still struggled with internal demons that were better off living in her room. I spoke with Ms. Nardo. Her appointment to adjust the meds was a month away.

Each day of the first week of assertive discipline, I explained the rules, consequences, and incentives. If a student broke a rule like talking out, she got a warning in the form of her name on the board. With the next infraction, she received a checkmark next to her name and had a timeout in the back of the room.

A timeout was supposed to occur in a spot where the student was seated away from the rest of the class. But a room made for twenty desks that was jammed with thirty-six did not have any wiggle room for students in need of cooling off. The next checkmark warranted a timeout and a phone call home. The fourth checkmark meant a trip to Klein and a meeting with a parent.

In small groups, they got tally marks for following the rules. At a certain point, the group got a reward, and if all the groups did well, the class would earn a privilege like the dance they wanted to have. They could earn the group rewards even if their personal record was not stellar.

The plan worked frighteningly well. Even during reading discussions they followed the rules. We settled in for our whole group reading lesson—the novel *Hatchet*. I was breathing like a normal person. The edginess I'd grown to feel with each transition had actually dulled a bit.

"Ms. Jenkins," Kenneth said. "I bet you think Jesus is white."

"All the pictures of him is white," Jamaica said.

"Are white, Jamaica," I said. "I'm not sure what color Jesus is."

"He ain't a *he*," Terri hissed.

"Yo mamma gone tan your hide, she hear you talking nonsense like that, Terri," Tanesha said.

"Blasphemy," Evette said.

"I believe in Jehovah," Katya said.

I pulled out of the conversation, envisioning the lawsuit that would result when one of them went home and reported it.

Allowing them to talk back and forth without having to raise their hands or wait for me to mediate was in conflict with assertive discipline, but this was what I liked to see in my class— thoughtful discussions about ideas. This was what learning was about.

If only I could get this kind of conversation to occur more around the texts, get them to decode more fluently.

"Ms. Jenkins. Is *He* white or black?" Kenneth asked.

"I don't know. I like the way you were all listening to each other's ideas, but we really need to get back to *Hatchet*. We're almost at the end." They actually listened. Wow, I was functioning like a real teacher. I felt light and airy as we went to lunch. I even called Jeep and left a cheery message on his machine. I knew he wouldn't be there so it was a risk-free call.

Peaceful, baby.

While I was awash in happy quiet at lunch, my kids, as was reported to me later, were swept up in lunchroom pandemonium. Chairs were thrown, plaits were yanked from heads, faces were scratched. My newly behaved children had turned into unrecognizable, unruly people. Worse than I'd ever seen. Or had I simply forgotten how bad they could be?

They tussled and pushed the entire way back to the room. They had their recess revoked and I was pulled from recess duty to tend my flock in the comfort of our classroom.

"In your seats. Heads down. No fun. No recess. Just quiet." I leaned against the front of my desk. As he did each day, LeAndre started the afternoon in my room to see if he could handle it. He slammed books around his desk, grumbling.

"LeAndre, your name goes on the board. Table three, I like how you're all sitting, reading. One tally mark for you."

"I ain't gonna be quiet," Kenneth screeched. Five cohorts backed him up. I listed their names on the board, then praised the students who were following directions. That group was dwindling in number.

I realized assertive discipline only worked if the students were willing to play along. These guys weren't afraid of a few squiggles and checks on the board.

"Seventeen of you have phone calls coming tonight," I said. "And your parents will have to meet with me at the school. No. Better yet. I'm going to *your* homes."

Silence.

"You coming to my house?" Kenneth said.

I savored the thought of showing up at Kenneth's, showing his family I was serious about his behavior, his education. I visualized Kenneth, all of them, coming back to school after my visit, sitting like angels, fearful of the next visit. I imagined my being at Kenneth's home, seeing him embarrassed then determined to shape up at school. They would hate it, but I was sure this added threat would do the trick.

"Yes, Kenneth, I am going to your house to meet with your parents."

Murmurs broke out around the room then silence settled in again. Me going to one child's house was having the impact I desired. That's all it took, apparently.

"Well, come to mine first." Tanesha stood and put four checkmarks after her name.

Evette followed her to the board, wrote her name and with as much gusto as I've seen a student employ at the board, she marked a series of checks.

The whole class followed suit and before long I had appointments pending at thirty-six different homes.

Now *this* was unexpected.

Chapter 19

Laura, Nina, and I decided wedding dress shopping should take precedence over normal post-school day activities just once. I never gave one second of thought to wedding gowns until Laura got engaged. Then, through the wonder of magazines the size of step stools, I was transported to another planet where flowing white gowns, sorbet-hued bridesmaids dresses and even mother-of-the-bride suits lived free and beautiful.

I doubted I'd ever get married, but I'd have to find a way to swing a wedding. Even if it was a phony one where only the bride was present. In a stunning, huge, white gown.

For a short, after-work trip, Elegant Day Dresses would do. It was the oldest store in our little section of town and its brochure claimed they'd provided beautiful dresses at affordable prices for generations of women. Affordable prices, I knew, were relative. Especially when shopping anywhere near D.C. Indeed, not one dress Sondra the storeowner brought out was less than twenty-four hundred dollars.

Laura started with a mermaid-ish type thing that was supposedly very popular that year. You'd have thought it would be perfect on Laura's six-foot stick thin body. No go. With that dress and a poufy veil, she looked like an animated cocktail toothpick.

It was weird to watch Laura parade around in those dresses. The serene expression on her face, the manifestation of what she was feeling was in her soul. She was separate from us now, consumed with thoughts of Paul reacting to her coming down the aisle, thoughts of their life together. We were being marginalized as Laura grew up.

Feeling pouty, I plucked a veil from the pile near the mirrors and snuggled it onto my head. Maybe I *could* buy into finding a mate. Maybe Jeep was the guy. So what if post-wedding depression caused an emotional downturn that would spur discord and divorce. Maybe the *one* day was worth it.

Nina joined me.

"Wow." Nina smoothed the tulle that flounced down my back.

"My H-Factor just hit a ten," I said. "I've only been a ten once in my life. A headdress is clearly the key. I'm wearing one on a daily basis henceforth. Could that work? The added height and pure color brings out my beauty. I'm glowing and I'm not even the one getting married."

"Let me try." Nina grabbed a lace-covered cap and slapped it on her head. Not great compared to my simple tulle number, but still.

"Jesus. Five point increase. Just like that," I said.

Nina smirked. "This can't be right." She put it back and grabbed a cream band-type thing that went around her scalp and had a little crystal thing coming down onto the forehead. She nestled it onto her head.

"Five extra points." I shrugged. "That one's horrible, too, but even so, your number goes up."

We preened like brainless princesses from millennia gone by. To be sure, none of us would escape this shopping trip without being plagued by white wedding dreams.

"Seriously, we could make the veil an everyday wardrobe staple." I said.

A loud moan, then screechy wails startled us. On the bridal pedestal, collapsed, was Laura. Nina rushed to her. I stopped and stared. Laura looked poetic. Crying amidst thousands of dollars of silk and beads. The sleeves that pouffed four inches off her shoulders and mounds of ethereal white silk provided the perfect contrast for her slight, perfect, V-shaped upper body, which sparkled with what from afar looked like stars plucked from above. Her straight black hair shone.

I wished I were an artist. I would have drawn her. How did someone manage that? To look beautiful while crying? Somehow her H-Factor soared even as her face crinkled, expressing some sort of invisible pain.

Sondra bumped me as she brushed by. I pulled her back to stop what I knew was going to be a scolding. "Give us a minute. The dress will be fine."

She pursed her bright pink lips. She seemed ready to explode, but turned away anyway.

Nina, still veiled, pulled Laura so close, she nearly sat on Nina's lap.

"What's wrong?" I asked. I couldn't go that close. Flaming emotions in people I loved were too much to handle.

"You guys weren't even paying attention. I found my dress and you two were over there jacking off with veils," Laura said. Her shoulders bounced with every word.

"Oh, my God," I said. "I've never heard you sound so Northern."

"We're so sorry," Nina said. "Carolyn got us all caught up in these veils—"

I bared my teeth at Nina.

Laura sucked in air, lips quivering. "I'm happy as a pig in right mud," she said.

"There's wrong mud?" I said.

Dirty looks my way.

"I can't quit crying. Paul's perfect. He loves me so much. I never thought I'd find this kind of love. And here it has fallen right into my lap. And I...just love you guys being here for me. Even if you're over there ignoring me. The veils do look great. Your H-Factors are soaring." She snuffled. "Happy tears. Just thinking of Paul makes me cry. I can't seem to stop."

"Tens all around." I pulled my veil off and twirled it above my head.

The depth of emotion Laura felt for Paul was tangible. I wanted that.

I knelt down with them. Maybe some of Laura's happiness would rub off on me. We bombarded her with ideas for the wedding as Sondra paced, hands grasped behind her back, as though that were the only way to keep herself from ripping the dress from Laura's back.

"We could have horse drawn carriages," I suggested. I settled my veil onto Laura's head and pulled a gauzy white layer over her face.

"And lobster for dinner," Laura said.

"Not if The Bike prepares them in his tub, we won't," Nina said.

"Agreed." I said. I straightened Nina's frightening veil.

Nina smiled and latched onto my arms, pulling me into them, nuzzling me until I insisted I loved her. For someone so confident, she sure made us say we loved her enough.

"You'd help me plan this?" Laura said. "My parents can't really help. Not with my father's health, you know. But, I'd rather plan it here, anyway." Laura wiped her nose on the back of her hand. Sandra dropped tissues over our heads and into Laura's lap.

I clasped my hands together. "Oh, yes. I can plan the wedding I'll never have."

Laura waved me off. "Please, Carolyn. With you in charge, I'd show up to a church with another wedding, have no food and no band. You can help with the little things, then just show up and look pretty."

I forced a smile. Hurt. Get your useless nose out of my wedding, Laura had practically said. I irritated her a lot, but she'd always included me, put up with me. Now with a wedding and a marriage, she had fewer reasons to do so.

After reassuring Sondra we would be back when Laura had her emotions in check, we went to the Olive Garden for dinner. Of the three of us, only Laura liked to cook. Although she complained about spending money on dinner when she had a nice rib rack and sweet corn bread ready for the oven at home, she couldn't resist when we insisted it was a post-dress shopping celebration.

As we ordered desert, Nina produced a cream kid leather journal from her purse. I couldn't even imagine where one found something like that. Yet, there it was. As though she was sealing the Maid of Honor position with this one wonderful gesture. I choked on my water.

Nina patted my back harder than necessary. "Okay?" They were laughing.

"Yeah. Fine," I said. I made people laugh. Not because I was witty, but because I was ridiculous. No one depended on me. I basically offered nothing extraordinary to the world.

But there was my job. My kids needed me. And yet I got so frustrated with them. Sick. Sick. Sick. I almost grabbed the lustrous leather journal and started listing all the narcissistic tendencies that gripped my very core. I couldn't escape myself. This wasn't like needing to lose weight or something. It was who I was.

"Carolyn," Jeep's voice sliced through my thoughts. Everyone hushed and stared.

"Uh… Hi," I said. I made eye contact with him, then shifted my gaze to see the girls grinning. I looked back at Jeep and pricked to life with nervousness.

"You remember everyone," I said. "From The Tuna a while back." I looked up at him, unsure of how to behave. We'd not seen each other since the fart episode.

"Aren't you a breath of fresh air," Laura drawled.

Nina invited him to sit.

"Hope I'm not interrupting. I called your house and Paul said you were all here. I wanted to see you, Carolyn. You're pretty tough to pin down."

I shrugged, confused—my most frequent state of mind. Everyone else seemed thrilled. We ate desert, they cleared it away, and after a cup of coffee they were calling him Bike to his face. Laura told him to keep June twenty-fourth open for her wedding.

"Hence the lovely white journal," he said.

"You're not a Secret Service agent for nothing, huh, Bike?" Nina said.

"My observational qualities are topnotch, as a matter of fact," he joked as he took the bill and paid it against our protests. He talked about his sister, MC, and her upcoming wedding, the way planning her wedding had been the happiest time of her life. He seemed to understand the uproar surrounding the event.

Jeep was up to something shady. All this charming the crap out of my friends was too good to be true. Some creepy plot to suck me in and screw me over. Who was he kidding? A man with six sisters. He had learned to play the game. Damn clichés. I couldn't get them to stop shuffling through my brain. I wasn't going to let him sweep me off my feet. Jackass.

"Carolyn. Mind if I drive you home?" Jeep asked.

"Okay," I'd bust his scheme wide open. It would be bloody and fun. With all my shallowness, I should be relentless in torturing him. He was building up to something shitty and I was going to beat him to it.

He started the car and set a small box on my lap. Another beautiful box. This one was plain, dark wood. I hated surprises I knew were coming. Like Christmas presents. This kind of surprise? This was good.

"Well. Open it." He pushed my hair behind my ear, causing waves to cycle through my stomach.

I creaked it open, heart pounding, wondering. I squinted in the darkness and lifted the box to catch the light streaming in the passenger side window. I drew back at the stunning sight.

The word "Beano" was printed on the teeny plastic green and white box. A note taped inside the lid read "May there Beano more gas, but much more nudity."

I buried my face in my hands as my cheeks flooded with heat. "Jackass. You're such a jackass."

"I figured since we've already seen each other nude and you've blown ass so loud it woke Mrs. Guthrie next door, we could laugh about it. Right?"

I nodded. "You are such an ass." And I loved it. Inside jokes and we were barely even a couple. Maybe I could have the kind of private, just-for-us type of relationship my parents shared. I looked out the window.

"Look at me." He pulled my chin toward him, then pulled my head to his and kissed me like he'd been waiting a lifetime to do it. Excitement practically blinded me. I officially suspended my pessimism. And my heart raced toward his, leaving me to believe it, everything that had to do with Jeep, was a very good thing.

Chapter 20

From the Beano presentation on, Jeep and I spent as much time together as we could. During those times, we enjoyed long periods of staring at each other in a crazy, fairytale way. He often had to be places late at night. Teaching absorbed my days, plodding lesson planning stole my nights.

When we weren't together, we talked on the phone. The abstract notion of a soul slip became a concrete thing. After we talked, I thought about what we'd discussed or discovered about each other.

I'd kept my promise not to have sex. And it didn't occur to me that it was strange he wasn't pushing. He was an adult. Every guy I'd ever known before was a boy. He surprised me often with quick visits in between his work assignments. Or with flowers, and notes. If I were even a little more like Laura, I'd be crying those happy tears.

At school, I had yet to break through my ill-fitting status to feel like I was a part of the landscape, that my efforts were valued. Klein wasn't in my room every day anymore, but like a seasoned saboteur, he didn't have to show himself to create fear.

Merely seeing his car in the lot each morning clobbered worry and disgust into our hearts. And now, the older teachers and people like Fionna weren't immune to his harassment.

Though there wasn't anyone in the school I'd wish Klein's evil deeds upon, I did experience momentary satisfaction at his dissatisfaction with Fionna's loose clothing code—I overheard him suggest that she shape that up. And there was the pissing-on-the-copy-machine incident.

The only student Fionna had sent to the office that year had threatened and swore at Klein. So Klein locked the kid in the copy room while he called his house, caging him like an animal. The kid peed on the copy machine.

Hearing that this had happened disturbed me in a different way than the LeAndre situation had. Locking an irate kid in a room was a stupid thing to do, even for Klein. And that a child would turn to that type of retaliation... I couldn't help being relieved the incident had nothing to do with me.

Leaving that day, Nina and I passed Fionna's classroom, where she sat at her desk, her expression vacant as she fingered a guitar. I poked my head in her room. "It'll be all right, Fionna. Call me if you need something."

She nodded at Nina and me. The intercom beeped. "Fionna. Come to the office. Now." Klein's terse tone crept over my skin as though it had come through the ceiling and taken human form right there in the room. I held my breath, waiting to hear him call me down, too. Guilt by association.

"Fucking dick." Fionna stormed away brushing my shoulder with hers.

Nina sighed as we started toward the exit. "Take a look at this." She dug in her bag and handed me a very academic looking article. Not your usual *Teacher* magazine font. No photos of children learning. Just teeny words crawling across the page. I hadn't touched something academic since my Masters program had ended seven months earlier.

"Harvard Educational Review," I said. "Lisa Delpit. Now that's a heavy hitter."

"She speaks my language," Nina said. "Make sure you read it. It could help you make some decisions about what to do with your class."

"Thanks, Nina. That's really nice." I wasn't in the mood to

read a theoretical article, though it intrigued me that Nina, the gym teacher, would read such a thing on her free time. I flipped through it then tucked it into my bag, too tired to give it another thought.

**

Nina went to TJ MAXX and I went home. Laura had a School Improvement Plan meeting so I had the place to myself. I yanked a mix-tape from my dusty Walkman and popped it into stereo system in my bedroom.

With an old photo album in hand, I collapsed onto my bed while music by Nirvana, Shiloh, Aerosmith, and Rusted Root filled the room. Tucked into the front of the album were some of my baby pictures. In each of them, my dad held me with one arm while my mom was nestled under the other.

I thought of my parents in Europe, living their dream, isolated, together. My mom would be reading incessantly. My dad would draw, tour and return to find my mom as happy as when he'd left. Then they'd play their violins or God knew what. I felt as though my relationship with Jeep was the beginning of what my parents had—that instant connection that grew with the ticking by of each second of every day.

Maybe with this relationship, I could find joy in what my parents shared, not feel so ostracized. And I surely wouldn't repeat that with my children. I'd never let them feel as though they were afterthoughts. Wait, kids? What was I thinking?

The pictures of college made me smile. I chuckled at the snapshots my suitemates had taken of my dog-crap encrusted shoe. The shoe that had given birth to the notion of "Crap Quotient." Oh how we'd laughed that day.

Photos of Greek Sing, Dance Ensemble and sorority formal photos all made old music dance in my head. I exchanged the tape with current songs for old tunes like the cheesy *I Need a Hero*, from Footloose. Before long I was pulling on my French cut black leotard, tights and yes, legwarmers. Who cared they were over a decade out of style.

I blared the music and danced back into my past with each

album, each group, each song. INXS, Whitesnake, the Dirty Dancing soundtrack, Violent Femmes, *867-5309*, *It's Raining Men*, *Maniac*, and *All I Want is You*, by U2. This was not a time for the grunge music of the day.

I was dancing to *All I Want is You*, feeling every inch of the slow music, releasing it into the world through my limbs as though I was the world's greatest dancer when it happened.

I did my signature splits–roll-chest lift-head toss-arched-back move, then, after a few seconds, released my arched back and began to roll back down to the ground. It was then I noticed feet at my now opened bedroom door.

Not one pair of feet. Three.

Nikes, black flats and cowboy boots. The cowboy boots almost made me puke. I rolled into a ball, wanting to yank off a leg warmer and pull it over my head. In the fetal position, with my arms latched over my head, covering my ears I could try to ignore them, their gales of laughter. I couldn't blame them. If I'd seen any of them in such a compromising position, I'd be laughing my ass off, too.

Laura bounced around singing, "Maniac, maniac on the dance floor," and I could feel the floor vibrate with what was likely a great imitation of the Flashdance number. My God, they'd been there for ages.

"Get out. Everyone. You must go. Leave me in peace to die like an old dog."

I heard the door close and Jeep squatted in front of me. I finally looked up from my protective ball into his grinning face.

"You were spectacular." He shut the door and lay down beside me on his back, his hands underneath his head.

"There are no words," I said.

"Spectacular."

"I didn't think there could be a fitting encore to the fart fest. But I outdid myself. My Crap Quotient knows no bounds."

Jeep sat up and paged through my CDs and tapes. "This is good. Very good," he said.

He pulled out a tape and slid it into the player. *Dancing in the Moonlight* came on. Jeep stood and pulled me to my feet. Our bodies touched, making me giggle. We sang and moved to the beat.

"After all this," Jeep dipped me and held me low, nuzzling my neck, "what's keeping us from having sex? What's left for us to discover about each other?"

He whipped me back to a standing position, wrapping my leg around his waist.

"From where I'm standing," I said, "a lot. I don't recall you blowing ass uncontrollably or seeing you dance solo with wild abandon in a French cut leotard and legwarmers." I buried my face in his chest.

"Nor will you. Look at me, Carolyn."

Scratching came from the hallway. "Now what? I'll bag the King Harvest and put on some respectable Pearl Jam. *Yellow Ledbetter*," I said.

"Yeah, sure," he said, walking toward the door. My roomies had shoved something under it. Jeep bent down to investigate.

"Um. Carolyn?" He held up blue square somethings. I walked closer.

"Condoms?"

"I guess Laura and Nina think you need some action."

"I live with sixteen year olds. That's why they're such good teachers. They identify with the students way too much." I stared at the condoms. "We can't have sex now," I said.

"We were going to have sex?"

"Not now. Not with them thinking we're having sex. It's like having your parents slip condoms under the door. Besides. I need to know you. Something. *Your* secrets." I didn't want to say I'd promised myself I wouldn't have sex again until married.

"Don't have any," he said, pulling me into him.

"The word 'secret' is in your job title. Who you are is about secrets."

He put the condoms in his jeans pocket and looked at the ceiling. "The night I met you at The Tuna, I had about two hours left to decide if I was going through with the marriage to Tess."

I looked at the floor.

"But then there was you."

"Me?"

"You're the reason I didn't meet the deadline."

Poker face fully employed, I nodded as if I heard stuff like this every day. "That's a lot to live up to." Saliva collected in my mouth. I had to force myself to swallow.

"That's your response?" His jaw slackened, like one of my kids.

My response was that I was in love. Utterly in love. Sex was less a gesture than saying that. But I couldn't do that, either. Not yet.

He sat on my hope chest at the end of the bed and snuggled me onto his lap. He smoothed my hair. "I have something to say to you."

My throat tightened. I forced my mouth to stay shut—to not ruin this moment with my silly words.

"But I'm not going to say it."

I shook my head, confused.

"It's not that I can't say it because I'm afraid it's not real. That *we're* not real. I've dated enough people that I know when a person walks into a bar and tells the most outlandish lies, acting like she's nothing she actually is, charming me every second of the way, that things are just right."

"You like me because I lie?"

"Carolyn. Listen."

Jeep pulled my hand over his chest, never taking his eyes from mine, but not saying anything else.

"I know what you mean." I was finally experiencing the love my parents had known forever. "I do, too."

His beeper went off. I pulled away as he looked at it. "Shit. I have to go. Hey, you'll be getting invitations to my sister's engagement extravaganza weekend soon. You'll come, right?"

"Uh. Yeah. Extravaganza? Sounds fancy."

"Just family and some close friends at my parents' house. I want you to meet them all. My six sisters. And MC's fiancé, Ford. You'll get a kick out of that guy." Jeep kissed me. "You'll come, right?"

"Jeep and Ford. I'm sensing a theme there," I said.

"You want a theme? Every one of my sisters is named Mary. Mary Colleen. Mary Faith. Mary—"

The Marys. I liked the sound of having a sibling. Six of them seemed even better.

His beeper beeped again. "You'll come?"

"Sure. Why not?" He kissed me and left the room. I watched him get into his BMW from my bedroom window. Why not? I didn't have to know what the hell a freaking engagement extravaganza was to know it wouldn't go well. But going well wasn't the same as things being right. And right then, the thought of Jeep, the thought of being with him with his family seemed as right as anything I ever heard.

**

"Phone, Carolyn." Laura startled me from replaying my conversation with Jeep before he got beeped and had to leave. "The dad of one of your students is on the phone. The one in Lorton."

I grabbed the phone. Prisoners only had so much time to talk.

"Miss Jenkins. This is Manny, Katya's dad."

"Hi, Mr. Toomer. How are you?" How are you? That seemed like an exceedingly bad question to ask a guy in prison.

"Fine, thanks. How's Katya doing?"

"She's coming along. Her reading is still below grade level and she's struggling with fractions in math."

"Who doesn't?" he grumbled.

"I sure did," I said. "Her behavior is awesome, for the most part. She's being swayed a little by a certain group of girls. But she isn't overly social. She clings to me a bit. Doesn't have a lot of friends."

"Good. Then she's listening. Nothing friends can do for a kid. Teacher's the one with answers. Her aunt and uncle? They got the answers and Katya loves them. Friends ain't anything but headaches, I tell her. Her mother's no help, neither." I thought that was an odd statement, considering he was in jail and Katya's mom wasn't.

"Well, if you've been asking her to hang out with me, then she's doing it. As for reading and math, it's not that she isn't trying—"

"She's slow. I know. Like me."

"It's looking as though she has some delays, yes. But not in the way that she can't function. She's working really hard. I can't say that about everyone."

"Well, good. My baby's doing good."

"She is." I said as the phone disconnected. I was beginning to see how "doing good," was relative.

I slumped onto the bed and stared at the phone as though I could see through the line to the man who had been on the other end of the call. How cruel that I was entrusted with such an important job, yet had no skill in performing it. Katya wandered at my heels at recess and during the day like a baby kitten. Her blond hair was sometimes darkened by grease, her hands sometimes dark with dirt. And she had me? Great. I was there— a mere skeleton of the teacher I should have been. I wished I could do something more tangible than offer her father flimsy reassurances. I wanted to make Katya a reader, an independent learner who could control her future. I reminded myself I was making headway with the class. I reminded myself I could only do so much, that I wasn't the parent.

Then I let my mind wander back to Jeep. I lay back on the floor, recalling the feel of his arms around me, the warmth and strength. The sensation was exactly what I needed to feel comforted. He loved me. I'd felt it in the embrace, in his skin pressed against mine. I knew he loved me whether he said it aloud or not.

Chapter 21

"Hey, Laura." I barreled out of my room, wearing the sailor suit she thought would be appropriate for the sailing event at Mary Colleen's engagement extravaganza.

"This outfit sucks." I plucked at the gold buttons that marched down the double-breasted navy jacket. "It's not gonna work at all." My person—body, face, hair—looked good. As in all good love relationships, I lived on the phenomenon of chemosynthesis. Simply being with Jeep, thinking of him, filled me with satisfaction and fed my body, replacing the need for food. The result was that I had no flab even without my daily running. But the outfit was another story. "Even these shorts lay funny. I look like I'm in the chorus for *Anything Goes.*"

Laura's face paled, making the black circles under her eyes look more pronounced. Her usual chipper demeanor had been replaced with my moody pre-Jeep one.

Her H-Factor: 2/10

Even considering I often scored her low because of her overzealous use of charm, I'd never gone near a two for her.

"What?" I lifted my hands and ignored her mood. This extravaganza was important business. "I'm just not sure about this outfit."

"Really? We spent ten hours shopping for this extravaganza thing of yours. It was the best sailing outfit available. The clerk agreed. Put it to bed already!"

I held my hands up. "What did I do?"

"Nothing. It's just that this thing has preoccupied you beyond even schoolwork. And to be honest, I've had it up to my six-foot head with you ignoring my requests to clean the house."

"I clean."

"Not when I ask you. And you've been changing everything around. You even painted that blood red wall—"

"You despised that paint," I said.

"The point is you don't have time to help out around here in the ways that benefit all of us and I'm sick of it," Laura said.

"I'm doing my best. With all the work at school, I do my best." I felt sadness filling my heart. Having Jeep in my life didn't even help temper the blue feeling that was suddenly flooding over me.

"Those are excuses for you to be lazy," Laura said. "Before you were moody and moodier, now you walk around all giddy but doubly distracted, expecting the world to fall into place for you and yet you're not willing to make changes. Think of Alex. All he wanted was a little bit of a domestic focus on your part. Just a bit."

I started to interrupt but she shoved her forefinger toward me so violently that I shut right up.

"You really think you'll find a guy who doesn't mind that you don't care about making a home, creating luscious meals or taking a toothbrush to the shower tile once in a while—that you're challenged in the domestic arts? All of them! This Jeep guy has been around. You think a guy from a family who throws an engagement extravaganza weekend won't mind that you don't put him and a home first in your life?"

I nearly fell over from my heart constricting so tight that no blood flowed from it. How could she say all those things? This weekend was scaring the hell out of me for all the reasons she'd just listed. I'd counted on her to tell me those things didn't matter, that I did.

"Oh, well, I guess I'm just doomed, then. And you're a compulsive, anal old woman who still likes ten-year-old little girly, humongous bows and frills."

"You best not be referring to my weddin' dress."

"Cut out the accent. You only use it when it suits you. Like to get Klein to back off you."

"It's who I am, so handle it," she said.

"Well, the slob thing is who I am. So live with it."

"Not for long, I won't. I don't have time to babysit you anymore. *I* have a life," Laura said.

My breath caught. I almost choked on the pain that statement caused.

"Fine," I said, slamming my door like a child.

"Fine." I heard Laura scream over the slam. She'd never screamed, ever. How could she be so angry? I'd been like this since we'd met. I guessed she'd simply had enough.

I stood inside my bedroom, acid filling my stomach, rising tears burning my eyes. I forced our argument from my mind. Everything would be fine with Laura. She just needed to cool off from whatever it was that had her so upset.

What I had to do was make sure the extravaganza went well, that I fit into Jeep's family, that they saw me as a piece of the whole that was them. I could do it. I could make them like me for who I was. There was no way Jeep and I could have the connection we did and not have it extend to his family. No way.

Chapter 22

Jeep and I were on the way to the engagement extravaganza. I practically pulled my fingers from their sockets as we crossed the bridge.

"Excited?" Jeep squeezed my thigh.

"Yeah, sure. I'm so sad about Laura. We really haven't talked in over a week. That's never happened to us before."

"It'll be okay. You're both under pressure with school. Her wedding. It'll be fine."

I wasn't so sure. I'd been trying. Wanting to show her I cared, I'd made sure she saw me wearing the stupid "boat wear" outfit she'd picked out for me. She hadn't responded.

Nervous thoughts had plagued me from the second I'd said yes to attending the shindig. All I could think about were the ways this weekend would be hell. Now I tried to focus on how I would be welcomed into the arms of the sisters I never had. This was my big chance.

The invitations had flooded in for several extravaganza events. Tea and lemonade on the porch at eleven a.m. Sailing at two p.m. Cocktails and dinner at six. That was just Saturday. Sunday was equally packed with activities. Each invite arrived sans preprinted RSVP card. Apparently it was the height of manners to hand write an RSVP to each and every event.

It was risky to trust the invitees to write a stinkin' note of reply. I had the world's worst handwriting. Lines and curves jutting out in all the wrong places. You can bet Klein had let me know that on more than one occasion. On that count, he was right.

I grimaced, imagining Mary Colleen ripping into the RSVPS, her handwriting analyst by her side. Dividing them into piles. Prom queens here. Serial killers there. Beauty queens here. Disorganized slobs, there.

I actually considered having Laura or Nina write my notes. But that didn't feel right.

We pulled into the driveway where his sisters stood in khakis, jeans and skorts. All normal clothing. Nothing resembling the Love Boat inspired costume I was sporting. Maybe Laura had been irritated with me longer than I thought.

The Marys all had straight, sandy colored hair. Nothing remotely like Jeep's dark chocolate, curly hair. They could have worked as a sixties singing group.

Sweat broke out all over my skin when I saw myself through their eyes, in my costume.

"Carolyn. So good to see you again." Mary Colleen folded me into a hug. Then hugs from the rest. Way too much physical contact for my liking, but hey, that's what sisters did, right?

The oldest sister, Mary Helen, was fifty-three. The same age as my parents. She looked about forty. Her unblemished face made me think she had lived a stress-free life. After Mary Helen, three more Marys were born. Mary Sue: forty-six. Mary Lisbeth: forty-five. Mary Faith: forty-four. Then Jeep, thirty-five; Mary Hope, thirty-four and Mary Colleen, thirty-two.

My heartbeats tumbled over one another and I tried to breathe evenly. The four oldest Marys looked nearly interchangeable. They were all gorgeous. Well, I probably wouldn't say that if I met them out somewhere. But here, in their element, their confidence and power resulted in peak H-Factors.

We headed to the massive pillared porch where iced tea, lemonade, teeny cookies, miniscule sandwiches, and fruit were being served. I didn't say much. They spoke quickly and changed subjects often, their words falling over one another like kids tumbling down a hill.

"The other day, old Humphrey stopped by," Mary Helen said. "And you know what that old coot is up to when he comes calling with his fancy cards and golden cane."

The Marys cackled. I forced a smile.

"Well, not this time. He came by saying he wanted Mary Colleen to put on a show for everyone on Sunday. A show that highlights her finer gifts." Everyone hooted. I nodded along and tried to look involved in the conversation without knowing what any of it meant.

"He wants Mary Colleen, or should we say, MC Flannery, to resurrect her famous Super Summer Talent Show dance." The sisters hollered and cajoled Mary Colleen to the center of the porch.

I nodded enthusiastically, thinking she must have been very talented to have brought old Humphrey—whoever the hell he was—to their home with a request for a reprise. My plastered-on smile was cramping my cheeks. I looked forward to having something bring a genuine grin to my face.

Mary Faith pushed the button on a boom box. "MC Hammer's *Can't Touch This* filled the air. A joke?

Mary Faith counted off and MC Flannery was shaking and pushing body parts to the rhythm in the least talented way I'd ever seen. I stifled a laugh with my hand.

The intense expression on Mary Colleen's face made me fully understand she was serious. I glanced around. Jeep and the Marys were cheering her so I clapped along, too. I wanted to fit in, bad. I wanted Jeep to still love me after this weekend ended—even in his "I can't say it yet" way. I even considered dancing with Mary Colleen just to show I was one of them. I wanted to be on the team. For the love of God, I did want that.

MC (which I was instructed to call her from that point on) finished her dance and chugged some lemonade. I was relieved to be ignored. Blending in. A fantastic strategy.

The Marys cackled and laughed and finished each other's

sentences as though they had never formed a life outside the one here. And as the conversation barreled on, I found that they hadn't. Even MC and her fiancé, Ford (who would be arriving with his family later Saturday), would live at the mansion once they married.

They called it Tara. As in *Gone with the Wind.*

I guffawed. "Really? Tara? You're joking?"

Silence spread across the porch. All I heard was the sound of MC pressing buttons on the boom box.

"It's so cute, I mean," I said.

Jeep smiled at me. "My parents were hopeless romantics. The house has been in the family for a hundred years. Seen good and bad."

"Oh. That's so sweet. Really. That's where you get it, huh? Your romantic nature?" I smiled at the Marys. They scowled. I pulled at my fingers again, praying for their mindless chatter to start up again. That was the only thing saving me. Them filling the awkward silence till it overflowed with the incoherent trains of thought only family members could thread together.

Jeep sat on the arm of the wicker chair I was perched in. He squeezed me reassuringly and kissed my forehead.

"Aw. That's. So. Sweet." MC's words dripped with sarcasm. I thought she had been suspicious of me at Jeep's house that one night. Confirmed. Her mocking words had the consistency of syrup.

Jeep laughed at something Mary Hope said across the porch. His eyes glowed with familial happiness. Suddenly I wasn't in the mood to weasel into their good graces.

Crap Quotient: 5/10.

"Carolyn," Jeep said. "Mary Helen was asking about your school."

"Oh, sorry." I looked up at her, feeling small. I stood and sipped my lemonade. "I love my work. Hard as it is." I wondered if Mary Helen looked like Jeep's mother. "How much can you actually do for kids like them? I mean, really?" Mary Helen said.

"A lot, actually. I don't know enough about what I'm doing, but I'm figuring out what doesn't work. It's a start."

"That's good enough? Thank God we went to St. Stevens."

I nodded. Not wanting to discount her experiences.

A maid in a black and white uniform pulled Mary Helen away.

"How about a walk on the grounds?" Jeep took me by the hand and we headed down the staircase that led off the side of the porch. "We're not due to sail for another two hours," he said.

I hugged his waist as we walked into the woods, relieved to have some time away from the scrutiny of his family.

We sat on a fallen tree and faced each other. We kissed a few times. I felt like a teenager.

"I love my sisters. But sometimes it's just too much."

"No, they're nice. I never had siblings so I think it's great." I wanted it to be great.

"But MC's dance? Embarrassing as shit," Jeep said.

"Like watching fish electrocuted in a bathtub or something. Does she know she's bad? Not that I know anything about bad dancing. And who am I to talk? Look at what I'm wearing!"

Jeep plucked at one of the gold anchor buttons. "You're adorable—sailor suit and all. You're so weird, but in a good way. This dance of MC's? That was just... wrong. That time, that day you were dancing in your room? That was right. All of it. There's no one in the world like you."

He pushed my hair behind my ear. I'd never felt so special. Being called weird never felt so warm and loving. I was elated that although Jeep was clearly close to his family, there was a special space in his life just for us—separate from them.

Jeep pulled me closer. He kissed me and I almost told him I loved him. But I knew I didn't have to. I knew he could feel it, that everything that needed to be said aloud was already, silently, fully understood.

Chapter 23

Jeep and I finally had to head back to Tara to get ready for sailing. Coming out of the woods, I had the chance to look at the home without being distracted by introductions and freaky dances.

Carved wood molding painted crisp white, surrounded the fifteen-foot high oak doors that were stained the most amazing deep sea blue. The wooden siding was buttercup yellow, which exuded such storybook romantic warmth I wondered if they needed to use the furnace in the winter.

MC pulled the fit-for-a-giant door open and Jeep and I stepped aside. The sheer size of the foyer caught my breath. It was bigger than my classroom.

"Wow, this place is stunning. Gorgeous," I said.

She rolled her eyes, looking bored. Mistake number two: being overly affected by the beauty of their home. I thought that was odd, that it might be nice to be told your mansion is breathtaking, but perhaps not.

Simple though sturdy oak pieces dotted the expanse. A roll-top desk stood to the right of the door and a twelve foot oak bench perched to the left of it. I imagined Jeep and his sisters sitting on it, waiting to leave for church. Each piece looked as though it had been there forever. The red wallpaper was actually understated, as it had faded with age. Only a wink of the paper behind the bench, where my luggage had been placed, revealed that it had once been screaming red damask.

"Circa eighteen-twenty." Mary Colleen took one of my bags and started up the gently curving staircase.

"Great era," I said nonchalantly. She glanced back, eyes squinting at me. "Monet." She pointed to an oil painting.

"An original?"

"The one and only."

"Spectacular," I said like an idiot.

"Jeep's room is down there. Here's mine. There's Mary Helen's. Your room is between ours. Mary Helen's was formerly my parents' room." MC pulled me into it.

She whispered with her hand to her mouth, "You have to see this closet."

It wasn't a little two-by-two foot thing. It was fifteen by twelve or something.

"That's a room where I come from," I said.

"Yeah." MC smirked. "Look at this. My wedding dress."

Moved that MC would show me these things, I felt more confident. "It's exquisite," I said. "The simple neckline. Nothing extra. Really beautiful." I made sure I didn't touch it. It was so different from Laura's bowed and beaded number with the puffiest sleeves known to woman.

She nodded. "How about this?" She pulled out a three-drawer wooden box from a bank of cabinets and slid one drawer open. Inside were piles of jewels. MC's slim fingers burrowed amongst sapphires, diamonds, rubies and things that shot light and color as MC exposed them, things I couldn't even name.

"Here." She held a diamond ring the size of a dime under the light. "Wanna try it out?"

"Noooooo," I said. "That's too beautiful to even touch."

She waved it under my nose.

"Well, okay," I said. "Just for a second." It only slid past the first knuckle on my ring finger. I held my hand out in that way no woman could resist doing when her hand was bearing monstrous diamonds. Like trying on the veils, the ring gave my H-Factor instant oomph. That, I could handle.

"That's mine." She pulled it off my finger as though I'd said it wasn't. She flung the ring back into the drawer and pushed past me. Three Marys were waiting outside the closet, glowering. Who could blame them? It was early in my entrée into the family—too early to show the family jewels, yes.

MC dragged me from the room, as though protecting me from the others. She wanted to befriend me? Or she decided I was a better option than the monkey nuts Marys for the time being. So what if MC was the first of the six women to get married? Big deal that she went by MC. Who cared that they all lived here from birth and the way it was stacking up, until death? Old-fashioned but cute. I thought I could get along with MC. One out of six wasn't so bad.

My assigned bedroom featured a curved bay window with a padded window seat. I imagined reading, lesson planning and dreaming there. The room was decorated in various shades of green. The walls were a barely there shade of mint. Pale, grassy-hued gingham pillows with complementary emerald, light pink and pale jade stripes were scattered around the room. A lush sea green bedspread lay over the double bed. Velvet drapes hung at both ends of the bay window. At least seventeen shades of green were represented in the room. Practically invisible sheers caught the light, casting an ethereal glow throughout the room.

I touched the fabric on the ruffle of one of the pillows. Thick. Custom made. Not the kind you'd see in Nordstrom's and not available anywhere except at one fourteen Salty Air Road. I imagined the room hadn't changed in fifty-one years.

"Hope you like it." MC sat on the bed.

"It's gorgeous." I sat on the mint settee. "Thanks for inviting me. I'm honored."

"Well, my brother gets what he wants. I adore him." She shrugged and left the room. I looked at the space where she'd had been on the bed, the crease she'd made in the bedspread. I smoothed it away, wondering what the hell that had meant.

I had missed my chance to ask what to wear for sailing. But

I figured khaki pants and a white t-shirt was more appropriate than the sailor thing. We met at the dock. Two forty-foot sailboats bounced in the water like excited dogs awaiting their walk.

Mary Faith held a basket. "Here are the papers that will assign each of us to a boat for the day." She handed out the paper strips.

She handed me a red strip for the red sailboat. Jeep got blue. This made me nervous. I wanted to spend time with Jeep. And I'd never sailed before.

But I came up with a plan. Stay out of the way. Offer help. Wait for instructions. Smile a lot and laugh at the Mary-speak.

I stood against the metal railing, wind whipping through my hair, feeling a little majestic, actually. The abnormally warm April day made me forget the bizarre family stuff. I was enjoying the motion of the boat as it moved in the water. This serenity was broken by panicked voices.

"Thrust the flank!" Mary Helen jumped up and down, face red, eyes darting all over.

I looked back and forth, trying to discern who was monkeying up the works.

"You!" Dozens of fingers pointed my way. "Carolyn! Thrust the flank!" A chorus of voices came at me like unexpected waves.

"What? Are you kidding?" I said.

"Flank! Flank! Flank!" Mary Helen screamed, bearing down on me, pointing at something.

"Thrust! Thrust!"

I pulled a rope.

"Harder! Harder!" She shouted in my ear like a drill sergeant.

My trapezoids strained—I swore they ripped as I pulled like a lunatic, raising blisters on my hands. Mary Helen barked orders at everyone on board. I kept pulling. My foot slipped, but I caught myself from falling on my butt. Mary Helen stood over me, screaming, with her mouth open, eyes squinting as though she could infuse what she knew about sailing right into my head if she screamed loud and close enough to my face.

"I'm pulling." I barely got the words out. Mary Helen stepped away to rail at someone else then came back toward me. It was then she lost her footing, latched onto me and swept us both into the bay.

I gagged on the waves of the Chesapeake. Then began laughing uncontrollably, which didn't help keep the water out of my mouth.

"Stop cackling. You. You little girl," Mary Helen hissed.

That stung, but I kept laughing. What had I done to this woman? She knew I didn't know how to sail. I should have been pissed at her.

Our red boat sped away. The blue one turned and started back toward us. Jeep's smile comforted me. He grabbed a life preserver and bent over the metal railing as the boat passed fairly close.

"Mary Helen. Grab on." Jeep climbed down the ladder part way and threw the ring to her. I finally quit laughing.

I was not pleased with the rescue order. He was in love with *me*.

Mary Helen used the ring to paddle to the boat and climb up. Jeep smiled, offering his hand to her. I could have swum over beside Mary Helen. I didn't really need the ring. Personally, it didn't look like Helen needed it either. That wasn't the point. For the first time this weekend, I didn't know if Jeep and I felt the same way about our relationship, about us, about that miraculous ring of love that shielded two people from the rest of the world. Did he even know it was there?

Maybe it didn't exist for us. I looked into Jeep's eyes as he reached down to lift me out of the water. He was smiling, not even realizing what he'd done. I was dying. This was never going to work. A girl with a man. A solid mass sat in my gut making me question my judgment. Maybe if Jeep didn't say he loved me, it was indeed because he didn't yet feel that at all.

Chapter 24

I tried to get Jeep alone, but from the sailing forward, his sisters had us scheduled down to the second. And none of it gave us an opportunity to alone. I had a tendency toward paranoia. Even allowing for that, it was obvious these women hated me. And the dislike had started long before they'd met me. Damn handwritten RSVP.

The next portion of the extravaganza included cocktails and dinner for sixty. The dining room seated twenty-six people. The rest of the guests would be seated at large round tables that filled the library and parlor.

I felt good about how I looked for dinner. I wore a dress Laura hadn't wanted me to buy. Thank God I hadn't listened to her on that one. And I scored a seat at the family table, in the dining room. It all added up to a soaring H-Factor. My slinky black dress fell slightly above the knee, was V-necked, fitted at the waist and skimmed my hips as though it had been made just for me. The dress worked because I wasn't huge-busted. In my mind you could get away with a more suggestive dress if you didn't have too much to suggest. I looked more classy than slutty.

I descended the staircase and was hit by a wave of green,

blue and purples—the wedding colors. The sisters and their friends stopped talking and looked at me suspiciously. Mary Helen finally nodded approvingly. Could they possibly think I wouldn't notice them doing that? They'd just given me the fashion-eyeball. I'd done it to other people a million times, but I didn't like it turned on me, not at all.

Jeep came to me and put his hand on my lower back. No kiss, but a warm smile.

"I want you to meet MC's fiancé. Ford, this is Carolyn. Ford is the first brave soul to join the family."

"Ow!" Ford shouted like James Brown. "We're back to calling Mary Colleen MC Flannery? Excellent!"

Finally someone to make me laugh.

"Nice to meet you." His handshake was friendly. He looked me in the eye and seemed to smile with his entire body. His slightly longish hair and easy mood won me over. No wonder Jeep's family had allowed this guy access into the fold. He was fantastic—the opposite of me, personality-wise. Not a trace of moody syndrome.

He smiled and threw back an entire glass of red wine. "It's wonderful to meet the great Carolyn. Jeep can't stop talking about you. I'd say you've hooked the man, but that'd be uncouth."

My face flooded with heat. Jeep smiled at me and kissed my cheek.

"Let me get you some wine," Jeep said, heading toward the bar, Ford following behind.

"Hi." A tall blond came up to me. Familiar looking.

"Hi," I said.

"From the bar," she said.

"Bar?"

"The Tuna or whatever that hole in the wall was called. I'm Tess," she said.

Ah, yes. The flaxen Cindy Crawford lookalike. The ex-fiancée. In a cocktail dress she was even more stunning.

"Nice to see you again." A server with a silver tray floated by and I popped a mushroom into my mouth. I needed that wine yesterday. I should've brought my own bottle to prime in the room before this event. I never imagined the ex-fiancée would be at the party. Or that if she *was* coming, Jeep wouldn't warn me.

"You don't know who I am, do you?"

"I know."

She put her hand on mine as though I were a child. "Don't worry about me. Jeep and I were never meant to be together. Like an old married couple before our time. We knew too much about one another. We know each other too well. In every way. You know?"

I remembered Tess's ultimatum to Jeep. "Oh. I'm not worried." I pulled my hand out from under hers and patted it as though *she* were the child. I had to rustle up my confidence, find that same feeling I'd had that first night at The Tuna.

I didn't know where Jeep got sidetracked to, but I couldn't wait any longer for my wine. I politely excused myself and got my own wine, mingled with the non-threatening types and resisted the urge to proclaim myself an FBI agent or vice president of Feminist Women in Politics.

After an hour of drinks and hors d'oeuvres, a stooped, silver-haired man in a tuxedo meandered through the crowd ringing a tiny bell, signaling dinner was to be served. Everyone ignored him but me.

Maybe it was the teacher in me, but I followed directions and went straight to the dining room. There, alone in the fifty-foot long space, I looked around. The walls were sage green with about eight inch molding at the ceiling, four inches of molding at the chair rail point and another eight inches' worth along the floor.

I located my place card (in the shape of a little ship with a red sail). Right behind my seat was a wall that featured a faded mural. Beautiful from afar, creepy up close. I think it was Jeep's whole family, including the parents, in white, gauzy clothing, sitting in the woods. As if it wasn't clear when you met the family in person, the mural seemed to be a reminder to everyone else that they were not part of the inner circle.

Across from where I would eat my dinner, an oil painting

of men hunting in red coats plastered the wall. One simple statement. Perfect. The third and fourth walls were the backdrop for oil portraits and sprawling mahogany buffets that complimented the dining table. The chairs were upholstered in sage green and red material and were beautifully faded like everything else in the house. It all went together perfectly.

The time it must have taken to pull this home together staggered me. The family must have procured the items in that room with the same gusto that I pursued the answers to my students' literacy problems. Based on what I learned from seeing Jeep's Cape Cod home, I'd already started rethinking my redecorating ideas. Non-ideas actually. Not that I was far in the thinking process. But I knew enough to know I knew nothing about home decorating.

Finally the crowd trickled in. Twenty-six of us around the dining table that burst with enough silver to fund my Olive Garden forays for a lifetime, probably. Even knowing the simple rule about starting with the silverware on the outside and working in, I couldn't even decide which piece to use first. There was silver everywhere.

The centerpiece was pretty. Sort of. The bluest hydrangeas, irises, pale roses, Gerber daisies and bluish greens I couldn't identify with a name. But the shape of it—a sailboat—made it clear that money didn't guarantee taste in every instance as even I could see it was a little tacky. It had a blue sail on it. Signifying the boat that "won," by virtue of not having dumped anyone in the "drink." It was a blaring reminder of the little adventure that had ended with me in the water. I hadn't even realized it was a competition.

The table was five feet wide. Many of my students could have laid across it with no limbs dangling over either edge. I had to peek around the centerpiece to see Jeep. I waved half-heartedly. He smiled reassuringly. I felt a little better. Secret communication. The sign of a good couple.

Ford was on my left and Tess on my right. Maybe the sisters thought I could handle myself fine. MC and Mary Faith sat on either side of Jeep. The rest of the guests were merely actors to me. I couldn't keep any of them straight or how they knew the family. I heard words like "lifelong friend," "island neighbor," and "his father started Lomax Corp, the company that changed the world of shipping, forever." I couldn't remember the facts. But the tone was clear.

Mumbling gave way to silence as Mary Helen called us to attention for her prayer. She even made us hold hands. That wouldn't have been so bad except Tess had been assigned to the seat on my right. We held hands awkwardly. Tess's hand was tiny. It felt like warm butter inside my chalk-dried mitt. I'd have to buy some better moisturizer.

"I'm tearing up." Mary Helen choked on a sob after finishing the prayer. "I miss Mother and Father so much. Tonight we'll honor them. As well as MC and Ford." She choked again and took deep breaths. "My parents are with us in spirit and in body." She held her forefingers like a stewardess and pointed over her shoulders at two urns, presumably, though not confirmed to be, full of dead people—the parents.

Ford threw his glass of red wine into the air, sloshing it onto what must have been an antique lace tablecloth. "Cheers!" he screamed, "To Motheh and Fatheh!" He winked at MC around the ship. She brightened.

Mary Helen began to eat, signaling we should start, too.

I stabbed my salad, unable to take my eyes off the jars that were full of Jeep's parents' ashes. I didn't have dead parents. Maybe this was what children of dead parents did.

Ford elbowed me. "Freak show."

"It is odd." I tried not to sound judgmental.

"I love MC more than anything in this enormous world. But freaky? Yes they are."

"So, Carolyn." Mary Lisbeth put her hand to the side of her mouth and shouted from the far end of the table. Twenty-four gazes shifted to her then to me, then back to her.

Shit. I thought the number of dinner guests would preclude talking to anyone but my immediate neighbor. Not that I wanted to talk to Tess.

"You're an educated woman," Mary Lisbeth said. "What are

you reading currently?"

Two dozen gazes ping-ponged back to me. "Not much. Teaching is overwhelming. But I love to. Read, I mean. James Patterson. I like him." I nodded. Visions of my parents came to mind, the two of them curled up on the couch, buried in blankets with *War and Peace* and *Emma* sticking out. I refused to read all classics in lieu of the fun stuff. Who didn't love Patterson? Maybe this would be my bridge into the family circle. Literature. Yes, that made sense.

Mary Helen scrunched her face. "*Patterson?*" She snorted. "He studied where? I'm afraid I'm more of a Jane Austen fan. Edith Wharton."

I nodded, hoping the literary inquisition was over. I'd never had a conversation with a roomful of people watching, waiting. I wondered if this was how I made my students feel when I grilled them about what they were reading. But school was school. Being put on the spot was expected in the classroom.

"I'm familiar with Patterson," MC said over the centerpiece. All gazes snapped to her. "But I don't have time to indulge." She recoiled as though someone suggested she shoot heroin.

Mary Sue lifted her wineglass toward me. "Yes, an indulgence. I sort of think of Sanford that way, too. Like junk food. For the brain."

What the hell was *this*—the literary witch trials? Couldn't we talk about what Dylan on 90210 had to be so moody about all the G-D time?

Mary Hope joined the inquest. "I like to work for my literature. Dig at what the author is trying to get at." Polite, tittering laughs, a demure bravo and nods were offered around the table. This didn't even qualify as conversation in my book. Who were these freak-nuts?

"Everything in moderation, right?" I said.

I silently begged Jeep to peek around the ship, to offer a reassuring glance or word of support. Nothing. Screaming "orgy at eight" it seemed to me, would have garnered less hostility than admitting to reading Patterson.

"Can't always be on an intellectual health kick, right?" I

said, trying to garner my own polite laughter. Nope. I felt my posture slump.

"I never tire of rereading *The House of Mirth*," Mary Hope said. "Lily. Searching for money and love."

"And finding neither," MC said.

"Sad," Tess shook her head and stared at me. "A lady should know when she's out of her league."

I felt the gazes as the dinner guests awaited my volley. I told myself I was being sensitive. The Marys and Tess *couldn't* be using a turn-of-the-century novel to talk behind my back right in front of me.

"Excuse me, Carolyn." Tess reached across me and clamped onto a water goblet. "You took mine." She flashed a condescending smile. I *was* out of my league in that house. My bones disintegrated under my skin. I didn't know what was keeping me upright.

"Getting a taste of something *better* is worse than never knowing the difference," Mary Helen said. "Lily certainly learned that."

Mary Hope seemed to stretch her neck, to draw out her words to make sure I heard her. "True words, sister. True words."

"What do you think, Carolyn?" Mary Faith said.

The staccato beat of silver soupspoons hitting china was all that broke the hush as I looked from one Mary to the other. Was I being too sensitive? Beside me, Ford slurped his wine as though drinking at The Tuna. I looked at him, emptying his glass with his head thrown back, not giving a damn what anyone thought of him. I felt a grin come to my mouth. If I was going down like a forty-foot yacht, I was going to have fun doing it. I could play their game.

I reached forward and pushed part of the centerpiece to the side to see Mary Faith clearly. "What do I think? Well, it sounds like Lily needs some remedy. Please. Seriously, My mother loves Edith Wharton. I know she thinks *House* is a great read. I read some Wharton in college. It could have been *House*," I said. "I don't know. Poor folks singing. Drummers marching. It's only life in the end, you know."

The dinner guests stole glances at one another. They knew something was wrong with what I was saying, the way I was saying it, but they must have been as unfamiliar with music as I with *The House of Mirth*.

Ford tapped my hand with his knife.

"What?" I smiled.

He swallowed what he was chewing. "*It's only life?* That sounds—"

"Well," Mary Lisbeth interrupted. "I suppose there are books for everyone. Different strokes for different folks. Isn't that what you might say, Carolyn?"

Jeep was buried behind the centerpiece. I was on my own. My head said to play along like a good girl. My soul disagreed.

I made sure my voice was light and casual when I spoke. "Mary Lisbeth, I don't speak in clichés. Not unless I'm aware I'm doing it. In which case I announce outright that I used a tired, worn out old woman of a phrase."

As though a signal were given, everyone at the table abandoned the group conversation and began to talk to the person on his or her left or right. Thank you, God.

"Song lyrics," Ford said. "You talk in *them*," Ford held his hand up above the table for me to high-five. "Neil Young, Indigo Girls, Black Crowes. 'Bout time we got some hot blood around here."

An ally. He'd caught on to what the rest of them hadn't.

"Inside joke. That's what that is, huh?" Ford said. "Between you and yourself. Now me. I'm in on it. Jeep told me that was the very second he fell for you. In the bar. Some inside joke you had between you and you. That sealed the deal for him."

I dabbed my mouth with the linen napkin. "He told you that?" I felt buoyed. I peeked around the centerpiece. Jeep was talking to MC, laughing at something she said. When he saw me peering at him, he waved and smiled. Jeep *had* felt the soul slip that night, too. The same as me.

I watched him, the way his shoulders bounced when he laughed, absorbed in the conversation at hand. Jeep lived in the moment and his face conveyed what I imagined was in his heart. He didn't overanalyze or wonder or muse. He just lived. I could use some of that in my life.

MC boomed around the other side of the ship centerpiece. "You must really love children. Teaching must be fun. Sort of like playtime for grownups." She lit a cigarette.

A cigarette at dinner? Shaving time off all our lives, with no regard.

"I wanna live." I shrugged. "I'm the kind of girl who's gonna give."

Ford leaned in. His Polo cologne filled my nose. "Neil Young...well sort of, anyway. Point made. You *are* fun, my little friend."

I smiled.

MC shot us a searing look. Her eyes narrowed so much they nearly crossed.

I felt my confidence surge. "I assure you, teaching is not playtime," I said.

"What?" Mary Helen said. "A little reading, painting, simple math facts. That's not child's play?"

Ford cleared his throat, raised his glass and sang. "Questions, lots of questions. Scattering kids in loads of crooked lines."

"That's right, Ford," I said. Who would have thought Ford could pull Indigo Girls out of his ass without notice. Well, the tune was right, anyway. He had the words half wrong.

Ford hummed a few bars of *Closer to Fine*. We leaned into each other, shoulders pressed together and did a quiet duet of the chorus.

The Marys passed uncomfortable glances, then recast their attention to the people sitting closest to them. I was finally at ease. I felt as though I'd known Ford forever.

He grinned and high-fived me again. "You'll be a nice addition to the family, for sure. I might even cut back on the booze if you move in."

"Don't toss the bottles yet, my friend."

"Here," Ford said. He whispered. "A family secret for you.

Jeep is named Jeep because he was conceived in one. The very conservative, virginal Marys hate that story. Their parents were horny as can be. Everyone knows it. Horn-dogs, pure and simple. This table?" He knocked on the tabletop. I raised my eyebrows.

"Let's just say Mary Lisbeth could have been named Mary Mahogany just as easily as Lisbeth."

My jaw dropped and I laughed obnoxiously and covered my mouth.

Ford elbowed me. "Bet you a thousand big ones you can't guess what's in those jars. And lest you think I'm not good for it, I have a gargantuan trust coming due upon marriage."

"The parents' ashes?" I said.

"We have a winner!" Ford leapt to his feet, shoved his glass into the air and sloshed wine onto the table. This startled the maid, who was re-lighting a candle near one urn. She turned and bumped the sacred vessel from the mantle, sending it the floor. The mishap drew gasps from all in the room. The abrupt silence was punctuated by the maid's breathy whimpers and repeated apologies.

Mary Helen stood and shuffled to the urn, her hands placed at her belly as though she was holding everything in, dinner and all. She took it from the maid and lifted the lid. From where I sat, everything was fine. The lid was intact so the ashes were safe, right? Guess not.

"There're no ashes in the urn. No *ashes*!" The rest of the Marys scrambled toward their sister. Fussing and pacing, they bumped into one another like clowns.

"Where are the ashes?" MC hissed at Mary Helen.

"I didn't do anything to them. I brought them down for this dinner. That's it!" Mary Helen scanned the table. A smile and a shrug passed between Jeep and Tess as he leaned around the ship to share a memory. He saw me notice, but didn't fill me on what exactly was happening.

"You usually keep the urns in *your* room," MC said to Mary Helen.

"I didn't *do* anything to the ashes. I don't know why they're missing."

"Mother and Father were never apart in life *or* death. You do remember Father only living one day past Mother, don't you?" Mary Sue screeched.

"Apparently they're spending eternity separately, Mary Sue," MC said.

To be sure, I thought.

I didn't think I could have been more skeeved out. I felt I should tell Jeep I was sorry this ridiculousness was happening.

Jeep gritted his teeth, trying to calm his sisters.

I went to him and reached for his arm.

He threw my hand off with an irritated shrug. "Carolyn. Let me handle this."

They stopped bickering long enough to focus on me, clearly agreeing with Jeep that I should butt out of the situation. Anger flashed over me. My heart shrunk around itself as embarrassment set in. I should have understood his agitation, his need to help his sisters sort out the case of the missing ashes. But all I felt was humiliation at his reaction to my attempt to comfort him. I backed out of the room before I started to cry.

Chapter 25

I sat on the bottom step of the curving staircase. Voices in the next room rose and fell in volume and pitch. Squeals of sisterly angst peppered the relative peace in the foyer. On the floor beside the bottom step was the basket filled with the colored tabs that assigned us to particular boats. I dipped my hand in the basket and picked up a few papers. Except for that one red one and one blue one, they were all blank. I picked up a few more, unbelieving. How ridiculous. They fell through my fingers back into the basket. This could not be possible.

They'd planned it. The Marys. The only two people who had a slip of paper with a color were Jeep and I. The Marys freaking set me up like a lab rat; it had been a test to see if I was deserving of their brother.

"Carolyn?" Jeep strode toward me. "I'm so sorry about in there. It must look so bad to you. And I'm sorry I was short with you. They just get so hopped up and bickering and I'm in the middle and then—"

"What happened in there is not as bad as this." I stood and dumped the slips onto the floor. He bent to inspect them.

"Doesn't take a Secret Service man to figure out that Marys one through six don't want me anywhere near you," I said.

I hated that my voice caught. I tried to channel the same resolve I managed with Klein from time to time. Don't cry. Don't cry.

"It's not the way it looks." Jeep looked up from the papers he'd sorted.

"Cliché," I said.

"It's true," he said.

All the insecurity I'd tried to tamp down all day was taking over. "Did you miss the whole *House of Mirth* conversation? I might not have read the freaking thing, but I got their point."

"They didn't mean it that way. They always talk about literature," he said.

"I better call the President and let him know your ability to read between the lines *sucks*." I crossed my arms.

"That's not fair." Jeep moved toward me.

I backed up. "It's family. I know. Yours is a freaking nightmare."

"That's not fair," he said again.

"I'm not throwing stones. Sorry for the—"

"Cliché. Jesus, quit using them if you don't want to commit to them. Your family's perfect? I notice you don't mention them much."

I grabbed his arm. "Of course my family's whacked, too. Whose isn't? But you need to know I wanted your sisters to love me. That would have been a dream come true. But your family is living in some bizarre—"

"Jeep!" Mary Sue barreled into the foyer, bleary eyed. "Mary Helen said to bring you this. MC needs a Valium. This party is going the way of the Titanic!"

The world slowed as I stared at the green and white bottle in Mary Sue's hand. I watched the bottle pass from her French manicured fingers into Jeep's strong hands. Beano?

I felt my breath leak out of my lungs. He told them? My eyes stung. Don't cry. Don't cry. Don't cry. Beano.

I tried to hold it all in. I tried. But I couldn't. I dashed up the grand staircase and down the hall to my assigned bedroom. Even mired in despair, I couldn't help thinking my exit must have looked very Gone with the Wind-ish, what with the sweeping staircase and all.

I got to the room and punched my home phone number into the olive green phone. One of them must be home. I wrapped the cord around my finger. Please be home.

"Hello?"

"Laura. Can you come get me?"

"Who is this?" I heard her say to Paul, "Someone's on the other end, screeching." Huge pause.

"Hello?" Laura said.

"Please. Don't hold our argument against me now. You can still be mad, but come get me. Please." I barely squeezed the words out of my mouth.

"Gibson Island?" Laura said.

"One fourteen Salty Air Road." I squeaked out the directions.

"Paul and I'll be there lickity split."

I threw my hideous clothing into the bags. Except for the boat outfit I arrived in. I laid it on the bed for the wicked, loony Marys to find when they cleaned my room. I yanked the last part of the zipper closed, hoisted one bag over my shoulder and trudged down the stairs with the suitcase in hand.

The suitcase thudded from the stairs to the wall. I pretended it didn't matter. I offered sarcastic waves to onlookers as I tore through the foyer and escaped onto the beautiful porch. It would have been such a nice place to spend my summers.

MC stopped me before I made it down the front steps. I tried to go around her, but she blocked me.

"Aw, come on. You really want to leave?"

"Yes." I clenched my teeth.

"This isn't the best way to go about this," MC said.

"Really? How should I go about this?"

"You have to ask?"

I moved to the side. She blocked me. "Please step aside."

"My mother's ring is missing. You didn't—" MC cocked her head. "No, of course you wouldn't."

That was it. I pushed past her.

The spring day had baked me in eighty-five degree heat, but the evening temperature had dropped into the forties. My dress left me exposed, but the cold didn't bother me a bit.

"What are you doing?" Jeep came up behind me, offering his suit coat.

I pushed the coat away. "Leaving." I set the suitcase down.

Jeep reached toward me. "I want to explain."

I stepped back. "No. I'm not blind or stupid. And I don't compete in games of love."

"But Tess and I are over. She told you that."

I crossed my arms. "I'm not talking about Tess. I mean the insane Mary posse in there. Your family has great distaste for me, Jeep. I'm not a moron. And though I might have to put up with crap like that at work, I will not under any circumstances put up with it in my personal life. And don't think I won't read *The House of Mirth* to find out *exactly* what they were saying about me."

"They didn't mean anything. They just come across unfriendly. They stick together like glue. They need to get to know you. *I* know you. That's what counts."

I waved my hand at Jeep. "MC accused me of stealing some ring that *she* forced onto my hand earlier."

"What ring?" he said.

I re-crossed my arms. "Some freaking dime-sized thing. Must have cost twenty grand."

"Uh, well, more than that."

I wished his joking tone softened my mood.

He pulled me into his arms and squeezed. I could feel his chin on the top of my head. "Look, I'm sure MC didn't mean to accuse you." I drew back to gauge his facial expression. "Sometimes you read between lines that aren't even there. You're over-analytical."

I turned away.

"Carolyn. Don't let this hurt our relationship. We haven't known each other long. But I feel like we've known each other forever. What's between us is right. It just is."

I wanted to agree with him. Looking back at his face, trying to read his intentions. I knew he wanted to show he cared about me. But I found myself shaking my head. Headlights flashed over Jeep's face. I was nearly out of there.

"You're wrong." I picked up the suitcase. "You're too close to see the truth. This is who your sisters are. Every time I look at you, I'll see a six-headed monster orchestrating your life. And that, my friend, is not something I'm interested in entertaining."

"Carolyn." Jeep grabbed my arm again. "I—"

I pulled away. He let me go and looked at his feet as I opened the car door. Before getting in, I turned back.

He shook his head. I shook mine in reply then shoved the suitcase into the car and got in myself. Tess came up behind Jeep. She seemed quite satisfied.

"Over him, my ass." I fell back against the seat, stuffing rising emotions back into my body.

**

Paul drove. Laura, beside him, turned to hand me Kleenex, pasted on an appropriately pitiful expression and offered me consoling headshakes. I wasn't blubbering, but a steady stream of tears ran down my cheeks. Such a disaster, I told them. I wondered why things couldn't work out for Jeep and me the way they had for Laura and Paul.

Within months, they'd gone from being friends to being affianced. Things for me had worked out the extreme opposite way. As if the universe had to balance itself out or something. I had thought our soul slip offered some sort of love insurance. How was it possible to have intermingled souls one minute and absolutely no connection the next?

"Caro," Laura drawled, "the sun don't shine on the same dog's tail all the time."

"I'm too pained to dig through the nuances of that saying right now. But it seems, on the surface, that the sun *always* shines on your tail."

Laura turned and dug her fingers into the seatback, her lips quivering.

I sat forward and put my hand over hers. "What? Is your

dad okay?"

"I'm pregnant."

"*What?*" I fell back against the seat.

"My family will skin Paul alive when they hear this. My dress won't drape right *at all*. The bows and bustle will lay like a bedspread on a lumpy old mattress."

"My God, Laura. You never said…" I mentally chastised myself for feeling left out about her not spilling the sex beans to Nina and me. Grow up, Carolyn.

I covered her hand with mine again. The lights from passing cars lit up her face, illuminating her fear.

"You'll look beautiful in your dress," I said. "And the baby. It's really, *really* wonderful." I squeezed her fingers for emphasis. I was happy and surprised to notice I felt nothing but joy for her. A baby. That was something else.

Laura pulled her hand away from mine and patted me on the head. "I know you're dying to know, Miss Nosey-nose, so I'll tell you. A month and a half ago or so. I figured engaged was close enough to being married. I'm sure about Paul and sure I want the baby, but my parents are gonna have my hide. Bad 'nough I'm marrying a northern boy."

Paul grinned at her lovingly. He laid on his best Southern accent. "Aw, come on now, your kin folk gonna love my Yankee ass."

Laura giggled. I nearly imploded from bearing witness to their affection, certain I'd never experience the same thing for any prolonged period of time.

"I think that's why I was so cross last week. I'm sick as a dog and worried. I simply focused on cleaning because I could control that. I lashed out."

"Yes," I said.

I slid back in the seat and rolled the window down an inch. I put my head against the glass. We lapsed into silence and every few seconds Laura and Paul would look at each other. Their faces shone and faded into shadow with the headlights of passing cars.

Paul held up Laura's hand and kissed it.

"You and Jeep weren't right for each other," Laura said. "It'll happen with someone." The last thing I wanted to hear.

"At least we can stop pretending we're not living together," Paul said.

"Oh, no, we can't. Not until the wedding. Besides. We *don't* really live together. You don't get mail at our house. So, officially, you don't live with me," Laura said.

"Well, he lives with me," I said. "I see him in his underwear every night. Creeping to the kitchen at midnight."

"Doesn't count," Laura said.

"Wouldn't it be better," I leaned up between the head rests again, "for your parents to think you were living together when you got pregnant than to think you've been boffing in various and assorted locations around town?"

I was glad to be distracted. Not that the weight of dread had left me. But being with Paul and Laura helped. If they'd just let me live with them after they got married I might be able to manage.

"It's possible I *could* convince my parents I'm pregnant by Immaculate Conception. They'll want to believe it so bad, they'll nod and say, 'That's nice, Sugar Doll, now about those table linens.'"

I forced back another round of tears. At least she knew Paul loved her. More than anyone in the world. The security. Laura could wrap herself in it, wear it all over the world. It would defend her from all things bad and depressing. To know someone was going to stand up and forsake all others for her. To be there every night. No matter what.

I never cared about that until recently. Until I had a bit of it.

"You need to forget about Jeep Flannery, double-oh-seven," Paul said. "A guy like him is unmarried at age seventy-two for a reason."

"No shit," I said. "Six reasons, actually."

"And from what you told us," Paul said, "there were far too many firearms around his house. Like the Goddamn Wild West." Paul looked back and smiled. "Besides, anyone willing to give you up deserves to be let go."

"Thanks, Paul."

Laura rubbed her belly.

I put my head on my arms, which rested on the back of the bench seat in front. "I'm sorry for the fight, Laura, for all the tension lately," I said.

Laura held her hand up. "Forgotten."

"No," I said. "I said you're compulsive and anal and an old woman with childish taste in clothing. And that you put on your accent to get what you want from Klein."

"That *was* mean," Laura said.

We drove silently for a few minutes.

"You sure you're pregnant?" I asked.

"What do you think?" she said.

"You took twelve tests and have your periods from the past decade mapped out down to the second," I said.

Laura nodded. "I'm sorry, too. That I said your sloppy habits were a sign you were lazy and an indictment of your H-Factor, that you were domestically challenged."

"The truth hurts, baby," I said.

"It sure as hell does," Laura said.

And so we drove home. Every time I took a deep breath to flush away my weakness, to suck in some strength, I felt smaller. Getting past the Jeep situation would be hard, but I had to do it. I couldn't roam the earth like a gaping wound, open to infection and possibly death. Death didn't seem so bad, but knowing me, I'd just linger at the edge of it, watching the world go by, feeling its pain, but missing its joys.

I pondered an action plan, a way to forget what could have been, what had been, if only for a very short time. I traced a heart in the condensation that had formed on the window. There was that whole save-the-world-by-teaching thing. I erased the heart with the palm of my hand. Hell, at this point, saving one kid might be enough to make me feel like living. Saving people was not easy work and it was exactly the type of challenge that might allow me to forget Jeep and what I felt for him. It was exactly the kind of thing that might just save *me*.

Chapter 26

Laura and Paul were increasingly intertwined, casting off waves of joy and well-being. Nina had run into Random Man a few more times and began spending planned excursions with him. If he came around three more times I would have to call him by his real name.

All that meant I was afforded the chance to focus on work even more than before. Jeep called several times daily. His voice on the machine sent waves of angst through my body, making me grateful for the piles of papers and series of home visits I'd arranged. I couldn't call him back. I wouldn't put myself in the position of being vulnerable, confused, messed with. I didn't know how to move forward with him. So I moved forward without him.

At school, I made more changes. I cut out the scads of ridiculous follow-up activities suggested in the reading manual. This gave the kids time to read new text rather than re-read the same one five times to no good end.

We created an environment where we looked at everyone's strengths and weaknesses, exposing the latter so we could actually work with them. Everyone knew Terri was an excellent reader and was available to work with Katya, who couldn't read a lick. Katya had begun to catch up in math, though, and so she worked with Jamaica and other students who weren't coming along as quickly. I knew this method was potentially dangerous. The kids could be vicious and this situation could provide them with endless barbs and clever cut-downs. But miraculously, it didn't.

My subversive curriculum was considerably more engaging than the county one, but my amateur attempts at getting the non-readers to decode fluently wasn't having an effect. Why could they read the list of rhyming words one day, but wouldn't know them the next? Why could they read the first letter of a word, but only guess at the rest? I don't know what the guys who wrote the manual were smoking, but they clearly hadn't used classes like mine when they did the research that informed the series.

Each child was dramatically more invested in his work. That felt good to see, but each day was still topped with at least one shining example of my inadequacies. Marvin was one example. I had made it three-quarters of the way through the year without fully assessing his reading ability—an appalling omission.

I hadn't even realized he had been held back two times until I read his file for the second time. I had only skimmed the information at first because he never got in trouble, was a natural leader and helped keep his peers on task.

The other students clearly didn't know he'd been held back. Marvin was smart. He knew how to draw attention away from himself. But one day when I asked him to read a list of names to me, I was stunned at his complete inability to read at all. He could name a letter here or there. Yes. But he had no sense of the patterns of letters within words, especially vowels.

I looked around the room at the students who were busy writing. Marvin stared at the paper I had given him.

"Marvin. What's wrong?" I put my hand on his shoulder. Tears splatted onto his paper—the wetness giving new shape to the letters in the words. Suddenly what I'd missed all year seemed stark and true.

"You can't read at all," I said.

He shook his head slowly back and forth.

I couldn't believe he'd masked this all year, that I'd overlooked the signs.

"Marvin. We'll fix this. We will." I kept my voice low and hoped my words would infuse him with the energy that had been spurred by my horror and despair. He couldn't just go on this way. But while I had worked hard to not view weaknesses as something to hide in the classroom, I thought this information was better left in the closet.

And so, Marvin's was the first home I visited—the visits I thought would scare them into good behavior as they would not want me showing up at their door. When I made the threat, I never imagined they would all *want* me to come to their homes.

Marvin and I walked to his house, just a hundred yards from the back door of the school. The house was a ranch and the yard was neat with nicely trimmed bushes and evergreen plants in pots outside the front door.

His mom, who looked about twenty-six years old, let us in and smothered Marvin with hugs and kisses. He lingered in her arms and smiled up at her like a toddler. He seemed so old at school, where he towered over the primary students.

"Ms. Jenkins. Call me Sharon," she said, reaching over Marvin's head to shake my hand.

"Thanks. I'm Carolyn," I said.

"Marvin, show your teacher into the TV room and I'll get some snacks."

Marvin beamed. He walked me into a room off to the right of the front hall. The walls were white with a grayish undertone that was depressing. There were no pictures anywhere—no posters, artwork, family photos, nothing. I knew from his file that he'd moved four times in five years. The denim couch was a little worn, but nice. There were beanbag chairs strewn around. I sunk into one and looked around the room. I was eye-level to the coffee table and a stack of worn Dr. Seuss books.

Sharon set a tray of vanilla wafers and orange juice on the table in front of us.

"Thanks. I rarely eat lunch. So this is really great of you, Sharon."

"I'm glad you've come, Ms. Jenkins."

"Call me Carolyn."

She smiled. "Sit on the couch."

"The bean bag's great. Comfy," I said.

"No." She reached for my hand and pulled me up. "I insist you sit on the couch."

"Okay. No problem." Her smile made me smile.

"I don't know why I never get to the school," Sharon said. "I get home from work before Marvin. I should stop in, but I...I guess it's partly that I don't feel comfortable there. I'm very happy to know you care about Marvin like this. To come to me."

"He's so smart. He's a great leader. We've kept it a secret from his classmates that he's been held back twice. He's not so much bigger than them that they notice. But it's Marvin's reading that is the problem. He can't read," I said gently.

Sharon sighed with her entire body. She played with a cookie. "I have him read every night. These." She stacked the Dr. Seuss books. "At the last school, they said the more he reads, the better he'll get. Even if it's the same thing over and over. He works so hard." Her voice was whispery. Marvin stared at the cookie tray, then at me. His irises swallowed up the pupils with their darkness and mirrored his mother's quiet despair. I was staring into his future. One without promise or hope or dreams.

"Whoever told you that was correct. To some degree. But it's not enough for him to read these books over and over." My voice caught—taken by surprise with emotion. "I can show you some activities that might help him with phonics. But you'll need to do them every day to get results. I contacted a professor from my college and she sent them to me. I'll figure this out for you both. I promise."

I felt as though my life's path had been laid before me, right then in that vacant living room that somehow overflowed with love between a mother and son. Who needed Jeep when I could become the best teacher in the world?

"Ms. Jenkins," Sharon said.

"Carolyn," I said.

"I don't want you to think this house means I don't care

about Marvin. It's bare, I know. I want to have a warm home. I work for families like you. I know what your homes look like. Books everywhere. But we move too much. My ex. We have to stay away from him." Marvin nodded with his mother.

I shook my head. "I...I don't think anything. What you imagine my house was like growing up is probably part right. But you know, the relationship you two have. That's special. And I'll find some way to help Marvin."

We talked for about a half hour more. I showed her how to work with Marvin with his reading book, how to ask questions about the stories. I shared the very rudimentary knowledge I had about beginning reading, using phonics. I also suggested she borrow some harder books from the library—books that were at his age and interest level. She should read with him. I hoped the combination of practicing discrete little skills and reading bigger, engaging stories would help make him literate.

"Thanks Ms. Jenk—"

"Carolyn," I said.

"I have to be respectful," she said.

"Oh." My faced filled with heat. "I see." If she knew the degree to which I was failing Marvin, she'd beat me to a pulp, calling me Carolyn all the while.

"See you tomorrow, Marvin."

He latched his arms around his mother's waist and hugged her close.

Sharon was right about my upbringing—about the books, anyway. But, even in their less than desirable economic status, she and Marvin shared a closeness I didn't have with my parents. Still, I'd been given the tools to function in the world. That was no small gift to be given. Everything had become complicated to me in the past year. Navigating layers and curtains and swags of gray was apparently, not my thing. And nothing seemed black and white anymore, even if that was exactly what I wished it to be.

**

Walking to the school parking lot from Marvin's home, I saw Fionna's car was still beside mine. I'd never seen her arrive earlier than two seconds before the kids streamed into the school or leave after anyone—including Nina. When I got closer to our cars I saw a pair of feet jutting out from between them. I ran and knelt down.

"Fionna?" I pulled her up into a sitting position.

"Oh, wow, that's crazy, man." Fionna giggled. "I've been having headaches and wow, that's something else. I passed out."

"Are you bleeding?" I felt around her head for the cut I imagined she must have gotten if she'd fainted to the ground full force.

"No, no. I'm fine, Carolyn. I guess I needed a little rest is all. Thank God I'm in my pajamas, you know?" She giggled again.

"I'll take you home," I said. "You shouldn't drive."

It took a while to convince Fionna to let me drive her home. But in the end she couldn't stay awake long enough to argue any more. I dragged her into the back seat and when we got to her apartment, her roommate carried her in like a sack of potatoes.

As I was driving home, I knew I had to talk to someone about Fionna. If she was this messed up on drugs she was going to hurt herself or someone else. One of the kids, maybe. They'd know she was on drugs, anyway. These kids were smart.

I was glad to have so much to focus on at work. It allowed me to push the thoughts of Jeep away, to numb the hurt and smother the love that wouldn't go away on its own. I was grateful when exhaustion set in at the end of each day, allowing me to forget that he was out of my life, that our souls, mid-slip, had slipped away from each other. Every day when I got home I would find a letter from him. This day was no different. He claimed to love me and said he needed another chance. He seemed sincere, but I couldn't let him back in. Visions of his sisters beat around in my head. Humiliated, I tried to forget the extravaganza.

And the times I would soften my heart and let my mind

wander to him, to the way every second with him, before the extravaganza, had meant something big, I would soon shake the images away and let sleep take over. The pre-extravaganza us hadn't been who we really were. I needed to accept that sometimes people worked hard at life and it still kicked them in the ass.

**

The days went on and I continued my home visits after school. I could see a difference in student behavior and focus after visiting each family. For instance, I could tell Marvin was reading at home with his mother and not only Dr. Seuss. I recorded data with meticulous notes, patching the holes in the students' backgrounds, replacing what I thought I knew about them with what was actually true.

Lying on my bed, looking for patterns in the information I'd collected, my muscles unwound and I started to doze. Someone knocked at my door. I ignored it. I didn't have the energy to talk and I wasn't in the mood to listen to how well the wedding plans were going, what was on the short list of baby names, or that Random Man was developing into a fine catch of a man for Nina.

Even with my eyes closed, I could tell the door had been opened, that the room had brightened considerably.

Someone sat on my bed. Nina. She put her head on my shoulder, I shrugged it off and turned on my side, fake yawning.

"You're awake, so don't bother with the 'I'm asleep already' routine," she said.

"Ummm," I said in my best sleepy voice.

"I know you're upset about Jeep," Nina said, "about things not working out. But he's not the guy for you and I'm worried that you're going to toss yourself from the Key Bridge tomorrow afternoon or something."

"I'm due at Terri's house tomorrow afternoon. I won't be available for body tossing until well into the evening. Then I'll be too tired."

"That's not funny. I think you're being self-destructive,

planning to go into these neighborhoods like some urban cowboy."

I rolled over so I could see her, gauge the intention behind her words.

I pushed up on my elbows. "I love those kids and if going to their homes makes a difference then I'm going to do it. I mean, what's the point if I show up to work and do shit that doesn't work for kids I don't understand and leave at the end of the day, happy that my bank account is one hundred bucks fatter."

Nina closed her eyes and hid a frustrated sigh. "We can fight over that later. It's the Jeep thing that really has me worried. You have to let go of him and move on. We'll go to the Green Turtle tomorrow."

I closed my eyes and let my head drop back. "I can't breathe, Nina. Every night, when I'm trying to sleep, all I can think about is his hands."

"The hands," Nina said.

"Don't make fun." I collapsed fully onto the bed and adjusted the pillow under my head.

Nina sat up, cross-legged and rolled her eyes.

"I can't help it. The nature of a relationship is conveyed in the casual, unplanned touch. Does he run his hand over your hair for no reason? Or rub your shoulders unexpectedly before eating his scrambled eggs? And the way the hands look. Purposeful, useless, or powerful. It's not hard to tell. It's all there. And I can't get Jeep's hands out of my mind."

Nina hit me playfully with one of the decorative pillows. "Have you tried thinking of the bad stuff?"

"I've tried."

"Ah, Carolyn. I can't stand to see you like this." Nina pulled me into her body and nuzzled me. I pushed away.

"Tell me you love me," Nina said.

"I barely like you at all," I said.

"I know you love me," she said.

"No," I said.

The phone rang. I reached for it.

"Hello?"

"Carolyn." A familiar voice. I waved Nina away. She left the room, blowing me kisses, making me smile.

"Alex." I shouldn't have picked up.

"I have some stuff of yours," he said. "I should return it. We need to talk."

"Consider the stuff your parting gifts," I said.

"That's cruel," he said.

"I've become hardened."

"Yeah, fuck. That was—"

"Alex. I have to go," I said. "I'm expecting one of my Lorton phone calls—"

"It's Thursday," Alex said. "I thought Thursday brought the calls from the Rikers parents."

"You remember that?" Maybe I didn't give him enough credit.

"I'm not a total ass. I really love you—"

"Alex. We're not—"

"Right for each other," he said. "I know. But what if I come down? You can make a great meal, we'll talk. Just have fun."

"You know I'll never be the having-fun-while-meal-making type."

"You don't want to try?"

"That whole housewife thing? I'm shuddering as I say the words."

"You're gonna have trouble, then. Finding a husband," he said.

"That's for sure," I said.

We were silent for a bit. I wished I could just hang up without another word.

"Oh, that's my call waiting. I have to go, Alex. Don't worry about my stuff. Really."

"Carolyn?"

"Alex. You are a great guy. The right woman is out there waiting for you. Just go look."

I hung up the phone, ignoring the call waiting. I snuggled deep into my bed, not undressing. I stared at the clock. Nine p.m. I should have been in the family room with Nina, Laura and Paul, watching *Seinfeld*. But they were all leaving me.

Nina and Random Man were talking about going on vacation together and in my mind that was just a half-step from moving in together. And of course Laura and Paul were moving out. I asked if I could be their pet. Or live-in funny girl. They said no. Maybe I could sign on as Fionna's keeper. If she hadn't had one foot in the grave and the other on a banana peel, if I hadn't been convinced she'd drag me into the pit with her, I would have asked.

There was no point in putting off my impending loneliness. Might as well get used to it and keep future, further disappointment as far away from me as possible.

Chapter 27

A week after finding Fionna passed out in the parking lot, and with three more home-visits completed, my kids took the state exam. The test was so hard, they couldn't even read the directions, let alone understand and perform anything on it. But they certainly played the roles of frustrated, tearful, and angry students—that they could do. Even I, an adult who was quite the comprehender, had to mull over the instructions several times before mapping out a strategy for each problem. This test might mean the end of my career and them.

Because the test was so hard, I made sure I visited Terri's home that week. She was one of the students who could do very well on the assessment if she focused. I needed her parents' support to make that happen.

Her house was a century-old, brick townhome overflowing with bookshelves and bursting with people. It was three stories high, with twenty-by-twenty foot rooms. A long, thin hall ran beside the rooms from the front door back to the kitchen. In a way, It reminded me of Jeep's place—even though it was a different style of home, they shared the same age, with similar intricate detail.

Terri's home was large and beautiful, but clearly affordable because of its location in a struggling neighborhood. The home teemed with loving conversation. Generations of relatives came in and out of the kitchen, which was painted a Russian Blue.

When I arrived, Terri and two of her cousins were sitting in the kitchen having their hair braided by Terri's mom, Ruth, and two aunts. Their husbands came and went, testing the sauce on the stove and delivering updates on their workdays before kissing cheeks, lips and foreheads and grabbing a Sports Illustrated or the Wall Street Journal from the pile on the countertop. They headed to the front room for some "peaceful reading time," as they called it.

Terri and her cousins were also reading as intricate patterns were braided into their hair. I almost fell over at the book in Terri's hands. Langston Hughes. Her cousins read the Bible and the reader from school. I had thought the braids a colossal waste of time. I think I might have even told Terri so. I think I was wrong.

Turns out the time she spent having her hair shaped into works of art were hours spent creating memories and fostering literacy and language development. Terri's great grandmother, Ms. Moran, manned the kitchen. Food was everywhere. The spry woman narrated every move she made, describing the recipes for ribs, burgers, and sweet potato pie.

They invited me for dinner and I stayed. My favorite part of the meal, the part I might actually have been able to duplicate in my own house was a delicate spinach salad with home dried cranberries and what Ms. Moran called her wedding day salad dressing.

"Could I have that recipe?" I asked.

"No child. No chance in Hell," Terri's tiny great grandmother said. "I haven't even given it to Ruthie."

"She gave it to *me*." Terri's Aunt Sasha swung her generous hips as she cleared the table.

"That's because you were on your death bed for five minutes," Ruth cut in.

"I'm alive and kicking. And I won't share that recipe for anything," Sasha said.

That was that for the recipe. After stuffing myself with culinary magic and laughing for hours, Ruth walked me to the door.

"Thanks for coming," she said. "You know I won't never show up in that insane asylum Mr. Klein calls a school."

"It's tough there," I said, wanting to agree, but realizing that would be disrespectful. Even to a man who didn't deserve any respect.

"It's Klein—an awful man. If not for my people living right here, for this house my grandfather built, I'd been outta here a long time ago."

I didn't quite understand why they stayed, even with the attachment to the house. But, I understood a lot more about them after spending time there. And that was a good start.

"I'll do what I can to give Terri what she needs at school. She could do great on these tests if she focuses," I said. "She's incredibly smart. I'm so glad to see how much reading she does here. But she acts like she doesn't care. Lots of talk about modeling and boys."

Ruth shrugged. "That's how it is around here. Better to be dumb and get the guys than smart with no romantic prospects. I'm trying to change that. Why you think we fuss four hours a night with these girls' hair?"

"I thought it was just so they'd look good. I'm sorry I thought that."

"How could you know?" Ruth said. "We braid them up to keep them ours, to keep them young as long as possible."

"I see that," I said. "Thanks for sharing your home. Your life." I couldn't stop myself from hugging Ruth and I didn't look to see her reaction before heading down the porch steps.

"Thanks for coming, Ms. Jenkins."

"No. Thank you," I said, looking over my shoulder as I headed down her front steps.

**

In visiting the first chunk of my students' homes, I realized the many ways school was the puzzle box for them and each student was the ill-fitted puzzle piece, tossed haphazardly into the mix. They were working within a system that might never offer what they needed. I had no solution to this overwhelming systemic problem, but hopefully, that small understanding would at least help me better bridge the gap between school and home. The families I'd met at their homes so far made me think it was possible.

Then I visited Katya's apartment. She answered the door with toilet paper hanging out of her ears.

"What's this?" I pulled the paper from her head.

"The bugs. They'll burrow in and leave eggs," she said without a hint of disgust.

"The bugs?" I asked. She opened the door and let me in. Empty. And not the way Marvin's house had been. This was moving-out-day bare. Only a mattress sat in the far corner by the windows. Sun poured in. No curtains. No blinds.

I was setting my purse on the counter when I saw them.

Roaches. Everywhere. Basking in the sun as though it was their last day on earth. No fear. My stomach turned. I gagged before I could stop myself. I was mortified for Katya. She beamed at me, her grin wide and loose as I'd never seen it in school. She handed me my purse. "You better keep a hold of your pocketbook. You don't want to take any of them with you."

"Oh, well, okay," I said. I smiled back at her, forcing my lips to curve into something that appeared natural.

"I'm so happy you're here, Ms. Jenkins. I been waiting for this," she said, hugging me. Over her head I saw the blankets on the mattress rustling. Then two heads popped out from under the covers.

"What you doin' here, *teacher*?" Katya's mom sat up, pulling the comforter around her boobs. Naked. Beside her, a nude man lit a joint.

"Um, I'm sorry," I said. "I sent a note home. You signed it, saying you were okay with today as a visitation day."

"What? You some uppity social worker? Vis-it-in' homes and shit? How 'bout you teach my Katya to read? How 'bout that, teacher-girl?"

I looked at Katya. Her face betrayed nothing.

"I...didn't mean to intrude," I said. My head was full of conflicting thoughts. Call the cops. Call Miss Tucker. Klein? Who the hell was I to show up here and do this?

The naked man emerged from under the worn blanket, stood and pulled on a pair of tighty-whities. Then he pulled two pistols from between the mattress and wall. Twirled them wild-west style. Trepidation slammed into me, closed my throat and made me aware of the blood rushing through my body. I pushed away the fear on behalf of Katya. He walked toward us, still twirling the guns. What the fuck was this guy doing? He set the guns on the counter behind us, then plucked Katya's chin in a harmless fatherly way.

I was shaking. My hand was sweating around the purse handle. Katya pushed her chin into the air. Her body tensed, but her face indicated she was fearless in the face of this man. There was definitely no manual for this situation.

"It ain't no big shit, you showing up here." Katya's mom reached for what looked like a crack pipe. Not that I'd ever seen one.

I looked at Katya. Poker face. I flicked a roach from her shoulder as though doing this was as normal as removing lint from a coat. She flashed an appreciative smile. It was then I understood the toilet paper in the ears. It was then I knew I had to take her with me. Where? I was stuck. I pulled Katya toward the door, ignoring her mother's wails and lawsuit threats.

I flung open the door. A man and woman stood in the hall. Katya's Aunt Mary and Uncle Jason introduced themselves. I almost covered them in hugs and kisses. Katya's mom was too far into her high to object to us leaving. The man didn't care.

We went to Mary and Jason's home. Turned out their townhouse was the one connected to Terri's. Before they'd let me in the house, I had to dump out my purse in what they referred to as a "roach check." Gut check was more like it.

I didn't talk much while there. I listened, grateful they had it together. They were nice and said they were pleased Katya had me for a teacher. Turned out they were in the process of adopting Katya. But their niece was still endlessly trying to win her mother's love and attention. It was Katya's aunt who had signed the permission form. Katya was supposed to have told me to show up at her aunt's house. But she'd hoped her mother would be having a good day and that she'd want to meet me. And somehow want to change her life. Somehow I'd convinced Katya one person could change the world if she tried hard enough. Now it seemed a cruel thing to teach a little girl.

The last step in the process of adopting was getting Katya's father's blessing. He was in jail and according to Jason and Mary, he loved Katya enough to see adopting her out was a good thing. He hadn't mentioned that on the phone, but I told Katya and her aunt all the good things he said about them.

When I left, Katya latched onto me. Her sour-smelling scalp, under my chin as she hugged me for five minutes, would forever be etched in the olfactory zone of my brain. That smell, her apartment, her life, would never, ever leave me. And, I didn't need to see decades pass to prove it.

**

After visiting Katya's family, I arrived home to find Laura crying.

"I'm worried," she wailed. "Paul's not home yet. I just told my parents about the baby and they weren't thrilled. I can't stop crying. It's like they were saying they didn't think I'll be a good mom. What if they're right?"

"Laura." I sat with her on the couch. She leaned against me and sniffled into my shoulder. I wrapped her up in my arms as though she were my child. We stared at MTV, with the volume barely audible, not really watching. "You'll be the best mother ever. She'll be so lucky you're her mom. I can't imagine someone better to be a mom than you."

Laura sniffled and played with her engagement ring. "Paul says the same thing, but I don't know. I'm scared to death. And, I'm going to look like a monster at my own wedding."

"Oh, please." I squeezed her. "It's documented in several sociological journals that the H-Factor of a bride, even a homely one, far exceeds any woman's within a one-hundred-mile radius. And after visiting Katya's place I'm convinced you don't have to do much to be a good parent. Parental Potential? I'd put yours about 10/10. You'll be great."

"I'm going to miss this," Laura cried. "You. All your stupid quotients and factors and potentials. I'm gaining a marriage, but losing this, losing you."

I shook my head. "Lose me? You think I'd let that happen? We'll still be close. We'll be at school together. You can't go crying on me about that. Tears give me anxiety and heartburn. So stop it." My own voice cracked. "After all we've been through, our lives have been imprinted with each other. You're stuck with me and all that comes with that." I spoke as emphatically as possible. I needed this to be true. Saying it aloud would help ensure it was.

"I know." Laura wiped her nose. "You're right. And you'll figure things out, too. You'll have a good life. I know it," Laura said.

I smiled at her and she buried her head against me. I thought about how different Laura and I were. I didn't want to change to be more like her, but had I been born more like her, life would be easier.

She seemed more suited for success than me. Take school, for instance. She was disappointed when Tichelle stabbed Clarence with his pencil, or saddened when six-year-old Jeremy was late to school because he couldn't read the clock to know it was time to go, but she suffered no guilt or feelings of failure about these things.

My theory was that because Laura cried incessantly, mostly about stupid stuff, she expelled any toxic crap that might make her truly sad. Laura had it right. No lofty ideas about saving anyone. She simply performed her duties in an orderly, teacherly way. That traditional teacher-y-ness was in her as much as it wasn't in me. It was why I hadn't been able to "figure things out" yet, as she put it. I lacked the algorithm where one thing led to another, neatly.

I'd tried to impose such tidy measures on my life before.

But laying a web of must-do's over my existence felt suffocating. The trouble was, I didn't have some scary great artistic talent to offset my willy-nilly approach to life. Any shortcoming can be hidden in the shadow of greatness.

Paul ran into the house, shouting for Laura. His boss had given him the message that Laura had called, that she needed him and rather than just calling her back, he rushed home to see her in person. He scooped her up, all six feet of her, and held her tight, not saying a word. Not having to. I almost burst into tears—like Laura!

I'd never have what they did. For a half a second, I considered giving up teaching to pursue becoming a housewife full thrust. Cooking, cleaning, ironing. The whole thing.

The phone rang. It'd been days since Jeep had tried to contact me. Who could blame him for giving up? I hadn't returned any of his calls or acknowledged his letters. But this day put me in the mood to reconsider. Maybe this was him.

"Carolyn?" My mom's voice startled me. My dad always called.

"Dad's okay?" I asked.

"Of course," she said. "He's on the pot. I thought I'd get the conversation going because we're due at the museum for an opening."

"Oh, fun."

"Your father. He loves an opening. What's new with you?"

"Laura's pregnant and getting married. I'm in the wedding—"

"Pregnant? Dear God, Carolyn, don't you go and do that. You're only 23. Life's too short. You've only been abroad once—"

"I'm not the one who's pregnant," I said. "Could you be a *little* excited for someone else's life-changing events?"

My mom always had a ready retort in these situations, yet this time she was still. I could hear her toying with the phone cord and imagine her face as she considered whatever it was that she didn't want to say.

"Of course I'm happy for Laura. Having a baby is

miraculous and if anyone can make this work, it's Laura. She's wonderful, nurturing, rule-based. Lives up to every standard ever set by society."

"Yes," I said.

She paused again. I sighed, wondering if we'd ever have a comfortable conversation.

"I shouldn't say this…" my mom said. Her voice was conspiratorial, unlike I'd ever heard her use with me—as though she was about to share the secret to life.

"What?" I said.

"This just took me by surprise. Took me back."

"Back to what?"

"Having babies. It got me thinking. That mother-child bond isn't there for everyone. I hope it happens for Laura. I hope her expectations aren't so high she can't adjust to whatever reality comes along with the child."

"What do you mean?" I felt sick. Was she actually saying she never felt bonded to me—that she'd never experienced any real love toward me?

"Sometimes when that bond isn't there, the child spends her life searching for that type of deep connection and love in others. Like your father and I."

I took a ragged breath. "Are you saying—"

"What I'm saying is my mother couldn't stand me." Her voice cracked. She cleared her throat. She'd never come across as vulnerable to me before. "I was the last of ten kids. She could barely keep her eyes open during the day. By the time I was born, whatever spiritual stores were available to feed maternal bonds were depleted. I was very lonely as a child, set apart from the rest of my siblings because they were so much older than me. Luckily, one day, like a clap of thunder, your father appeared."

We sat silent on our ends of the line. A soul slip—she'd had one with my father. I'd known that my whole life, but I never knew how badly she'd needed that kind of love, that she was anything like me at all.

"What about us?" I asked before I could stifle the question.

"I love you, Carolyn. I feel so different toward you than

how I imagined my mother felt toward me. There's no comparison. You have to know that. I know you understand how much I love you. In your skin, deep in your heart, you know. If you stop and close your eyes and stop thinking so much, you'll feel it." Her voice caught again and cracked over the last words.

I felt as though she needed me to reassure her. "I know, Mom. I think I know." I didn't understand exactly she was saying, but we'd never talked like this before. She'd never confided anything in me especially not anything related to her emotions. I still wasn't convinced she'd felt that magical bond so many mothers did.

"But Mom? Are you saying you didn't feel that bond with me because you didn't have it with your own mother? That there was no way to experience that with me? That someday I'll have kids and not feel it?"

"Course not. That's the exact opposite of what I said. Oh, here's your father." My mind was only beginning to wind around her reaction to Laura's pregnancy, mothers and babies, their bonds. They fumbled the phone hand-off. The thought that I'd had many times over the course of my life—that my mother hadn't wanted to be pregnant with me—kept stabbing me despite what she had just said.

"Hello Caro! How's my baby girl?" I could hear my dad's smile.

"Hi Dad. I'm okay. Mom says you guys are having fun, heading off somewhere or other."

"We are, we are. And we're thinking we should come see D.C., see you, see your place. Would that be good?"

"Yes, when?"

"You tell us."

"Okay, let me see what's coming up with school and well, maybe as soon as possible?"

"Great, let us know. And Carolyn. We adore every inch of you. We always have. We're just not sentimental."

"Except with each other."

"Not really. We're just together all the time. That's not

sentimental, it's just the way it is, proximity. You've always been sensitive, Carolyn. Listen, I know how hard you're working. Don't get down on yourself, not about anything." Clearly he'd overheard my mother's end of our conversation.

"Okay. Love you, Dad."

"Love you, Caro. Mom does, too. You know she's not one of those girly, demonstrative types. She's always been different that way. Why do you think she only had one child? She didn't want you or any child to ever feel what she did. She might not say that in words, but that's true."

We hung up and I felt disconnected in every way.

I let my mother's revelation sit with me, bothering me, pushing me to pick the phone back up and dial to ask more questions. No answer. I shifted back on the couch and arranged the pillow under my neck in just the right way.

Even at a young age, I must have known my mom was ambivalent about me on some level. Without even being conscious of it. She wasn't smoking crack in front of me or letting bugs nest in my ears, but I'd always thought that something about me, her child, must have filled her with a sense of duty, rather than love. And there wasn't a moment in my life I didn't know that in my bones. Until today.

I closed my eyes and replayed the phone call. I imagined how lonely my mom must have been as a child, even with older siblings. I tried to reorient my perspective toward her interactions with me, my interpretation of them. She'd chosen to have one child so she wouldn't be the kind of mother hers was.

It hurt to imagine my life all over. Like a flame curling the ends of my very being, I felt my center—who I was—scorch with every word my mother had said. I opened my eyes and stared at the ceiling. The hurt was there, but in that small, quiet moment alone with the bruised feelings, I realized if I fully experienced it, the searing pain could clear-cut the dead, bad emotions, leaving room for new goodness to grow.

I could choose to fight the family narrative my parents put forth or believe in it. I could trust my father's reassurances, take comfort in them rather than question them. I wound through his words again and again and in the end I found true compassion for my mother, for the woman who knew her limitations. And for the first time, I felt sorrow for her instead of anger. She'd done the best she could. In that one conversation, my mother had uncovered a huge part of who she was and shared it with me like never before.

I pulled the afghan from the back of the couch and tucked it around me. Perhaps this new thread my mother revealed was for me to take and work back through our relationship, strengthening it.

Lying there, I knew that my future could be shaped in whatever way I saw fit. Happiness was a choice I could make. I let that idea surround me and rest in my heart. Things would be different now, even if just a little at a time. I felt closer to my parents than I'd ever thought possible and that alone was enormous.

Chapter 28

One Friday Laura and Paul went back to Pittsburgh to close Laura's college bank accounts. Random Man, aka Donald, was visiting some friends at the shore. So it was Nina and I drinking beers at The Tuna.

We slipped off our jackets and slid onto bar stools.

"I forgot this was where I met Jeep," I said.

"Oh, please. You for-got. My ass. Don't ever go back to him. He doesn't deserve you. His H-Factor's zero out of ten."

"If he was a piece of crap as you suggest, I wouldn't feel this way," I said.

"I'm tired of hearing you cry in your room," Nina said.

"I don't cry in my room." I raised my hand to the bartender to signal we needed our beers.

"What're you doing in there, then?" Nina asked.

"Thinking," I said. "Okay, crying a little, but only inside. Just until I fall asleep."

"He's a jerk. Forget him," Nina said.

"That's like saying to forget I have an arm attached to my shoulder. One that doesn't work—paralyzed, maybe. Useless, maybe, but still dangling, reminding me that once we were together in a good way."

"That's stupid. You didn't feel like that. You were always insecure about him."

"You can't tell me how I felt," I said.

"I can. I'm your best friend," Nina said.

"I never said that."

"You love me," Nina said as she nestled me into a hug.

She wouldn't let go until I told her I loved her.

The bartender finally brought us our Coors Lights. "You wouldn't believe the difference in the class since I started going to my kids' homes," I said.

"You need to stop that. You could have been killed at Katya's place, with that man with his guns, all of it." She shuddered.

"If it's not too dangerous for my kids to live there, how's it too dangerous for me to visit? Why don't you come with me?" I said.

"No way," Nina said.

"Humph," I said.

"Don't humph at me, thinking you're better than me. I know what you're thinking."

"Ooooh," I wiggled my fingers at Nina. "Tell me, what am I thinking?"

"That I'm black so I should be willing to do all the crap you've been doing."

"What? Are you crazy? This doesn't have anything to do with race. You don't have to worry about the kids the same way I do and it's not as though we don't have white kids, too. Katya's white and her situation is worse than most," I said.

Nina shook her head as though my comment was unsatisfactory. "I don't care like you do because I'm black?"

"No. It's the gym teacher thing."

"It's not easy, Carolyn."

"Not easy. Just easier."

I didn't want to argue about this for the hundredth time. It didn't matter. We sipped our beers silently. Ten minutes passed without us talking. When we finished our beers, the bartender slid us fresh ones without even asking if we wanted them.

"So," I said, "Terri wants to be a hairdresser. Can you believe that? Smartest kid in the class. Could be a lawyer, a doctor. Anything."

Nina stared at me with eyes so filled with anger, they seemed to vibrate in their sockets.

"What?" I pulled back slightly.

"I can't believe you just said that. Have you learned nothing from your little home visits?" Nina said.

"What? Terri could be anything and yet she wants to sit around and braid people's hair? I get the braiding thing on many levels, but not as a future career for her. Not her."

"You're so… You're such…" Nina let out a growl that drew the bartender's gaze.

"What?"

"Who's Madame C.J. Walker?" Nina said.

I ran my finger over the frost on my bottle. "I've heard the name." But I couldn't remember where.

Nina grabbed my wrist. "The first female African American millionaire. And guess what she was, great white genius?"

"A hairdresser?"

Nina threw my hand down. I massaged where she had gripped my wrist.

"It's different in the black community. It's not something bad to be a hairdresser."

"Not bad, but for someone so bright… In my community, it was the fallback. A sign of someone without many options. That sounds worse than I mean it to."

"Well, that's your race's problem, isn't it? This is why you shouldn't be gallivanting all over Capitol Flats like you're running for Mayor and you're about to hand out scholarships to Harvard for a bunch of kids who can't even read."

"This," I said, "from the person who teaches her kids how to play lacrosse."

"It's a great sport."

"So *you* can teach them a sport that only ivy-league colleges and two dozen state schools in the country play but I can't have the same high literary hopes for the kids? I'm supposed to smile nicely when the smartest girl in the school says she wants a life of parting hair and weaving beads into the scalps of cranky twelve-year-olds?"

"I played lacrosse at Salisbury. Should I only teach dodge ball? Football?"

"You went to Sidwell Friends not Lincoln. So, yes, teach football. Yeah, throw in a skinny post play here and there. That's essentially what you're telling me to do. Lower my standards." I said.

"I disagree with everything you said." Nina sipped her beer.

"These kids," I said. "They have to actually learn to read to function and know how to think. I have to give them texts that challenge them. I've got nothing against lacrosse, but you can't put me down for doing the same thing as you. I have high expectations. And if that means walking into their neighborhoods and homes to learn more about them and to reach their families, I'm going to do it."

"Yeah, well, you better check it before you do it again."

"What? Like someone's gonna try to kill me and right before he does, he'll give me a shot at freedom… if only, I'm proficient in African American trivia?"

"You're no different from the people you think are racist, you know." Nina sipped her beer.

"That's not true." I sipped mine.

"Racist Potential: seven out of ten!" She raised her beer in the air.

My mouth fell open and I felt dizzy as my blood rushed to my feet.

Nina stood.

"Racist Potential? Well, your Jerk Potential? One-hundred out of ten." I drew the numbers in the air.

"Listen," Nina said, "I have something to tell you. I've applied for the Educational Administration program at University of Maryland. It'll give me a real chance at changing things. You're not the only one who wants to change the world."

I pulled her wrist and squeezed it. "You want to be a *principal?*"

"Don't hiss at me. I'd make a good one."

I let go of her. "Principal—instant asshole. Just add water."

"What does that mean?"

"You know. You're planning to be one of them—"

"First of all," Nina said, "don't embarrass yourself by making statements I know you don't believe. I'm not like Klein, but if you can't support me then... You know what? Just read the Delpit article. I gave it to you to help you not be such a crackpot, not to use it for toilet paper."

She slammed some money on to the bar and stalked away. I clenched my jaw and stared at her back as she left.

Racist Potential? That was harsh beyond words. Ignorant? Clearly I was. That was the whole point of visiting my students' homes. Everyone was ignorant in some way. But me, racist? Her, a principal? She's a freaking gym teacher. I had no idea what I was doing, but she knew less than me. She'd gone too far. Not to mention she'd left without me. I'd have to charge her for cab fare later. That much I knew.

Chapter 29

Ignored by Nina, and realizing more every day that Laura was pulling away from me. I pouted when it became clear that the little pep talk I'd given Laura about us staying close may not have made it so. In my angsty state, I finally read the Delpit article Nina had given me so long ago. I thought reading it would show her I took her seriously, even if I didn't think she knew as much as I did about educating children.

It took me a few tries to get through the whole thing. At first I couldn't get past the part that essentially said most white people, even well meaning ones, do nothing to further the education of black kids. Why'd she give me this piece of crap? To help me decide I should quit? She couldn't really think I should. Could she?

The article made me less excited to do my home visits. But I'd promised the kids and there was no way around it now. Kenneth's home was decked out in Jesus artifacts and poster size photos of Martin Luther King, Malcolm X, and assorted local heroes: athletes, politicians and family members.

Kenneth's mom and dad were warm and sure about the message they wanted to send their children—education was important and so was their history. His parents worked for congressmen and both were taking college courses at night. Dinner was lively, replete with references to current events, religion, and relatives who were from all social classes, backgrounds, and races. If I hadn't visited his home, how else would I have known Kenneth was constantly immersed in complex discussions about everything under the sun?

An entire month spent educating myself in my kids' lives. Something I should have done long before April. Despite what Nina thought, I'd made headway. Behavior had improved, but mostly, I felt I could at least enlist the parents—most of them—for help when I needed it. In many ways the white children's homes were no different than the black children's.

If the parents were drug-free, mentally healthy and consistently made an argument for education, the kids did fairly well in class. Even if the Terris and Kenneths of the class camouflaged their smarts to be cool, they still had what they needed from their parents and relatives. The things my parents had given me.

Unfortunately, Katya was not the lone case of neglect. More than half had similar, if less extreme, living experiences. Many parents wouldn't let me in the home. That was fine. I could do without crack pipe demonstrations, nude people, and roach infestations. But I had to attempt each visit.

A quick stop at Ms. Nardo's restaurant often capped off my home visits. LeAndre spent more time in Miss Tucker's room than he did in mine. Still, Ms. Nardo and I spoke almost every day. She did an amazing job with him. And I felt at home in her restaurant.

"Hey, Ms. Jenkins."

"Can't you call me Carolyn yet?"

"Better not to."

"Why?"

She leaned over the counter and peeled off her clear plastic gloves. "You're a teacher."

"None of the parents will call me Carolyn."

"Do they call you blockhead, cracker, fat ass or white bitch?"

"Not to my face."

"Well, that's all that matters."

Ms. Nardo was buried in paperwork that needed to be filled out before she could move up LeAndre's psychiatric appointment and get his medication adjusted again. She said she needed to get some wings done or her customers would be calling her names, so I helped her fill out the forms, writing all the answers she gave verbally.

"I'm not that different." I tapped my pen on the form.

"Come back here and help me bread the wings. I can't hear you," Ms. Nardo said.

I washed my hands and put on gloves. She handed me some wings.

"You ever hear yourself speak?" she asked.

"I guess so." I said.

"Last week when I picked up LeAndre I saw you. You were lining the kids up near the front door. You know what you said?"

I shook my head.

"You said, why don't we all think about lining up. It's time for lunch," she mimicked me. I laughed.

"Yeah?" I knew I probably said just that, but I wasn't sure at all what she meant.

"With those words, with the way you phrased them, you gave them permission to decide whether they were ready to line up. They heard you say, "When you find yourself in the mood, why don't you line up. I'll wait for you."

"Oh my gosh." I shook a chicken wing at her. "I read something like that in an article. By a woman from Harvard." I dumped the wing into the breading and swirled it around.

She nodded at me. "She must know her shit."

"She must." I sighed.

I knew I had to re-read the Delpit article. My language patterns… Ms. Nardo had noticed them. Delpit discussed them in her work. It was time for me to take a closer look at how my background might make learning harder for my students whether I wanted to or not.

Chapter 30

A little over a month had passed since the extravaganza and I was exhausted. The home visits had taken a lot out of me, but they'd had an impact in the classroom. Even the kids whose homes I hadn't visited came in with better attitudes because I'd made the effort.

I'd also been following Fionna around, watching her every step. She'd started to go to A.A. Even though I didn't trust her I felt sorry for her. Her giggling had gone by the wayside as she'd absorbed the full impact of her parents' deaths and the realization that she'd snorted away her entire hundred thousand dollar inheritance.

I had summer meetings lined up with a few professors who seemed to know a thing or two about reading instruction. I'd found that some of what the Delpit article espoused, I was already doing. I'd tried to make learning meaningful and direct.

For example, having kids speak in book language as well as street was direct. But I had to work on habits that had arisen as a result of my being immersed in what Delpit considered the dominant, middle-class culture of power. Habits that had come to light from not just from reading the Delpit article, but also from talking with Ms. Nardo.

I tape recorded myself teaching for a day. And transcribed the tape. And there it was in black and white. My words. My intentions for one action, the kids hearing something totally different. It mortified me to think *who* I was might keep me from ever being the kind of teacher I wanted to be.

Why hadn't Nina just told me this or talked through the article with me? Simply saying my race was part of my problem but not explaining what she'd meant hadn't been helpful. Maybe she hadn't known how to explain it. Or maybe she'd known I hadn't wanted to hear it from her—the gym teacher. I felt chastised by Nina, without her saying a word. I was embarrassed that I'd not listened more to her.

We continued to ignore each other. I searched for more literature that might inform my teaching. Shirley Brice Heath's book showed me the specific ways economics and the home lives of different social classes influenced learning in school. It was exciting and new information but I wasn't sure what changes I should make in the classroom to reflect this new understanding.

Even with all the work, I still felt lonely. I missed my friendship with the girls and I missed Jeep. The end of the year was upon us. And we were all making arrangements for new housing. I attempted to talk to Nina, to ask her to look for an apartment with me but I was met with her shoulder shrug. I grabbed her arm and offered an apology that she rebuffed. It probably wasn't that great of an attempt on my part.

But I was sick of working at every aspect of my entire life. I picked up the phone to call Jeep a thousand times and hung up every time. I walked down the hall to see Nina every day, but something always made me stop. Perhaps it was all the work involved in being a good girlfriend, a good friend. Perhaps my inaction told me everything I needed to know about myself, about what I really thought was important.

Chapter 31

One Friday, Nina asked me to go to The Tuna. I thought this was it. That she would accept my apology and I would accept hers. I couldn't wait to tell her all I'd learned from the Delpit article. And from Ms. Nardo—how her observations had totally changed my teaching process.

One beer into the night and Nina and I were bickering like never before. Things started off badly when I asked what had given her the idea to become a principal—just some friendly jibber-jabber before launching into the whole Delpit thing. Turned out she and Klein had been having meetings discussing her future as his Vice Principal—a position developed just for her.

I shivered at the thought—that she'd shared a secret and significant relationship with the man responsible for the shit I stepped through and every minute of every school day. An act of treason. And there was no way Nina could guide teachers instructionally—not unless they were starting a magnet school for the athletically inclined.

A voice came from behind me. "Carolyn." Jeep's voice. I didn't turn. I sipped my beer.

He sat beside me.

Nina rolled her eyes and left.

"She doesn't have the car keys," I said.

"That never stopped *you*," Jeep said.

I stared into the mirror the way I had the first time I met him. I felt the same excitement I had that first day. But that was better—excitement without expectation.

"Remember the night we met here?" he asked. He ran his finger over the back of my hand.

"Sure," I said.

"Bullshitting me about every inch of who you were," he said. "So young. Interesting. Honest. About who you were. Even if the facts were lies. You weren't like me. My friends. My family."

"The opposite of that."

"Yeah. I said that."

"I know. I remember every word. Every touch. Everything." I stared off at the clock.

"You have to give me a chance," he said. "My family is *not* who I am. I love them. But they're just who I shared the first half of my life with. The next part of my life was me alone. And now, I want you to share the next part. The rest of it," he said.

I couldn't look at him. "Don't fool yourself. Your family is who you are. You come from a true-blue obligate family."

Jeep squinted.

"Oh, sorry, the term isn't in *The House of Mirth*. Let me explain. Your family is only capable of existing under singular circumstances." I sipped my beer to quench my dry throat. He sipped his, too. I pointed my beer at him. "To change anything would destroy your family. If faced with a person who requires something new from one of its members—well, that's simply unacceptable. It would be the death of the family. For whatever reason you managed to escape most of their raging lunacy, but they will always be there, part of you. And you'll always be there for them, making things better. Sharing jokes at my expense."

He scrunched up his face further.

"Oh come on," I said.

He lifted his shoulders in response.

"The Beano? Hello? I'm supposed to believe you didn't tell your sisters about my farting that first night? They just happened to have a bottle of Beano on hand and they thought you might need it?"

He laughed and ran his hand through his hair.

I flinched.

He took my hand. I pulled it away.

"It wasn't *Beano*. That was MC's Valium. She's a little addicted and we need to hide it from her. Mary Helen keeps the Valium in it. I never told any of them about the farting. Is that why you were so mad for so long?"

"That's part of it. You let them skewer me. That's unforgivable." I pushed my beer away. "And I read *The House of Mirth*. I'm not into having to break the literature code that seems to rule your family dinners. They hate me, I know that."

This was just never going to work. These complications may have been stupid, but if stupid things were a problem early, what kind of problems would arise later? I got up and left, feeling as though I was making the right decision. No matter what he thought.

I trudged to the car where Nina was sitting, scowling.

"What the hell are you doing?" I slid in on the driver's side, starting the car.

"Waiting. Testing you. I knew you'd drop me if old Ten-Speed showed up. I was right. Took you half an hour to come looking for me."

I shifted into reverse and pulled out, not engaging in this conversation.

"I don't even think he really works for the Secret Service," she said. "Have you actually seen his ID?"

"What is your problem? I'm not with him, am I?"

"I'm tired of seeing you mope. You've always been a grumpy person, but you were self-deprecating. Now you're just miserable," Nina said.

"I'm not talking to you," I said. "I'm still pissed about the racist potential comment, and Klein? How could you? So don't get the idea that this is one of our cute arguments. I'm so mad I can't even muster an angry word to hurl at you."

Nina stared out the passenger side window.

We got home and I parked the car. I was so tired of being told by everyone I knew what was wrong with me. I slammed the house door as I went in. Just to make sure Nina knew I was serious.

I ripped open the refrigerator door and took a six-pack to my room.

I pushed the door open and flicked on the light. A body was in my bed. I juggled the beer, I was so startled by the sight.

"Alex!"

He sat up and waved.

"What the hell are you doing?" Acid tore into my stomach. I thought the amputation had been complete. The last thing I needed was to be forced to explain myself to Alex.

"Sorry." He gestured to his body. "I'm not feeling well. I didn't think you'd mind," he said.

"Not to be a total jerk, but then why're you in my bed? I can't afford to get sick. With Klein always up my ass—"

"He's still riding you?"

"Of course. No. I guess he's eased up a little." I sat on the edge of the bed, not so angered anymore. "But I probably just jinxed myself by saying that. He'll be all over me Monday for sure."

"Aw, come on. Tough girl like you. You can handle it," he said.

"I'm sick of having to handle stuff. I want things to be easy." I held back a rising sob. What was I going to do? Pour out my feelings of humiliation at the hands of Jeep to Alex? He'd love that. I settled back on the pillow, suddenly comforted by Alex's presence.

"I want you back. I want *you*." He shimmied up to my body and pushed his pelvis into my butt.

"What the hell, Alex?"

He chuckled. "Come on."

"You can't be serious," I said. I sat up, swinging my feet off the bed. "We haven't even seen each other for months. For months before that, things weren't good. Years before that, you were torn between being in a relationship with me and wanting to live it up with every chick in town. What in God's name would make you think I'd sleep with you?"

"Just hoping, I guess."

Someday, he'd see "Just hoping" was not a reason to do anything.

A knock at the door further sparked my irritation. I flung the door open, thinking it must be Nina. It was. And behind her stood Jeep.

I looked back over my shoulder at Alex. Shit. I thought I could see the hair on each man's head stand up on end.

"Is this the guy with the number on the coaster? The Bus?" Alex sprung out of bed, naked. What balls this guy had. "Where are my boxers?" he shouted.

"*How would I know?*" I said. "I wasn't even here when you slithered into my bed."

When I turned back to the doorway, Jeep was gone. I ran out in time to see the front door close. I felt panicked. My chest tightened as I barreled outside and made it to Jeep's car before he could pull away. "Jeep!" I screamed and pounded on his window. He rolled it down.

"Please. Don't leave. I didn't know he was here."

"Somehow I don't believe that. I can't believe you let it slip your mind that your ex still had a key to your place."

"That's *exactly* like me. You *know* my disorganization knows no bounds."

He shook his head. "Look. I believe you, Carolyn. I do. But I think you were right. Together, marriage, would never work for us."

He rolled up the window, shaking his head, tires squealing away. For the first time, I realized I had been stupid to ignore his pleas to talk and try to work things out. Had he really said the word marriage? It didn't matter. It was over.

Back in the house, Nina was filling Alex in on the Jeep saga. That was the lowest thing I could imagine a friend doing. But the way things were going, us being friends didn't seem to be a reality any more than Jeep and I were still a couple.

"Carolyn, I can't forgive you for this," Alex said, leaving the house. Mentally, I began to argue with Alex about why his forgiveness wasn't needed or wanted and didn't even make sense because I'd done nothing wrong. But there wasn't any point in discussing it. He could leave with the advantage. Fine with me. Now Nina, I cared about.

"Thanks, Nina." I flopped onto the black leather couch.

"What? I didn't tell him anything that was classified."

"I think you enjoyed telling Alex how much my love life sucks. I saw your gleeful smile."

"That wasn't glee," she said.

I turned to the back of the couch and pulled the afghan over me, tucking it under my chin, squeezing my eyes shut. "It was glee. I know it when I see it."

"You see what you want, Carolyn. It's just how you are."

I heard her feet shuffle away and her bedroom door slam. I wondered why things had to be this way. I was grateful for sleep when it finally began to settle over me—that gentle time just before completely drifting off. My new favorite time of the day. If only I could stay inside that bubble of peace forever. If only.

Chapter 32

There wasn't much more time to go in the school year. In my hands was a newly minted, ulcer-inducing list of the fifty things we had to do to be checked out of school at the end of the year. It might have been nice to have seen the son-of-a bitching list at the beginning of the year. Yeah, right. As if I would have filed it away and checked it periodically.

It'd be a nightmare. Sitting in front of Klein, having him tick through some obscenely detailed list, narrating all my failures. It was too much to think about. So I put my name first on the list of people he'd see. The sooner I got out, the better. Even if it meant I didn't sleep until I got organized.

My plan was to try to steal time from the school day to get started on cleaning up. It was against the rules. The kids were supposed to have instruction until the last clock tick of the last day of school. But it wouldn't be my first lie of the year. I thought of Sissy. "It's about survival," she had said during a meeting. She had been right. That much I knew.

**

Kenneth came in one morning and tossed a heavy book into my lap. "Here."

I looked at the title and almost flipped it onto the floor. If he had dropped a bag of dope into my lap, I wouldn't have reacted more strongly

"Kenneth. We can't use this," I said.

"You said we could bring in a book that was important to us." Kenneth squared his shoulders.

"I did, but it's a Bible," I said. My head pounded at the thought all the trouble a Bible in school could cause.

"Here." Evette dropped her Bible into my lap, too.

I stood and set the Bibles on their desks, patting them. I didn't know what to say. I couldn't believe they had actually brought books from home to read, but still, Bibles could not be read in public schools.

The kids clustered around Kenneth and Evette. They paged to their favorite passages, discussing them, sharing them. It was as though my subversive curriculum had suddenly leapt to life.

There were kids who still couldn't decode a word, but that didn't stop them from talking about what the others read out loud. A miracle. I covered my mouth to hold back an abrupt surge of emotion. Tears filled my eyes.

If I allowed them to proceed with this, I could end up in big trouble. Even with parents who rarely raised a stink about anything, this could be trouble.

I thought I heard the click of the intercom—Mr. Klein possibly listening in—and panicked.

I took a deep breath and interrupted. "We can't use these."

"I knew you ain't down with Christ," Kenneth said. "Because He black?"

"Kenneth," Evette said. "We had this argument before. Ain't no one know what color Jesus is. He's sans color, like Ms. Jenkins always say. Sans this sans that—sans color. That what *I* say,"

"He a *She*. That what I say," Jamaica said.

Kenneth popped open his Bible. "It says right here. He. He is *not* a She."

I should have stopped them, but I couldn't. The moment was too precious, even if the text was contraband. They went on for half an hour excitedly building ideas from what was in the text. I stared at them. How could I not take advantage of this enthusiasm?

Such a simple thing to educate children, but oh, somehow it never played out that way, not really, not for the people who worked and were schooled at Lincoln Elementary. Not for us.

**

Once May started, each morning turned into a steaming hot afternoon that left my hair matted to my neck. At one staff meeting, Klein said he'd be putting window air-conditioning units into the classrooms in the old part of the building. Everyone except me. Money was tight that year so *I* wouldn't be getting an air-conditioner.

I laughed out loud when he said that—guffawed with the gusto an asylum patient might employ once he realized that he could never leave, that he might never find peace. Everyone stared at me. A surprised look crossed Klein's face, as though he was confused.

I realized I'd never really expressed my professional opinion of him in a forceful, confident manner. I had been stifled by a lifetime of giving authority figures the respect they deserved. I had kept my mouth shut. Then it had gotten to be sort of fun implementing my subversive plans.

While being a thoughtful, purposeful teacher, I was silently screwing Klein over. Each day I got through *my* plans instead of his, I felt like I was giving him two middle fingers straight up. Even if he didn't know it.

So there we were, melting in that classroom, losing all enthusiasm to learn and teach. Sunshine poured through the broken blinds, broiling us like chickens in a roaster. Klein was in no rush to fix them. So I did the only thing I could. I shut the lights off every afternoon. And he did what he couldn't resist doing—he put a letter in my file every evening saying it was dangerous, that kids might trip and fall if I turned off the lights.

Too bad. Over the course of eight months, my sixth grade girls had become seventh grade almost-women. In terms of physical development, some were a lot more woman than I. Although most of the kids had been given deodorant at home, it barely took the edge off the stink by the end of the day.

The Bible discussion had been our last good one. The students could barely function. But how could I hold Cedrick's lack of effort against him when his face was so sweaty, it looked as though he'd just emerged from a pool? How could he be expected to construct meaning while half dead from heat?

Tempers were a problem, too. One sardonic grunt or sarcastic retort resulted in bodies on the floor. They were too moist to land punches, though. They were so devoid of energy, they'd give up fighting before I had to intervene. Assertive discipline didn't have a caveat for sweat-soaked, heat-crazed kids and their teacher.

The cloakroom, being dark and relatively cool, often beckoned the off-task kids. It was the perfect spot for chicanery. And with the heat taking its toll, there was more misadventure in it than ever. One day, with the students herded into their seats and me at my desk fishing around for some materials, I heard a ruckus in the cloakroom. That freaking cloakroom.

I never entered the cloakroom with students. It had been rule number two at the new teacher workshop. Never spend even a half a second alone in an enclosed space with any student for any reason.

I did a quick assessment of who was missing from his or her seat. And came up with two names. Terri and Cedrick. Nightmare scenarios flashed through my mind as I raced there. I imagined one of them strangling the other, a death on my hands. I craned my neck, peering into the cloakroom, holding my breath.

I couldn't believe my eyes. I felt a temper tantrum coming on. How could they do this? After all we'd been through this year, all the progress we'd made, how could they jeopardize our damn progress?

Terri, a good five inches shorter than Cedrick, stood with her spindly arms up around his neck. His were looped around her waist. Their bodies were molded together like a school dance cliché. They looked at me, unmoved. Not embarrassed. As though this was the most normal thing a teacher could stumble upon in the world.

"Get out. Get out now. Don't touch each other. I will not have any kissing in here. Out, out, out." They came out of the cloakroom and everyone hooted. I shooed them to their seats and went to sit in mine.

I envisioned telling Terri's family about this. I was grateful for having made significant connections with them. Telling Cedrick's mom? That could be tricky.

"Ms. Jenkins?"

I jumped. "Yes. Evette?"

"Don't look so upset. They weren't doing nothing wrong. Just a little kissing," Evette said.

"You guys are way too young to think about this stuff. You need to focus on school. Reading. Writing. Math. We've discussed this. Go to college, then worry about kissing people in cloakrooms." It was the weakest pep talk of the entire year. I was tired. Tired of trying to understand. To teach. To learn about teaching.

"I'm gonna have me a baby in tenth grade. That what I'm thinking about," Evette said.

I stared at her. And although they were way past saying things just to shock me, they knew much of what they said did just that. They were waiting for a lecture about how this plan would impede the pursuit of financial and emotional health.

"Come on, Ms. Jenkins," Terri said as she stood and began to imitate me—in voice, manner, even the way I pushed my hair behind my ear when I talked. "Babies are wonderful. But wouldn't it be nice to go to college, have fun, empower yourself before having children? Have babies when you have the life you want. Now's the time for work..." She lost steam when I didn't react. The other kids had their heads on their desks, too tired to hoot at the pseudo-lecture.

"You know exactly what I think." Who was I to tell them anything? Why couldn't I have been assigned to first grade where no one asked if every man we passed in the hall was my boyfriend. "You guys do what you want. If you want to learn. I'm here. Otherwise, just sit there," I said, knowing that was stupid.

Even after the kids were gone for the day, their odors lingered. For the hundredth time that year I picked up a couple of organizer thingies that were supposed to be used for paperclips and I don't even know what else, then put them down again.

That made me think of Jeep, the way he had seemed to appreciate my shortcomings. The sudden appearance of him in my mind drained me of every last bit of energy. Had I ruined things with him for good? He had liked me in spite of the way I tended toward disorganization. No, it wasn't whether he liked me, it was whether I would allow him to treat me the way he had in front of his family. That was important—it was everything.

I sighed and settled deeper into my chair. A page of song lyrics I had been using as reading material before the hot spell set in fluttered onto my lap from the desk. Neil Young's *Helpless*. Could there be a better anthem for the day?

I spun my chair and pushed play on the tape recorder. I spun back, put my feet up on the desk and closed my eyes. The *Helpless* lyrics poured into the room, relaxing me. Making me smile.

I sang, eyes shut, feet on desk.

"Ms. Jenkins?"

I flew upright, feeling disoriented.

"Marvin. What's wrong?" Ben stepped into the room behind him.

"I let him back in the building," Ben said. "Said he forgot his reading book."

Ben scratched his chin. I turned the music down. They were both grinning.

"What?" I asked.

"You look funny," Marvin said.

"Funny, huh? What do you think you look like when you're singing up a storm at recess?"

"I look good," Marvin said.

"That's a good song," Ben said. "I love jazz, myself. And some rock. But that, I like that."

"It's Neil Young. Kind of bluesy, I guess."

"We read that yesterday," Marvin said. "Didn't we? I recognize those words. It's a song?"

"Yep. I was going to play it today, but as you know, we didn't get around to it."

"Could we listen to it tomorrow?"

"I don't know. We'll see," I said.

"We appreciate it, you know. We just can't always be like you want. Believe that, though. You have to." Marvin grabbed his book and walked back toward Ben, who was nodding.

"Marvin?" I said.

He stopped at the doorway and turned back toward me, eyebrows raised. I was too tired to ask him the flurry of questions that ran through my mind in regard to what he'd just said.

"See you tomorrow," I said as they left the room, each lifting one hand to wave without looking back.

Believe? I turned the music back up and sank back into the chair I so rarely ever sat in. And then I saw the faded words I had put up on the bulletin board at the beginning of the year. Believe.

I didn't want to give up on Marvin or any of the students. Had Marvin told me they appreciated what I did two months earlier, I'd have been ecstatic. But with the heat, the cloakroom incident, my friends moving on and Jeep's absence, all I could think was, *Damn, Marvin, I am just too exhausted to believe right now.*

Chapter 33

The very next day, energized and ready to try again, we dove back into Neil Young's timeless songs, *Helpless* and *Heart of Gold*. Marvin must have spread the word that the "poems" were actually song lyrics. He must have told the kids to pay more attention because they were ready and quiet. And I, of course, almost died. I was excited again. I might have been too optimistic. Not that it was a habit with me or anything.

"What do you think about these words? 'I've been searching for a heart of gold?'"

"Boring," Tanesha said.

Lots of shrugs.

"Come on. What's the writer telling us?"

"God," Jamaica said.

"Searching for the Lord," Kenneth said. God, again. "He's been looking so long, he's wondering if the Bible's just some jacked up pile of—"

"Blasphemy!" Evette scolded.

"I'm not saying that's what I think. I'm saying that's what the writer thinks," Kenneth said. The others nodded.

"Like the other one, *Helpless*. He's searching for the Lord." Terri shrugged.

Tanesha sucked her teeth and rolled her eyes.

"At least I'm using my brain," Terri said. "You chocolaty chipped, nappy haired, horse."

"Terri. Speak in a respectful and kind way," I said. "You can express your thoughts constructively. You know how to do that."

"I ain't respectful to people who can't keep a secret," Terri said.

Oh no. Fighting words. I stood to prevent a brawl.

Tanesha and Terri sprung from their seats (they were faster than me) and began to claw at one another. Terri yanked out one of Tanesha's extensions. This prompted Tanesha to scratch Terri's cheek with a fake nail, which Terri then pulled off. I finally muscled in between them. They huffed and puffed, but looked relieved I'd stopped them.

Meanwhile, the class had dispersed to opposite corners.

Marvin buzzed the office so Ben and another janitor could escort the girls to Klein while I wrote the discipline referral. From that point on, the lesson was done. No one could concentrate.

How could we go from discussing God, a forbidden topic that had emerged out of a discussion of another forbidden text that most likely had nothing to do with God, to a brawl that sucked the energy out of everyone in the room? We had teetered on the edge of reason and all it had taken was one wrong word to send it all careening into insanity.

I sat there, hoping to disappear somehow. And to reappear in Aruba or Pittsburgh or in someone else's existence where there was serenity and control, happiness and ease.

Fifteen minutes later, Tanesha and Terri returned to the classroom, ignoring one another, but calmer.

Terri shoved the discipline referral sheet back at me. "Mr. Klein says we supposed to give you this back. Ain't detailed enough."

They sat back in their seats and we stared into space: me tired of trying; them, tired of acting up. Both sides officially on strike.

And so I daydreamed. About Jeep. But then that got too painful. I wondered if I could join my parents in Europe for the summer. They were going to visit me before flying out. I could just go with them. Space between my entire life and me might be exactly what I needed.

Thoughts of Laura's wedding ran though my mind. It was two weeks away. Yes, that was a good topic to focus on, because although sometimes Laura's happiness made me miserable, mostly it made me think it was possible for me to find someone to love, someone just for me. Trouble was, that line of thinking always wrapped back around images of Jeep. He was who I wanted. He was who I loved.

Chapter 34

Three days had passed since I'd gone on strike in my classroom. I must have had some kind of professional death wish. It seemed the entire year had been an exercise in slow-cooked suicide. It had finally become too much. The heat had suffocated our final attempts at being productive even though things had gotten much better after my home visits. The end of the school year had left the students and me to quietly accept the idea that our progress would be halted with the end of the school year.

I even started to use my planning periods to sit on my ass and drink coffee like a good veteran teacher. I was looking forward to summer giving me an opportunity to consider whether I should even teach the next year. I couldn't imagine facing such difficulties all over again.

After an especially useless planning period, I sauntered back to my classroom, where I knew Nina would have returned the students after gym. I grasped the doorknob and stopped, my will drained all of a sudden. I would have given anything to stay out of that classroom.

If I hadn't needed to pay my bills, I might have just quit then and there. What difference did it make if it was I teaching them or some substitute who thought magic tricks would keep them focused? Our methods resulted in the same failure.

There was not a peep coming from behind the door. Nina must have worn them out in gym. She would have that annoying smirk on her face when I entered that said, 'See how every kid is at his desk? See how well they behave for me?'

Outside of school we still weren't talking much. She didn't seem to be as bothered by the end of our friendship as I was and I couldn't completely blame her. I really hadn't known what I was doing as a teacher. But she should have given me credit for trying to figure it all out.

She was still ticked at me for being, well, me. I was pissed at her for deciding I was an unknowing racist and for being mean to me about Jeep. I wasn't going to apologize for being a suburban, middle-class girl with a broken heart.

I turned the doorknob. The lights were off. I thought of all the letters in my file. Were they still at gym?

I walked further into the room.

"Surprise! Happy Mother's Day!"

I slapped my hand over my mouth. What was all this?

Nina beamed at me and waved from across the room. I waved back, shaking my head. What were they doing?

The girls circled me as they had so many times that year but this time they hugged me instead of offering fashion and hair-style critiques.

"You're the best teacher and other mom we could have," Terri whispered in my ear, echoing an enormous banner that stretched across the blackboard—the banner they'd made. She guided me to my chair, which they had decorated with paper flowers and handwritten poems, and sat me down.

Terri pulled a stack of books from under my chair and settled them into my lap. They were tied with strands of yellow yarn.

"We wanted you to have something you could read to get to know us better the way you had us read to get to know you better. All that *Bridge to Terabithia* and *Hatchet* and songs you like. That was so we'd know about you, right? So Ms. Parker let us make lists if we were good in physical education and she helped us get everything for you. The books, the decorations, everything."

I was paralyzed. My eyes burned, I was so moved I could barely breathe. I just stared at the books: the Bible, biographies of Malcolm X, Martin Luther King, Jr. and Oprah.

"That one's from Ms. Parker and Terri." Tanesha turned the stack so I could see the bottom book—Madame C. J. Walker's biography. I shook my head and swallowed a sob. Of course that was in the stack. Of course it should have been.

"You know you love me for that one," Nina said, hugging me around the neck from behind, looking at me over my shoulder.

"I might love you," I said, "but I don't really like you."

"Mutual feelings, baby," Nina said, standing back up.

Katya came to me with a paper bag. I pulled it open and peeked inside. A paperback book. I pulled it from the bag, not able to imagine what it might be.

It was *Coal Miner's Daughter.* "My mom saw the note from Ms. Parker and said she thought it were a stupid thing to buy you anything, but then she shoved this book into my bag. Said you best learn her history, too. Not just black history."

I wasn't sure what she meant in terms of *Coal Miner's Daughter* being her mother's history. My face must have shown it.

"She was a singer once. She wore flour sack dresses. She had dreams. Like that girl in that book." Katya shrugged and stared at her shoes. My insides buckled. I held out my arms and she stepped into them.

"Thank you, Katya. What an incredible, incredible gift."

I held her hand and squeezed it. "I can't take this, though. If it means what you said then she needs to have it and *you* need to have it. But the memory of this moment…" My words caught in my throat and tears welled again "The thought is priceless. You can give—"

"Ms. Parker gave my mom another. She has another. She didn't want you to think she was always in the dumps. She wasn't always like you seen her that day a while back." Katya squeezed my hand to reassure me.

My eyes burned as I considered Katya's mother's unrealized dreams. I glanced at Nina. She nodded, vouching for the story. So Nina had not only orchestrated this party with the kids, she had met up with the parents to make it happen.

The boys worked their way over, hugging me. By the time the last hug came from LeAndre, I couldn't keep the tears from rolling. He pulled a book from behind his back.

"Not least, but last," he said. I turned the book right side up. *Homestyle Hash*, it read.

"A cookbook?" I said, laughing. "Oh, my, LeAndre, your mother knows me well." I knew the gift had been given to me only partly because I couldn't cook. Mostly, it had been given to represent a piece of their lives—the type of cooking Ms. Nardo did at their restaurant.

And so the day went on. My kids dumped cards in my lap and served me food and drinks as though I were a queen. They had moved the desks back to create a dance space and blared their music. They even went so far as to not include anything overtly sexual or violent. They had really thought this through.

Part of me wanted to get up and dance with them, but I just sat with Nina and watched them. They were now fully engrossed in dancing, interacting as though they were the best of friends. It seemed they were actually capable of monitoring their own behavior, sharing space and treating each with consideration when they had some control over what they were doing.

I looked at Nina, whose Cheshire grin was daring me not to thank her profusely. "I can't believe you did all this. It's unbelievable."

"*I* didn't do any of it. Except clear this whole thing with Klein. The kids planned it during gym class and after school. They were worried you didn't care anymore." Nina hugged me in one of her this-won't-end-until-you-say-you-love-me deals.

"I read the Delpit article. You're right," I said, still in her hug. "But I'm *not* like the white teachers in her article—not exactly. I did some stuff right. But I was wrong not to read it right away and I got stubborn and angry that you didn't just come out and say clearly what that article said. And I was so rude about you being a gym teacher and…"

"Okay, okay!" Nina let me go. "You did a lot right. Not that you didn't need to learn a lot. But I was a jerk, too. I'm sorry. I hated seeing you feel so bad over that rich guy, the Cadillac. Random Man and I weren't getting along. And it all came out with the hairdresser thing… and I was just pissed."

"Why didn't you tell me you and Random—Donald, we should call him Donald at this point, shouldn't we? Why didn't you tell me you were still having problems? That it mattered to you?"

"That's not me. To dwell. I fixed it. And it doesn't matter if I'm with a guy or not. I'm complete the way I am," Nina said. She cocked her head. "You are too, you know."

I nodded. I knew she was right. I had learned that the hard way, but I was glad I'd learned it. I was proud of my progress, my independence.

Nina turned to dance with the kids. I pulled her back by the hand.

"And Nina, you'd make a wonderful principal. That must have felt terrible, to have a friend think you were an ass for looking into the future, for planning. You're a great teacher—phys. ed. or not," I said.

"Well, I did more than that. I was going to wait until after school to show you this."

Nina reached in her back pocket and pushed a bright blue pamphlet toward me. I took it and read. It was a mockup to advertise a summer reading, math, phys. ed. and leadership institute at the University of Maryland. Nina's name was boldly printed in the introductory paragraph as one of the first teachers to help develop and teach a course at the institute. I felt so proud of her. I ran my finger over her name.

"Nina. That is incredible. I was running around the neighborhood visiting parents and you were developing a summer institute for learning." I hugged her. "You're amazing. You'll be brilliant."

She grinned. "Turn it over."

I flipped the pamphlet and saw the list of faculty on the back. There I was, my photo looking back at me, my position listed as New Teacher Liaison. I looked up at Nina.

"What?" she said. "You think I'm some sort of dumbass? I know a teacher who knows her shit. There's no way I would have done this without knowing you'd work with me."

"I couldn't have learned so much without you," I said. "That article. Everything."

We huddled around the pamphlet, discussing the learning components outlined there. We both admitted we would need a lot of help—neither of us was an expert in anything yet. But Nina had secured the services of several professors from University of Maryland and Towson to assist us. According to Nina, two of them even recalled my requests for assistance and were excited to be a part of "our" plan.

"You're right," I said. "We are good together." We flung our arms around each other's shoulders and watched the kids enjoy themselves. I finally understood why Nina didn't just tell me what I was doing wrong with my students. I wouldn't have listened. I needed to learn the hard way.

I looked at the kids. No matter what their test scores ended up being, right then it didn't matter. I thought again of displaced puzzle pieces. All my kids seemed to have come from separate boxes, but had been tossed together as though it didn't matter, and they should still fit together.

In fact, a new puzzle had been created, but one that didn't need to have every curve mesh perfectly with a corresponding crest. The spaces left in between the pieces that didn't fit, I'd realized, were as much a part of the picture as the pieces themselves. It was the spaces that yielded the unexpected, the rich marrow that might go unseen by an overwhelmed novice or jaded expert.

I felt a yank on my arm.

"Mr. Klein?" I said, looking at where his claw gripped my arm.

"There's a fire drill," he said. He punched off the tape recorder. "And you're in here. Did you just ignore the fire alarm?

What are you thinking, pulling this kind of crap?"

I resisted cradling the spot on my arm he'd crushed.

Nina stepped up to Klein. "I told you the kids planned this. You said it was fine. And you wrote the date down."

"I think you're mistaken," Klein said. "Now get your class outside."

We hadn't heard the alarm with the music on, obviously.

Nina and I lined up the kids. I was mortified for them. They'd worked hard to show me how much they cared and Klein had stomped on their efforts. As he did everything he came into contact with.

The students whispered words of encouragement as they filed past me, down the marble steps to our fire drill spot. Nina was silent, finally fully witnessing the depths of Klein's craziness. She slung her arm around my shoulder and we exited the school with all the other classes watching. I wondered what they knew about what had transpired.

Laura's eyes were, as usual, spread wide open in dismay. I forced a smile her way, shrugging. And the minute my class was outside lined up, Klein signaled us back in. What a dick.

**

Back in the classroom, Nina and I helped the students reorganize the room. I tucked each poem into a folder I would keep forever. I stacked the books each student had given me on my desk, my fingers running down the spine of each one as I placed it on the pile.

Nina helped us fold each decoration, roll each streamer back up, push every desk back into place. She'd given up her planning period to help. Then she gave me a few minutes to collect myself.

As I walked to the bathroom. I tucked the good feelings and thoughts associated with my Mother's Day party inside my heart. I tried not to let Klein's garbage infiltrate the good that the students had done.

I knocked on the teachers' bathroom door. No answer. Some gurgling, though. Fionna? I hadn't seen her at the fire drill.

It made sense that she might be in trouble so I kicked in the door with one shot.

And there she was. On the sink, her nude legs wrapped around Klein's ass.

They stopped grunting and thrusting, though neither moved to cover up. She smiled at me over Klein's shoulder and waved her fingers at me. Klein shook his head, his grey boxers around his ankles, ass hairy as a gorilla.

"Oh. My. God," I said as I turned and left.

I used the girls' bathroom near my room and wondered what I was supposed to do with this information. I didn't like knowing what I did and after the initial smugness, I just felt gross by association. The school was a disaster and these poor kids were paying for it.

Back in the classroom, I whispered to Nina what had happened and she left the room, gritting her teeth. I warned her to keep it a secret until we could find the best way to handle it. But she was pissed about the way Klein had treated us earlier and she didn't seem to want to go with my wait-and-see approach. Even if Fionna didn't deserve the benefit of the doubt, something made me want to help her. More emotional stupidity on my part, I guessed, and wondered how the hell a person got rid of that.

**

What a day it had been. The highs of the Mother's Day party, the lows of Klein holding an unannounced fire drill when he knew we'd never hear the alarm, the even lower lows of seeing Klein's naked ass humping Fionna.

I chose to focus on the highs. Waiting for the end-of-day announcements, I hoped my students would take the lessons they learned into the future—to build solid lives for themselves. That they saw me, even in a little way, as a mother figure was beyond humbling.

"Ms. Jenkins. Announcements are late," Kenneth said.

I looked at the clock. Fifteen minutes late with announcements? Another trick, no doubt. I stormed to the door and flung it open, expecting to see the halls crowded with kids and teachers, snaking their way out of the school.

It was empty except for a man dressed in head-to-toe black at the other end. He had a holster, backpack, boots, and weapons draped over his body. A sharpshooter. He pointed me back into in my room. I covered my mouth, palms instantly sweaty, shaking. I pressed the intercom button.

"Yes?" Bobby Jo's voice whispered.

"What's happening here?" I asked.

"Just stay in the middle of the room. Blinds drawn," she said.

The kids spoke in hushed tones as they moved, following directions. I told them whatever was happening was probably a minor thing blown out of proportion, but the kids were not reassured. I thought back to the time at recess when gunshots had come from beyond the playground. The kids hit the pavement, hands over their heads, and I stood there, telling them it was just a car backfiring. I stood there like an idiot, convinced it couldn't be possible. I had never heard a gun go off before, let alone expected to hear one at school.

We were safe in the room—that much I had to believe. "Let's get the rugs and sit up by my desk like we do for group reading." I no longer thought schools were completely safe, but I also knew I needed to proceed as though everything would work out fine.

"We have to get home before dark," Kenneth looked up at me, his expression like that of a helpless puppy.

I waved him off. "Oh, it's May. You'll be home long before it gets dark," I said, noting it was kind of cloudy, but not even close to nighttime.

"I can't be outside once the sun goes down," Evette said.

"You'll be home soon. You live two blocks from here," I said.

"Two blocks of crazy bullet-dodging sidewalk."

"None of us are allowed out after dark," Evette said.

"Before dark at my place," Terri said.

"Flashlight tag," I whispered.

"Flashlight tag?" Kenneth said.

"Yeah. You hide in the dark and the way you get tagged is the guy with the flashlight finds you and shines it on you," I said, smiling at the childhood memories.

"Sounds stupid," Tanesha said.

Everyone stared at me. Waiting for a lecture, I was sure.

"Sounds nice to me," Kenneth said.

Everyone stared at him. Eyebrows raised. Waiting for his punch line. "I decided the other day that I'm going to be a cop," he said.

The class rocked back on their butts. "You? You don't like nobody. How you gonna work with people who come from everywhere?"

I looked at Kenneth expectantly. He shrugged. "I can do it. I like all races sometimes. I like people. I do. Even the white people," he said.

"Ms. Jenkins," Evette said.

"Katya," Kenneth said.

"Crystal, Jimmy," Tanesha said.

"Kenneth shouldn't talk about whites like that," Marvin said. "I just realized it would...Ooooh...it would have made me so mad if whites talked like Kenneth about us."

The squawks of police radios outside the window cut into our conversation.

I scrambled to my feet and went to the window.

"It's okay." I watched as two men were wrestled to the ground, handcuffed and then stuffed into a police car. Other policemen still stalked the perimeter of the school. What the hell was going on?

"Talk Pittsburgh for us," Kenneth said, leaning against my arm when I sat back down.

"Yinz guys goin' to the Iggle for some chipped ham 'n at?" I said. They howled, rolling back and forth.

"Now you talk in street," I said.

Evette straightened and whipped her head around, "I ain't jonesin for no nasty, piglet ham." Everyone hooted.

"Okay, now in book language," I said.

"Are you folks going to the grocery store to buy some savory, tasty chipped ham? I, myself, am not in the mood for ham, thank you very much," Kenneth said with a grin.

I leapt up and did a dance with the Terrible Towel I had used to dab the blood from my foot after the shooting back in October.

The kids cheered. I felt like we were a family that had slogged through some tough stuff to finally see we worked better as a group. The opposite of how I'd felt just a few hours before on my planning period. Too bad the end of the year was near. Suddenly, I felt like I was just getting started with these kids.

Five 'o' clock rolled around and we heard a crackle over the intercom. "We are free to go!" Klein's voice was relieved and jubilant.

The kids scrambled to their feet and bolted from the room. All they cared about was getting the hell home before the first sign of darkness.

I stood at the top of the magnificent stone steps and marveled at this amazing day, this amazing year. I was finished being afraid of Klein. He did not know everything. Far from it.

I knew stuff he'd never even considered. I looked forward to working with those professors, to have them teach me instructional methods that actually worked.

Helping my students in social and emotional ways was not the goal of my work. Giving them the tools to navigate the world was. Effective instruction was what I couldn't offer, what I needed to figure out, Klein or no Klein. And I knew, when I finally had the secret, my teaching would truly be spectacular.

Chapter 35

After all the kids had left, Klein held a meeting to fill us in on what happened that day. He glared at me and I glared at him as I entered the library. I was sure he got my message: I was not afraid to use the information I had on him.

Fionna wasn't there. God knew where she was hiding. Klein's voice cracked before he steadied it, telling us that two armed drug dealers came looking for "someone," who owed them money here at the school. He claimed it was a mistake, that the person they were searching for was not in the school. I shook my head, knowing instantly they had been looking for Fionna. He claimed the only way to have kept us safe was to have locked us in and that he was some sort of hero.

I looked at Nina and Laura. We nodded at each other. Mistake, my ass. I wondered if Fionna had been hauled to jail. I doubted it; Klein was vested in her in more ways than one. He couldn't let this come out.

"Timothy?" Betty Sue said to Klein. "I think this is the perfect time for a visualization technique. Like the one we did the last meeting."

"Yes. Good idea. Everyone on the floor," Klein said. I glared at him. His shirt was pulled out of his waistband, his tie askew.

Laura and Nina rolled their eyes at Betty Sue but got on the floor without a word. It was carpeted in orange Astro Turf. I'd seen kids spit on it and the stain would disappear, leaving no trace. Which made it all the more fun for them to spit and try to make a stain. The thought of lying there made my stomach churn. I wouldn't lie down for Klein any more.

Betty Sue looked at me, motioning to the floor. When she saw the anger on my face, I guess she decided to ignore my non-participation.

"Okay, close your eyes. Imagine, a lovely, calm, safe place…" Her voice made me shiver. I looked around. Everyone's eyes were shut. Maybe they were sleeping. What was the difference at this point?

Klein had the balls to growl at me, shoving his finger toward the floor as though I should listen to him and get down, as though he didn't remember I'd seen him with Fionna. I shrugged. I'd just wait for the charade to end.

But then the anger welled inside me, growing and making me pay attention to it. I would not let him do this, pretend I was some sort of failure-slash-idiot when it was he who had failed this year.

I pushed my chair back and sprinted across the floor toward him. When I reached him, I grabbed his arm and dragged him past the prone bodies, avoiding a leg here, a foot there. The teachers just ignored what was happening.

We stopped at a set of doors on the far side of the room. All the resentment I had stuffed away all year was now enflamed.

He wrenched his arm from my grip. His beady irises fired around their sockets as though they didn't know how to focus on the wimp who had finally had enough. He crossed his arms.

I breathed so hard, my shoulders rose and fell with each breath. Somewhere in my mind, I knew this was a very bad thing to do. I rubbed my forehead, calming myself before I spoke. I forced my words into whispers. "I've had it with you, Klein. I might not be the greatest teacher on the planet. But I care deeply about those kids and have made great strides with them this year.

Have you seen their writing? Talked to them about the books we're reading? Because we blew off the reading series a long time ago. Nothing you told me to use did any good. And Fionna. You're partly responsible for today's debacle. I know who those criminals were looking for. You let her carry on the way she did and she drew those people here with her behavior. What're you doing, screwing her like that? She's fragile, dammit."

I paused, waiting for him to pounce. I ran my hand through my hair.

He stared at me, arms still crossed, jaw tensing. Unease and fear flashed over his face. No verbal response. So I went on, going back to the educational aspects of my beef with him.

I poked at his tie. "And I'm not trying to disparage anyone, because I sure as hell didn't know what to do, either. But I've been researching, and talking to professors at three universities. And guess what? *They* don't seem to think I'm a freaking moron to have ignored your suck-ass curriculum. I might stink at teaching, but at least I know it. Unlike you, who has no idea you're a failure."

Beads of sweat dropped down his forehead, directly above his right eyebrow, as though one side of his body was seething while the other remained a cool thirty-two degrees to ensure his cold heart maintain its proper hardness.

I smiled at the signs he was uncomfortable. "Anyway, I'm tired of being treated like a child. I don't need a freaking union behind me to mess you up. I'll do it myself."

With that I turned and began to navigate my way through the still prone bodies before realizing I wasn't done with him. I went back.

I gripped his arm. "It occurred to me that last statement was mildly threatening. I didn't mean physically mess you up. What I meant was, even though I can't teach for crap, I can write. There are plenty of newspapers that'd love to hear my story, I bet. So go ahead and fire me. I have power, whether you know it or not."

I was dizzy with dismay. Mixed with elation. I'd done it. But didn't know what to do next. I turned and began to walk over the bodies of my fellow teachers. No one did anything to show they were even alive. Hopefully, no one had heard a thing.

I was halfway across the library when I noticed. Every teacher had a thumb pointed right up in the air. A silent Lincoln cheer. For me.

Chapter 36

The final days of school passed and I kept looking in my mailbox for a pink slip, expecting an angry confrontation with a horde of Klein's personal lawyers. Nothing. He was ignoring me for the first time all year. I wasn't sure how I felt about possibly being fired. A clean break might be nice. Though not getting the chance to use what I learned this year at Lincoln would be infuriating. Either way, I wished he'd get to it. Nothing was worse than waiting to be fired.

Nina, Laura and I still hadn't decided what to do with what we knew about Fionna and Klein. I did sneak into his office and peek in his picture frame. The person folded out of the frame was Fionna. She looked up at him as though he were her prince charming. Maybe it was more complicated than I thought. I didn't want to hurt her further. She was at a rehabilitation center. She wasn't sure she would return to teaching but according to Bobby Jo, that wasn't a problem for Fionna at this time. She had other options. Whatever that meant.

At the end of the second to the last day of school, I was packing the contents of my room and throwing stuff out. Each paper told a story of a year in my life as a teacher. Writings from the beginning of the year revealed students who could barely write three sentences about a day at Busch Gardens, or a visit with their cousins. Most essays were less than four sentences. Then I pulled a second pile into my lap. This pile consisted of papers they had just turned in.

The writings were on fire with the passion of students who were not happy with the violence ruling their lives and their inability to do well on tests. (Though they managed to write vividly, they still lacked the reading fluency I had counted on.)

"Carolyn." Jeep's voice echoed off the now bare walls. I jumped at the sound. The papers in my lap fell and cascaded over the floor in front of me.

"Jeep." I gathered the papers and piled them on my desk. I couldn't look at him, couldn't decide what I thought of him just appearing in my room without notice.

"I was hoping we could go to dinner. Clear things up," he said in his familiar, gentle way.

"I can't." That came out before I could fully consider what I actually wanted. I'd missed him so much over the past weeks and yet with him standing there, I wasn't sure how to react. I closed my eyes and considered what I was feeling. Inside the anger was…what? Love. It was there, but my loving him wouldn't negate the relationship he shared with his nutty sisters.

"Can't," he said, "because you have to mine through mountains of garbage? Or can't because you… can't."

"Don't make fun of my sloppiness now. It was cute when we were a quirky couple, speaking in bad cliché's, loving every minute of it. But then, well, so much has happened. Or not happened."

He flinched. "I thought, maybe, I hoped enough time had passed that we could figure this out."

"That's very mature of you. It must be the fifteen-year age difference we share." I was feeling irrational, but couldn't stop the words. "Last time I saw you… You didn't even let me explain about Alex." What was I doing? Did I want him back or not?

"There was a naked guy in your bed," he said.

"I didn't put him there. *I* was fully clothed and *not* in the bed, if you recall." I stared at the ground. I knew it wasn't Alex that had kept us apart. Jeep had said it himself. It had been me as much as anything. Yes, I had needed to focus on my work, but looking back, I jumped into that work pretty quick once we hit an obstacle. It had felt better to blame it all on something else, someone else. I started jamming papers into a garbage bag. What was I doing? I did want him. Why couldn't I just say it?

I reached for his hand and started to tell him I wanted to talk things out, but his beeper went off.

"I have to go," he said and as quickly as he'd appeared, he was gone.

I looked around my war-torn classroom and collapsed into a chair. No, I didn't want him to leave. *Get up*, I told myself. *Go get him*, I thought. But I couldn't move. This was just not meant to be.

I put my head on the desk and let a year's store of tears pour out. I cried because of the school year. And him. Him. Him. After what seemed like an eternity, I sat up and rubbed my temples, still unable to quell the sadness. The tears dropped onto some of the students' papers and blurred the ink on their final copies.

"Ms. Jenkins?" Ben's voice interrupted my thoughts.

"Ben. Sorry. I was just…" I looked away and wiped my tears.

"Not seeing, again."

"Huh?" I turned to him. I would have thought I'd be embarrassed at my display of emotion, but I wasn't.

He pushed his broom in a brisk movement toward me. "You have trouble seeing past what things should be to what they are. Sometimes things can be good enough. Not exactly the way you want. But good enough."

I sniffled. He was right. "What're you doing in a place like this, anyway? You should be running a counseling center for wayward post-college, almost adults."

He stopped and put his chin over his hands that covered the end of the broom. "It's home to me. No matter who's in charge and what kind of—"

Klein shuffled into the room. Ben drew a Kleenex from the box on my desk and handed it to me. Klein cringed once he got close enough to see me crying.

I wiped my nose with the Kleenex.

Klein looked at the ceiling and shifted his weight. "Oh... I, uh... I was..."

Ben began pushing his broom again, making Klein hop out of his way.

Klein scowled, but didn't scold Ben. Klein folded a paper he was holding into a tiny square and shoved in his pocket.

"I've been thinking about the professors you mentioned. That's a good idea, Jenkins." He sighed. "Carolyn. What you did was wrong, with that curriculum of yours, the way you did it." He cleared his throat and tore another Kleenex from the box, tossing it toward me.

I took the Kleenex and dabbed my eyes. "I don't normally break rules. Of any kind."

"I know that about you," he said.

His kind words and compassionate tone felt awkward.

He turned on his heel and walked away. I felt my shoulders release tension and I blew out air.

When he got to the door he turned back. "Why are you crying?"

I shook my head. I certainly couldn't delve into my love problems with Jeep.

He looked nervously at everything in the room but me. The perfect opportunity to tell me what a mess the place was. I felt my body tense again.

"Well," he said. "Things take time. You know." His face puckered as though the sentiment was sour in his mouth.

"Baptism by fire," I said, unsure whether I even understood what we were talking about.

"Maybe." He bent down and tied his shoe, as though stalling. I shuffled the papers on my desk and squared the piles.

He stood back up after tying his shoe and leaned on the doorjamb.

"You know, Carolyn. Sometimes when I'm here late at

night, thinking about you teachers, the notion of junk DNA comes to mind. You know—the idea that most of what makes up DNA serves no purpose. I wonder if ninety-five percent of the teaching pool serves no purpose. I suspect most teachers don't contribute anything of value, they're just there. I try to figure out how to change that. I do."

I didn't know if he considered me part of the garbage DNA or not, but I bristled at his dismissive view of teachers—professionals he so poorly mentored.

"No." I stood. "I think the ninety-five percent you wonder about just haven't been encouraged correctly. Recognized for their worth. Given the support to do their work well."

"Or that," he said giving me a thumbs-up sign. It was a weak version of the Lincoln thumbs-up, devoid of his usual verve. It seemed as though he'd finally realized the idiocy of the gesture.

I didn't return it.

He left the room.

"Mr. Klein." I chased him into the hallway.

He stopped but didn't turn back.

"I still haven't decided what to do about the whole Fionna thing. It wasn't right. Especially in light of all her problems."

He put his hand against a locker and leaned on it as though my words had impact. He looked over his shoulder at me. "It isn't what you think. You have no idea."

"Maybe not," I said. "But, you're not a good person, Mr. Klein. You're cold and callous and—"

"And you have no idea, Carolyn Jenkins. Do what you have to, but know that you don't have the whole picture."

He shuffled down the hall, the scuffing cadence of his feet filling my ears.

I hadn't been fired. Even after what I just said. I recalled the paper he'd folded up and tucked into his pocket. Son of a gun. *It was the tears*, I thought. The tears softened him toward me. Damn it. I should have just balled like a baby the first day of school, like Laura. Who could have known that was all it took to get a little support.

Chapter 37

Jeep. I should have told him how I felt. I should have made him ignore his beeper and continue talking with me. But, Klein would have interrupted anyway. Another moment had slipped away, gone forever. Walking to my car I saw two figures in the parking lot. Jeep and Kenneth sat on the hood of the BMW.

I stopped at the sight. He didn't leave. My breath wouldn't come. I forced my feet in their direction. Kenneth saw me and hopped down, coming toward me. "Remember this man? He's telling me how to become a real live Secret Service agent. That's what I'm going to be. Not just some plain old cop."

I loved Kenneth's enthusiasm. "Keep working hard in school and you can be whatever you want," I said. I patted him on the shoulder. "But you already know that, don't you."

Kenneth high-fived me then dashed away. "See you Monday, Ms. Jenkins! Last day of school!" He radiated the joy every kid, everywhere felt at the thought of the last day of school.

Jeep watched me with that sly grin that lifted one side of his mouth and caused his eyes to squint just enough that the little lines brought his face to life with stories I didn't yet know. "Are you crying?" His expression grew concerned.

"No, no, no, no," I said. "It's a little dating trick I have. Special makeup applied to create an extra special needy look. Works wonders…"

His eyes shone with what looked like the beginnings of tears.

"Well, *you* can't cry," I said. "Neither of us is romantic." I laughed, thinking of the wonderful boxes he'd gifted me with. He was the most romantic person I knew.

"Any girl who farts on a first date is decidedly not romantic," Jeep said. "And the guy who thinks it was the funniest thing he's ever heard can't be romantic either."

I covered my mouth, feeling tears coming back. All the anger I'd felt for him, the resentment that had been hardening over the months, shattered. I was weakened by the onslaught of love I'd tried to ignore. I leaned against the car so I wouldn't fall.

"We've already got the hard stuff worked out, don't we?" Jeep said.

I shook my head. I knew he was kidding, jumping past any real work we might have to do.

"My family," he said. "I didn't mean to be so stubborn. You are my first priority. Not them."

He got off the hood, took my hand and held it up, intertwining our fingers. My stomach turned in that delightful, love-struck way stomachs did. "But I have to ask one thing. I have to know. About your ex."

That was an easy one. "He left for Pittsburgh and I figured it was over. I was not at all what he wanted in a wife. I'm the complete opposite of what he wants."

"I'm not asking what *he* wants," he said.

I looked at our hands woven together. I squeezed. "*I* don't want *him*."

He squeezed back. "I'm just not up for games, Carolyn. I'm too old. I hate to say that. Because saying 'old' in your presence might bring it to your attention and seal the deal in the wrong direction. But I'm serious—"

He took my face in his hands and moved his fingers into my hair, making chills roar through me. He stood so close I could feel his heartbeat. He laid his forehead on mine and closed his eyes. Then he kissed me, gently, almost as if it wasn't really happening. I returned the kiss, remembering how wonderful it was to be with him like that. Some yells from kids up the street reminded me we were in the school parking lot. We stopped.

He wrapped me tightly in his arms. "I have never loved anyone the way I love you," he said. "Never, not in any way."

I nodded. He felt the same way I did. It was like a miracle visiting me, right there in the parking lot.

Still, the love I felt for him was tempered by reality, by the notion that love is often not nearly enough. I had some questions I needed to ask before we could move on as a couple. A couple. Not just a pair of college kids who had some chemistry and proximity in common. Now was the time to know for sure.

I crossed my arms. "What about your sisters? And the secret look that passed between you and Tess when they found the empty urn? That felt like playing games to me."

He crossed his arms. "My sisters suck. I can admit it. I love them dearly. We'll have to spend time with them. They're nuts about the memory of my parents—who gets to be the keeper of the urn and shit. But now that one of the urns is empty because Mary Helen spilled it when she was dusting, that's less of a problem for them…"

I turned away. I wanted him to be serious about this.

He spun me back around, untangled my crossed arms, took my hand and pulled it to his lips. "Tess and I were just laughing about my sisters. She knows how strange they are. Tess means nothing to me. I have no secrets with her. None. I am very, very serious. My sisters will not interfere with us. I promise." He opened the door to his car, next to mine.

"I have my car," I said. I believed that he was done with Tess. She no longer felt threatening to me. But I wasn't satisfied with what he'd said about his sisters. I wanted to be a part of his family, but it wasn't going to work if his sisters were central to our relationship—if I had to hear how much he loved them all the time.

"Follow me, then." He kissed me lightly, his lips brushing

mine before he tucked me into my car.

"Where're we going?"

"Home," he said as he popped into his BMW and pulled out of the parking lot.

I followed him to his place, but he drove right past it. I figured he'd changed his mind and wasn't ready to take things forward. I felt my breath catch at the thought of losing him forever, finally. Still, I followed. He wound around his tree-lined street for a minute or so before he turned left onto another street and then pulled into a driveway.

What was he doing? The house was adorable—a sweet cottage with flower boxes and a picket fence. I was not in the mood to have dinner with his friends or family.

He opened my car door and helped me out. "What are we doing?" He pulled me down the driveway to the front door. "Whose house is this?" He pushed a key into the lock and opened the door, inviting me to enter.

Once inside, I was no less confused.

"It's yours," Jeep said, spreading his hands open. "Ours. Throw everything out. Keep it all. I don't care."

"I don't get it." I turned and stared into the living room.

When I turned back to Jeep he was on his knee holding a ring up to me. No box.

My mouth dropped open. I leaned forward and cupped my hands over his. The ring. The big dime-sized thing MC had shown me at the extravaganza. I straightened and put my hands on my hips. "What?" A smile burst onto my mouth, fueled by excitement I'd never felt before. He pushed the ring up toward me.

I bent closer to it. It was perfect. Even in the dimmed light of the foyer, it harnessed and refracted so much light it looked like fireworks. The band was delicate, platinum filigree and diamonds.

"Bold but delicate," I said, barely aware I did.

"Like you," he said.

My gaze snapped from the ring to him. "Like me?" I pulled him up to standing. Could he be serious with this? "You can't just say you love me, come bearing this extraordinary ring after not speaking to me for forever. Is this a ploy to have sex with me? It's not sane," I said.

"Since when have you required sanity for anything?" he asked.

I turned the ring in the light. "Well never, but that's—"

"It *is* the point. If you're not sure... I'm sure enough for both of us. I'll take the responsibility of being wrong. But I know I'm right. I promise my sisters will not interfere. This house is a new start for us. I will give up everything for you, anything for you," he said.

I looked at him. His eyes glowed with love. How stupid could I be? Stupidity Potential. A new scale. The girls would love it.

Jeep pulled me into him. "Carolyn. Stop thinking about it. Trust me."

I nestled into his chest, the smell of his soap filling my nose. Feeling as though I'd had a spot in his arms for years, I knew he was right. To be sure. He was definitely that. All that was left was for me to say the words he wanted to hear. Yes, indeed, I loved him. I believed him. He'd said everything *I* needed to hear. And, with that, my heart ballooned with all the love that had lain there, dormant, waiting for me to trust enough to let it out.

Chapter 38

Laura had traded in her dream dress full of bows and other crap I didn't know the names of for a simple empire waist deal that didn't even hint at her pregnancy.

H-Factor: 10+

Crap Quotient: 0

As I walked down the aisle in my lilac, off the shoulder, bridesmaid's dress, I caught a glimpse of my ring shimmering under the bouquet. I smiled at Jeep as I passed him.

H-Factor: 8 (It can't be as high as the bride's. It simply can't happen.)

Crap Quotient: 3 (Klein and Bobby Jo were in attendance.)

Standing at the altar with Nina and Laura, I felt different than I'd expected to. I had thought I'd be sad that our lives were changing, that our friendship was evolving. Instead, I'd come to understand that we'd be together in one way or another forever.

That wisdom was cushioned deep in my heart, as true as any fact I knew. How could we have gone through what we did and ever really be fragmented? I knew in the best and worst of times, we'd lean on each other, even if we saw one another less and less. Everything was better about us when we were together. And I had learned there were lots of ways to be together.

Laura's students sat in the front row, dressed in their Sunday best. They made me think of my students. Those kids. They'd taught me so much. Mostly about what was missing in me as a person. And what they had to offer, what *wasn't* missing in them. Any old chili pepper could see that.

And that day at the altar, watching Laura cry, hearing her say her sugary vows, I realized being sure of who we were and where we were going was all that mattered. To be sure. If only for a short time. That was huge. And that just might last a lifetime if I let it.

THE END

Acknowledgments

Yes, *Love and Other Subjects* is fiction, but I drew heavily from my years in education to shape the school portions of the book.

Thank you to all the teachers I've worked with and learned from throughout my life—that includes students. Every time I'm in the position to teach, I learn more than I impart, I'm sure of that.

Thanks to my Maryland colleagues who were new when I was. I couldn't have done it without you. I don't think of you without smiling, even sometimes laughing right out loud. The truth is stranger than fiction…

Thanks to my father, mother, grandma Arthur, Beth, and Jamie—a family full of educators—I've learned so much from all of you.

Isabel and Moddy—working with you at Learning Research and Development Center at the University of Pittsburgh, I learned something new every single day. I appreciate every lesson, especially the ones I didn't want to learn. I wish I could replicate that environment in every aspect of my life. Isabel, your continued support is priceless.

Cheryl, Missy, Gayle, Darlene, and Shelley. The years with you at LRDC were the best. You were all great teachers—all in different ways. I miss being there more than I can say.

To Kate—your collaboration on projects and all things PhD, made the process bearable. The Cooper School is amazing and I wish I shared your energy and guts to create a school that fits my educational philosophy. It's an exquisite success—a living, breathing miracle.

Meryl and Linda—two teachers who never stop giving.

Thanks to the teachers, administrators, and staff in Duquesne. Some of the hardest working, least appreciated professionals I've ever seen in my life worked there. Even in the most difficult environments there are blinding bright lights. Also, resilience and humor—there is always that.

Many thanks to all the administrators in schools all over the country who choose to mentor the new teachers and collaborate with the experienced ones—it's a gift and a priceless service to all.

As always, thanks to Bill, John and Diana, my sisters and brothers-in law, Gran Jan and Pap Pap, Mrs. Nickerson, Lisa McShea, Catherine Coulter, friends, and readers. I can't say how much it means that you help shape my writing, show up at signings and spread the word about my work. Thank you a million times over.